SUMMER WITH THE ENEMY

SUMMER

WITH THE

ENEMY

SHAHLA UJAYLI

TRANSLATED BY MICHELLE HARTMAN

Interlink Books

An imprint of Interlink Publishing Group, Inc.
Northampton, Massachusetts

First published in 2021 by

Interlink Books
An imprint of Interlink Publishing Group, Inc.
46 Crosby Street, Northampton, MA 01060
www.interlinkbooks.com

Originally published in Arabic as *Saif Ma'al Adou* by Editions Difaf, Beirut, Lebanon

Library of Congress Cataloging-in-Publication Data
Names: 'Ujaylī, Shahlā, author. | Hartman, Michelle, translator.
Title: Summer with the enemy / Shahla Ujayli; translated by Michelle Hartman.
Other titles: Sayf ma'a al-'adūw. English
Description: Northampton : Interlink Books, 2021.
Identifiers: LCCN 2020057365 | ISBN 9781623718671 (paperback)
Subjects: LCSH: Women—Fiction. | Families--Fiction. | Syria--History—Civil War, 2011—Fiction. | Syria—History—Civil War, 2011—Refugees—Fiction. | War stories.
Classification: LCC PJ7966.J39 S3913 2021 | DDC 892.7/37--dc23
LC record available at https://lccn.loc.gov/2020057365

Printed and bound in the United States of America

Dedicated to the Raqqa of my memory

Profound thanks to
Carmen, Abdulrahman, Nadia, and Samir

A SILENT CRIME

He reached behind the white organza curtain trimmed with embroidered silver roses to close the window. The long edges of this
white wood-framed, rectangular window run down the wall like
two columns. The glass is divided into a grid of eight thick square
panes. A cold southern wind was blowing in from the Rhine,
carrying on it the mingled scents of metal riverboat ferries, char-
coal-roasted fish from nearby sidewalk cafés, and the humidity of
the previous night's rainfall. The river could be spotted between
the domed bridges running along Rhineover Street.

He leaned his body slightly forward to reach the edge of the
window and his chin brushed against the top of my forehead.
Though almost theatrically smooth, his sudden movement startled
me. I had been in a deep sleep, my body cradled in his right arm
and my face nestled in the crook of his neck, which gave off the
warm scent of musk and mulberries. I tried to ignore it, searching
for his natural scent, redolent of my faraway childhood.

Actually, so that we could have some time alone before I
left for Munich, I'd rushed to meet him so quickly that I didn't

even have time to dye my hair. White roots have started to peep through again and this is totally incompatible with how old I feel and the youthful spirit I harbor inside me.

I hadn't realized that Abboud lived right across from the municipal building on Port Street. I've passed by here every day for three days. I've walked down the sidewalk, following people setting off to work on foot or bicycles. Cologne had very few cars for such a big city. You never felt you had to leave early because the traffic would likely make you late for an important meeting. Many different kinds of tourists regularly descended on the old city, as did the foreigners—I had decided to call the refugees foreigners.

The day before, I'd sat in the café that the very window I've just described looks out onto. I enjoyed a delicious coffee and lunched in the restaurant next door. It was an excellent restaurant and the meal wasn't pricey. I usually sat with my back to the old brick building beside it, and looked out at the bridge instead. I've always loved bridges—they make return a possibility no matter how much time has passed! As I stood up to leave, the building whose third-floor apartment I am now staying in captivated me. I was taken by the little crystal pendant lights emitting a diffuse yellow glow, the classic organza curtains I was now resting behind, and the Opaline chandelier on the first floor that must have been produced at the beginning of the twentieth century. It illuminated a table with a white tablecloth, atop which passersby could spot a bowl with untouched red apples and green grapes, so perfect they looked plastic. I was secretly jealous as I wondered: Who lives there? It must be locals, settled people—Germans with families nearby. They own their apartments, having bought or inherited them. They have relatives and friends who visit and they spend pleasant evenings together on the riverbanks. Foreigners don't live in the center of the old town—their places are far removed, on the outskirts of big cities, in little villages, virgin forests, lands where there are few people. These are neutral places we regularly pass by, be it by habit or chance, which have no particular appeal and hold no special meaning for us. We may like them or hate them, or want to go in and buy them. We may even fear them. Then in the blink of an eye they can even become our own special places, and we create our own stories about them.

Abboud apologized for disturbing me and nestled me in his arms again, cradling me back to sleep. But I started rambling, telling him I'd seen him in my sleep, in a dream:

"Do you remember Bushra?"

"Bushra…? Oh yes, Bushra, of course, Khalil's wife?"

"She passed away…"

"Oh God! May she rest in peace," he said, voice full of sleep.

He didn't ask me how she'd passed. I didn't volunteer any information because most of the people we knew who'd passed away recently had died for reasons related to the war. But he and I were surely thinking the same thing. The day Bushra and Khalil got married I was ten, and Abboud was two years older than me. Like most other summer nights, we were playing outside with the neighborhood children when the wedding party arrived, clapping and singing in the street. We followed them to the party, clapping along. When we got too close, Amm Ismail, the father of the groom, shooed us away from the dabke troupe with his cane, to allow the circle of professional dancers to join together. We were all in the wide open-air courtyard facing their circular garden, filled with orange, apple, and lemon trees, as well as red and white Damask rose bushes. This courtyard was surrounded by their five-room house. Some of us rushed to mimic their dabke dance at the edge of the patio area where there was a large bathroom, a half bathroom, and a kitchen. But our dabke ended up a chaotic swirl, some legs thrown up in the air and others landing hard on the ground with no attention to rhythm, like children's dabkes often are. The newlyweds went up to their private chamber just after midnight.

The next morning, at perhaps six, I awoke and looked out at the neighborhood. Abboud was sitting outside alone on an iron barrel my father had left in front of the house. Our place was on the corner of a street with three other streets branching off from it. My father had left the barrel there to prevent speeding cars from running into the wall and damaging it. I washed my face and got dressed quickly to go out and catch up with Abboud. We entered through the main door of Amm Ismail's house and walked up the still-untiled, unpainted concrete staircase leading to the roof. Khalil had built three rooms for himself on top of his parents' house. The window was open and we peered in to spot the two of them naked. They were holding each other and sleeping peacefully. Bushra's body was pale, white, firm, beautiful—it was the first time I'd seen a naked woman, except for Granny Makkia—one of our elderly neighbors—whose body was tiny and flaccid. We'd started helping her shower in our bathroom after she had no one left to help her out.

After their honeymoon, when Khalil would leave for work, we'd steal in and sneak peeks from behind the door at Bushra bidding him farewell. We'd glimpse a wisp of a shiny silken nightdress—red, pink, or blue—and sometimes we'd make out a section of eggshell-colored thigh, or a freshly manicured crimson toenail. We'd each silently wonder: how could Khalil leave such beauty and go off to work? Would he ever find it mundane to spend the night with her?

I looked over at Abboud's smiling face, his eyes closed. He laughed his old laugh, while trying to conceal an endearing boyishness and instinctive embarrassment. It came out stifled and halfhearted, and I surmised that he was thinking about that night. Abboud and I share many secrets, and what we saw of their wedding night-nakedness is not even the most risqué.

As soon as summer came, we always scattered through the neighborhood, like birds escaping their cages. Nothing and no one could stop us—not the neighbors' shouting at us to move away from their cars or out from under their windows, nor their scolding us for walking with our muddy shoes on their freshly washed sidewalks or on the still-wet, newly laid pavement. We took those shouts and threats as friendly warnings, and responded immediately. We would slow down and lower our voices. But then we'd forget and start darting around again a minute later.

We ran through the streets, drew with chalk on the sidewalks, and rode our bicycles around. Two of us in the front, three in the middle, and two behind, then we would switch places. I liked being with Abboud even if we didn't talk at all. I always felt like he was on my side, that he understood me and would defend me if the need ever arose. He knew everything about my difficult family life and never used it against me, whatever bone of contention might have arisen between us. I was curious about his feelings for me, and I wished I could ask him about it, but our conversations never led in that direction. We simply played together. We were always on the same team—cops or robbers, it didn't matter. I admit that back then I loved him a lot, and at a certain point he became the only thing I thought about. It's not uncommon: younger children are often taken with older children, always trying to impress them. I don't remember exactly what I used to do to get his attention, but I tried many things. Perhaps he didn't notice any of it, though I can't be sure because boys think in ways unfathomable to even the most experienced girls. This confusion persists even after we become mature men and women, and then later old people. But it was because of him that I paid attention to music and Einstein, or "Ayn Stayn," in the American way he used to pronounce it.

His mother allowed him to come out and play only for short periods, and strictly forbade it on school days. In the summer, he could only play with us for two hours in the afternoon, according to her rules, but he'd often ignore her and come outside anyway. He traveled with her to his grandfather's house in Czechoslovakia for a month every summer. That's when life became bleak and summer vacation would turn into a nightmare. Everything felt empty and boring even though there were other boys and girls teeming around the neighborhood like ants. When the university students returned to Raqqa from Aleppo and Damascus, they would sit around on moonlit evenings and talk about their studies and faraway girlfriends. Men and women gathered and chatted in front of their houses until dawn, but I missed Abboud, every single day from morning to evening, and waited on tenterhooks for his return.

Abboud's father, Doctor Asahd, had studied veterinary medicine at Brno University, southeast of Prague in Czechoslovakia. He brought his beautiful colleague Anna back home with him as his wife. Everyone loved her, including me. I really admired her, even though she was the one who made me feel the distance separating me and Abboud, and pushed me away from him and their world if I got too close. She dragged him upwards, to Europe, and left the rest of us to wade through the muddy 1980s in our developing country. When he used to show me pictures of them on the Charles Bridge or at his grandparents' house in the old city of Staré Město, my heart would pound in my chest, sad about our impending separation. I decided to study hard so I could get a scholarship and follow him wherever he went. Then someday, I would be able to stroll with him along all fifteen bridges that crossed the Vltava River. He'd drape his arms over my shoulder as we meandered down the Saints' Road from the old city to the castle. We'd take a picture as a memento which we'd display on a table in our house, as well as a picture of us next to the statue of Christ on the cross on the Charles Bridge, written above him in Hebrew: "Holy Holy Holy is Jesus Christ the Messiah." These words were a punishment for a Jewish Rabbi who'd ridiculed Christ, refusing to take his hat off in front of him, Abboud told me.

The men who'd studied in Eastern Europe in the 1970s formed a sort of commune, their own little private club, in Raqqa. They had gone to the Soviet Union—Czechoslovakia, Hungary, Bulgaria, Romania, Poland, and East Germany. All of these countries were friendly with Syria, and they offered each other mutual support in their liberatory struggles for socialism and democracy against capitalism and imperialism. These men married beautiful women, who bore them lovely boys and girls we called the "foreign women's children." They were clean, tidy, polite, and serious in their studies. They cared about music and literature, and usually had some kind of pet—a dog or a cat.

Those Muslim children went to church with their mothers and celebrated their birthdays at home in their small modest houses, near the al-Thakanah or al-Dariyiyah neighborhoods. Their homes were cozy and displayed a mix of elegance, good taste, and practicality. Everything was in its place and there was no excess. These families would visit each other regularly and spend evenings at each other's houses—we would hear about it from their children at school. Their food had a different taste than our Arab food, and their drinks weren't like araq or whiskey, which people bought from Abu Ibrahim's liquor shop wrapped up in brown paper bags. They brought wine back with them from the Caucus Mountains in Georgia, and vodka from cooperatives in Moscow. When the vodka ran out, the doctors, engineers, and pharmacists concocted similar things locally, thereby transforming themselves into winemakers and creating a carnivalesque atmosphere of laughter, song, and friendly quarrels. They brought home lots of potatoes, boiled them, mashed them, then added barley to them. Everything was produced locally in Raqqa, the best there was. They would stir the mix, let it cool a little, and then add yeast to it. After a few hours, when the first carbon dioxide bubbles appeared, they would cheer and shout. About four days later, they would prepare some filters for the distillation process and Doctor Asahd would begin the work he was known for, as an artisan of good taste, repeating the process until the purity of the drink was deemed satisfactory. He reduced the sharpness for those who preferred it lighter by treating it with baking soda.

During the season, Abboud and I used to be tasked with rushing to blind Attar's shop in Suq al-Sharqi to bring the men anything that was missing in their recipe: yeast, baking soda, barley, dried orange peel…This whole process allowed the men to travel back in time to their days studying in the land of snow, fur coats, and sweet potatoes! Abboud used to tell me that Mendeleev, the person who created the periodic table of chemical elements, was the one who calculated the relative ratio of water to alcohol in order to create the best vodka. This kept evolving until it was patented in 1894, with the name Russian Standard Vodka—greatly contributing to the development of the Russian economy. I nodded my head, taken by the colors of Abboud's world. Like him, I grew to love perfumed tea and despise Coca-Cola. Those families gave our little town of Raqqa wings!

After each of his trips to his grandfather's house he brought me back gifts. Once it was a little ceramic traditional house with a pointed roof that broke a week after I got it, another time a silver necklace with a picture of the Virgin Mary with a sad, downturned head that I lost with the passing of time. Yet another time he gave me a doll dressed in traditional Czech clothes—a bright white cotton dress with a royal blue velvet dress over it embroidered in gold. She had two thick black braids and wore a velvet cap. We called her Natasha and I kept her by my side right up until I left Raqqa. Once he gave me a silver ring with a green gemstone that his mother had left behind and I considered it a token of our eternal bond. When we broke up, the ring stayed in an old, empty powder box. Later on when I came across it by chance, I barely even remembered Abboud or the reason I'd kept this rusty tin ring.

My mother was always busy battling my father and my

grandmother, so she left me to my own devices, and I spent my time with Abboud and our other neighbors' children. We passed our days out in the streets, which were self-contained and usually safe. This made me feel that I didn't have a good upbringing compared to boys and girls who weren't allowed to leave their houses. This in turn led to my isolation, especially when Abboud went to Prague with his mother in the summers. That's when I always really felt a loss. So I decided to take revenge on everything around me and started to live a secret life. I began accompanying our neighbor Farhan, who drove a red taxi, on his calls to drive at wedding celebrations.

Farhan was tall and thin, his thick hair always set in place. He combed it over from the part on the right and swept it upward so his head seemed taller than it was. He was twenty-something and had no worries in the world. An only child, he lived with his parents in a small apartment in the same building where his paternal uncles and their families lived. He gave his red taxi more care and attention than he would have given a girlfriend. Farhan used to wash his taxi every day at two in the afternoon. He pulled the hose from the faucet by the entrance to their building and poured Ludaline-brand dish soap on it. He rubbed down the wheels and then dried them while wearing white cotton underwear, his chest bare because of the intense summer heat. I didn't follow the car washing ritual in the winter because that's when we hibernated like bears in their den.

Normally, the car would be ready at 5 PM, and half an hour later I would climb into the backseat like a princess and accompany Farhan to the wedding celebration he'd been hired for. We would always first go to the groom's house in a nearby village, and pick up some of the other celebrants there as well. We then would pick up the bride from another house or even another village. No one in these places knew me—the bride's family thought I was from the groom's family, and the groom's family thought that I was from the bride's family. No one ever guessed that I was just the driver's neighbor going on a regular evening outing. I participated in the wedding celebrations of people I'd never met and who weren't from my social milieu. I'd do as they did and wave a colored nylon scarf out of the car window. Sometimes they'd reprimand me, because they wanted to sit in my spot and wave their own scarves out the windows. Rebuffed, I would pile in with the children and women who smelled of sheep, laurel-scented soap, and cheap perfume. There would be seven to ten people sometimes in a car that could barely fit five.

Farhan never meddled in my business. He thought my family knew I was with him at these parties, but I never told anyone. I always waited for the day the bride would get into the same car as me, but she never did. She rode in a private taxi with no children in it. We walked through the fields looking at the verdant beauty everywhere in the villages surrounding Raqqa. We drove down the main road where the bridge crosses to al-Kasra, and were met there by linden, oak, and willow trees; poplars lined the farmlands, the tops of their crowns communicating with the heavens. We passed by the tents of the Nawar community—barefooted children with matted blonde and red hair, shabby clothes, and faces darkened by the sun, leaving them with a unique appearance, dark skin and light hair. They tied brightly colored red, green, blue, and purple scarves together to make swings that they then hung on tree branches. One girl made a pillow the seat for her swing, and another pushed her. I wanted so much to join the girls in the game and ask them about the threads looped through their earlobes instead of ear-rings. I wanted to ask Farhan to stop and leave me with them. But I sensed that he wouldn't, and I never asked for things that I knew in advance wouldn't happen.

Farhan sold the taxi and left to work in Saudi Arabia. The neighborhood lost its color without him. Weddings took place in all the nearby villages without me. Of course no one noticed my absence, nor that of the scarf that I waved out the window and eventually lost. Perhaps my mother had gotten rid of it—she always told me it was just an ugly old Nawar scarf. During the three hours I would spend at weddings no one ever missed me, and I never asked about anyone. I was always there in my own world, with new people who I saw at their very happiest, dancing and trilling with joy. I would trill right along with them, clapping my hands and singing local wedding songs, like *Ya chauffeur doos doos*.

I liked to roll the window all the way down until the hot breeze smacked me in the face. I'd confront it, opening my eyes until they teared up, and the leaves on the trees outside looked blurry, as did the yellow fields waiting for the harvest, and the trucks passing by; images of people were undefined, paintings executed by an unsure hand. I wouldn't get out of the car when they'd enter the bride's house, rather I'd wait with Farhan for them to come out, and we would take the guests over to the groom's house. Then we would return to our own neighborhood, my pocket full of candies they'd thrown at the bride. Farhan would always ask me, "Did you like the wedding?" and I would answer, "I did!"

When Farhan married a young woman from a nearby farm community, I didn't go to the wedding celebration. Many yellow taxis came to collect people, and he drove a Mercedes that belonged to one of his friends with a Saudi license. He used to come back every summer with gifts for the entire neighborhood. Every household had a bottle of Hawaii perfume somewhere, as well as gold-plated Seiko watches, and pillowcases embroidered with flowers and expressions like, "Good Morning" and "Sleep Well." After this, he totally disappeared. Then suddenly, twenty years later, he returned as one of the leaders of the revolution, inciting people to demonstrate in the public square and accusing the local people in our neighborhood of collaborating with the regime.

Anna was constantly in conflict with Asahd because they lived in our neighborhood, in an apartment right above his family's house. She wanted him to move them to the west side of town, near what we all called the Eastern European encampment. But as he was a veterinarian committed to working on government-run farms, his financial situation was less established than that of his colleagues. He also needed to support his mother and unmarried sister who lived together. This same sister used to tell her friends that her brother and others like him had pigged out on pork when they lived abroad. According to her, their blonde colleagues, who had helped them out over there and later became their wives, were fleeing from lives of poverty and debauchery and had only come here to cover it up. They'd all grow mustaches as old women, she claimed.

Asahd was a broken man and a drunk. He was hard on Anna and sometimes hit her. She didn't find what she came to Syria looking for. She wasn't able to work in her specialty, veterinary medicine. She tried to give piano lessons, which she was very talented at doing, like many of her compatriots, but there wasn't anyone who wanted to study the piano in Raqqa back then. Even if she could have found someone they wouldn't have been able to pay much. So she became a seamstress. Once she made me a dress of red velvet that had a dark blue satin belt tied with a bow in front. I used to watch her pale, blue-veined hands moving nimbly over the thick fabric, a measuring tape draped around her shoulders. She'd grown really thin! My grandmother said that when she'd come she'd been full-figured, sturdy, and attractive. Worry and lack of money had made her strangely hunched over.

Anna excelled in her close attention to detail. In fact, she excelled in everything she made: jams, sujuk, qashqawan cheese sandwiches with salami. She gave me a little bit of everything whose delicious aroma emanated from their house: cakes, pies, basterma, and cannelloni, with a sauce either she or one of her friends would bring specially from their country. Sometimes, she asked the taxi drivers who travelled regularly over the border to Turkey to bring it back for her, until the day when she could find it in the shops in Raqqa. Everything she made tasted different than the food I was used to, even though most homes had access to the same ingredients. When I asked my grandmother why this was, she told me, "Every woman has her own spices." But I felt that it went beyond spices. My mother told me that culture was the reason for the difference. Anna taught the neighborhood butcher how to prepare her meat specially. He cut steak and prepared filets from the veal, which Asahd brought him from the cattle farm, differently than the usual large chunks of mutton with bone or little cubes that we called "ras al-asfour." Anna knitted elegant wool sweaters, turtlenecks, and V-necks with thick raised braids, in sober colors: gray, teal, and beige.

These sweaters made Abboud appear a confident young man, and offered Asahd ways to cover up some of his random behaviors fueled by his drinking and incessant smoking. The difference between her house and her mother-in-law's house on the ground floor, like the difference between a house in Prague and an ordinary house in Raqqa, really just boiled down to that: difference—nothing more, nothing less. Despite this, Anna failed in her relationship with Asahd. The love they'd shared in her homeland was highly influenced by their youth and studies, by him being away from home. That changed completely in our country, where love is influenced by the routine of work, the small family circle, and the authority of local women. Everyone was wrapped up in Asahd's business, Asahd who abandoned the woman with thick, wavy, chestnut hair and eyes the color of the clearest sea when seen from afar. He left her to marry another woman—an employee from the ranch where he worked, a thin young girl, with deeply tanned skin and henna-dyed red hair. Whenever I saw her, my nose filled with the scent of manure and clover. Her name was Safaa; she was impetuous and paid attention to no one. Her harsh-sounding, throaty laugh rang out everywhere: in the street, on the steps to her building, in the clothing shop, at the market. Men truly have strange taste. Anna had difficulty dealing with Asahd's belligerent Bohemian side. In Syria, she quickly grew accustomed to obedience, loyalty, and stereotypical understandings of the family, as they are expressed in idealized Arab settings, while he rejected everything domestic in favor of flirtations with young shepherd girls out in the fields and farmer women bent over clover fields with their pruning shears. He never denied himself their ample backsides, which he described as mythical. Before we ever saw Safaa in the neighborhood, my grandmother had already helped Anna to leave, by giving her enough money to pack up her few things and go back to her country.

Abboud stayed in Raqqa with his father. The injustice that had befallen his mother forced her to give up her child. She told my grandmother that he would soon grow up and come back to her. But for now she wouldn't be able to afford his living expenses in Prague. Her father couldn't support him either, because the economic situation there was very bad—people were dying of starvation. The authorities in the airport in Syria would also have prevented her from taking him without his father's permission. Running away with him was impossible. I never told Abboud about how my grandmother had helped his mother, but I was happy that he was closer to me after Anna left. I felt that I possessed him. But he lost a good deal of his radiance when she left. The shell of self-confidence that she had created for him was gone. I started feeling compassion and a sense of responsibility towards him, and our sadness was the same. Abboud and I were equally miserable with our family troubles.

Abboud was suspended between us and Anna, Raqqa and Prague. This showed the most in his awkward jokes, as successful joking requires that your spirit belong to a place and knows its contradictions. This also seeped through his accent, which wavered between the heavy Bedouin pronunciation of letters, needed to speak Arabic here, and the sounds of his mother's Czech language, which always made people laugh. He liked to speak to Eva, Layla, Candy, and Marwan in Czech; it made him feel closer to them. But after Anna left, they stopped being friendly with him and started to make him feel small. They would take his letters to her in Czecholslovakia every summer vacation when they went to their mothers' country. They also came back with the gifts Anna had bought for him: boxes of chocolates, fancy overcoats, shoes, and hats. When his maternal grandmother died, he wept many tears. But none of the other children with foreign moms visited him. He came over to our house instead; we understood him and didn't make him feel inferior like his former friends did. We made sure he was never alone and set up a room in my grandmother's house for him to receive condolences. I sat and cried with him and served traditional, bitter funeral coffee to the guests.

On holidays after Anna left, I woke up early in the morning and sped through my morning routine: washing my face, brushing my teeth…I rushed outside before eating breakfast, sometimes even still in my pajamas, but of course with shoes on. I always put on proper shoes and never went out in my house slippers. I stood in front of his house in the alley parallel to ours and knocked lightly on the iron door. My knocks resounded thunderously because of the thin sheet of metal that they shut inside it to cover the cracks in the door between the wrought iron. This sheet didn't fit very well; it was partly broken and shook constantly. That's when I would give up trying to go in and wake up Abboud, avoiding his grandmother's side-eyed looks and his nosy aunt's questions, telling myself, *Don't wake him up, poor thing. Let him sleep as long as possible, why wake up a child who will never find his mother at home?*

It was now our turn to give him snacks, soups, and sandwiches. The sound of music was missing in their house—no opera, no concertos, no piano, none of the things that had allowed him to transcend to another world. Abboud forgot how to play and he no longer listened to the cassettes that Anna had kept organized in a box in the little cupboard next to the piano. That cupboard was made of shiny brown cherry wood; she'd shipped it here from her country. There was a pull-down desk inside of it. It had a golden lock and she sometimes wore its ornate key on a chain around her neck. She lined up the cassettes on the upper shelf, and on the lower shelf kept many variously sized wooden boxes with mother of pearl inlay, colored crystals, and ornately decorated porcelain, and with portraits of princesses from ancient times, wearing medieval robes and elaborate feathered hats. I was always curious to know what was in those boxes, and never found an answer. Anna put her favorite sheet music in a large box under the cupboard. No one was allowed to come near this sanctuary, even Asahd. Despite his thoughtlessness, he always respected this particular rule.

They sold the piano. A buyer came from Aleppo and took it while Abboud was at school. I didn't know if the departure of the piano would mean anything to him. He'd become extremely taciturn. I was afraid that my questions would hurt him rather than relieve the pressure on him. So I declined to ask him how he felt, but I did ask him about the tapes. He wrapped them up in a red ribbon and gave them to me on my birthday. Whenever I listened to them, they transported back me to that state of reverence when I used stand behind the door of their living room, and tilt my head around it to catch a glimpse of Anna. She was brilliantly beautiful, all alone in the room, sitting at the piano in her best clothes. In the summer she wore a purple muslin dress, her chestnut blonde hair parted down the middle, wound into spirals on the side of her head, the ends tucked in at the base of her neck. It was like a crown encircling her head.

A pearl necklace hung around her pale throat. These same large pearls served as earrings.

In winter, she wore a long, black, high-necked velvet dress, embroidered with gold filigree. The sleeves of the dress were puffed up at the shoulders and gathered at the wrists, embroidered with the same golden thread. She lifted up this heavy dress to prevent it rustling against her body when she moved. The movement of her feet in their high-heeled golden shoes was refined and elegant against the piano pedals: bass, echo…

Beautiful, beautiful, Anna, sad Anna, so solemn and grand with her long, tapered, innocent fingers, the color of quince. The nipples of her small breasts showed through the tight bodice of her velvet dress. She had earrings made of one large crystal stone, refracting the light pouring in from the streetlamp outside the window. That colored beam, emanating from the crystal like a spell, stole me away along with her favorite composition, Rachmaninoff's second concerto. Once it became mine, I never shared it with anyone. I memorized the movements of this concerto, every sensory burst born from the melody, flying above the Altai Mountains, plunging down into the depth of Bohemian crystal mines. It was as if I were the one chasing after notes she played through the institutes of St. Petersburg, Moscow, and Prague. This madness overtook me after I took possession of Anna's cassettes.

Anna had hung a picture of Sergei Rachmaninoff in her special music corner in their large living room. In order to avoid any sarcastic comments or condemnations from those in a milieu where people would not have understood such veneration, she used to say it was a picture of her father—even though there were other pictures of her parents, siblings, and friends on the piano, and none of them looked anything like Rachmaninoff. It was a black and white picture of him in middle age. He appeared to have emerged from an immortal paradise with wide, alert eyes, like someone fully dedicated to the composition of music who had not yet completed his prophetic mission. He wore a classic dark suit, a striped necktie, and held a black pen between his elegant fingers. Abboud told me that Rachmaninoff's secret was in his fingers. He used to be called "big hands" when lived in America after he left Russia permanently in 1914. He was six foot-five inches tall and had large palms, which imposed complete authority over the piano. He could touch two notes thirteen keys apart on the keyboard at the same time. He locked himself away like a crystal forming in the depths of the harsh winters of the uncharted Siberian forests. All of this led people to refer to him as "a six-and-a-half-foot Russian scowl."

Abboud no longer had spellbinding stories to tell after Anna left. He went from being a levelheaded child into a witless one. He turned naughty, but he was not truly bad; his naughtiness was feigned. This was how he tried to please us, to prove that he belonged to us—with silly jokes and hostile humor that would oftentimes turn violent. His genuine reserve and spontaneous charm, both of which Anna had cultivated in him, had always distinguished him. He had previously emobodied a courteousness, passed down for hundreds of years from Czars in their summer palaces to ordinary people in the alleys and public squares of their country. The rest of the children of the slums of Raqqa enjoyed their lives, like the small, blind fish in the Euphrates. Once caught in a fisherman's net, they live by their instincts. But to me, anything Abboud did was acceptable, including the worst possible things. I always made excuses for him, defended him, and laughed with him even when he wasn't being funny at all.

✳

Though she was nearly eighty and it was starting to be risky for her to spend time alone, my grandmother liked to sleep at her own house. I would always beg her to stay with us; I wanted to discover the secrets that she was still keeping from us. Her house was just across the street from ours. An interior staircase with a black wrought iron balustrade joined the two floors. The ground floor had two living rooms, which opened out into each other, a bathroom, and a kitchen leading to a small interior garden. On the upper floor there was a small lounge with three bedrooms and a bathroom branching off of it. My grandfather built this house exactly as he wanted it and it was the nicest house in the city. It retained its ancient pride until a coalition bombing of Raqqa.

I was my grandfather's only grandchild, but nonetheless the upper floor was forbidden to me after he died. The rooms were locked, the upholstered sofa set with its small comfortable chairs was covered with musty white cloths, and the whole place was filled with the scent of mothballs. I completely abandoned this floor of the house; I even doubted that my mother had once been raised there or that I'd spent my childhood among those beds and chests of drawers. It's hard to believe that I would inherit this house one day. My grandmother's household décor changed after she started suffering from sciatica and then knee pain. She could no longer walk up the stairs so she transformed the downstairs living room into a bedroom, sitting room, dining room, and guest room. She set up a folding bed, which she pushed against the wall under the window that opened onto the neighborhood. The house's central heating system no longer worked after my grandfather died; it was very expensive and needed maintenance. So, she installed a large kerosene Aram-brand sobia heater and used it together with a fireplace to heat the open space. She also installed an electric hot water heater. The house lost some of its aristocratic grandeur because of these patchwork improvements.

My grandmother opened the windows at night to entreat the stingy summer breeze to enter. Our neighborhood was safe and no one took care to lock their doors or windows. People stayed up late, all the way until morning, in front of their houses. Every house was sure to have a faucet with a hose wrapped around it behind the door and people sprayed water on the ground in front of their houses in the evening. They put thin colorful cloth mattresses on the pavements next to low, straw stools, so we could sit on them and listen to stories about ourselves, someone we knew, or someone we didn't know. What we used to call gossip, sayings, proverbs, admonitions, or confrontations, today we call freedom of expression and transparency. One time, our gathering expanded and some people had to put their chairs in the road. A car sped by, the driver lost control and ran over Hajj Muhammad Nour who was sitting in his little chair on the street. He broke his leg, precipitating his death a few months later.

My grandmother could distinguish between the people outside her window from how they cleared their throats, coughed, or spat. Abu Mu'ataz spits quickly and violently. He gathers up all the saliva in his mouth at one time and then shoots— akh…ptooey. Abu Said who suffered from tuberculosis long ago breaks your heart: he coughs, he coughs, he says "akh" out of pain, then expels what he has managed to feebly collect, and sits on the sidewalk to rest. Abu Wadud's relentless smoker's spit is full-bodied. He collects his phlegm multiple times, "akh akh akh," and then a long, carefree ptooooooey follows. In the evenings, we would be able to make out Saree's mellow voice, as he tried to inject empty words, ancient expressions, and poetry into conversations with whoever was there. He always found a way to talk about a book he was reading. Then there was Abu Maan's booming voice, which matched his pretentious personality, and also Mrs. Khadija Maarouf, who was known for plastic house shoes which dragged all of the dirt, gravel, and tree leaves they'd picked up along the street. She'd come back home with bread and yogurt before going out again to buy vegetables. At dawn, Hajj Sharif came from a faraway neighborhood to pray at the big mosque at the edge of our area. As he walked by he called out everyone's names to wake them up for prayers. They used to ask him not to do it, but he ignored them and kept on calling out names every dawn. Then some people beat him up and he stopped coming. In the still of night, drunken voices coming from Abu Ibrahim's pub would either sing or swear or deliver speeches on politics. We could also make out the voices of young lovers who'd fallen for girls in the neighborhood. They used to come and go under the windows of their houses and pass in front of their doorways. Some of them were fancy and elegant; others were simple and reeked of cheap cologne. We might find the owner of an pickup truck, swanning around under the balconies of his beloved until one of her relatives came out threatening to kill him or to dump a bucket of water on the young lover's head.

My grandmother used to sleep while we were running around in front of the house or sitting and talking under her open window. Her bed was directly below the window, her medicines, mirror, eyebrow tweezers, a glass of water, and a pack of Kents on a low bedside table. Any passerby could have reached right in and taken them, but no one ever did. I used to listen to the children's conversations, the oldest of whom was fifteen. They talked about the neighbor's pigeons, trading marbles or "gulal" in our dialect, the models of cars people had in the Gulf, and football teams around the world. They discussed the trips one of them had taken to Damascus and Aleppo. They never talked about girls, but mostly told stories about funny things that happened to them. We never stopped laughing. Distressed, our neighbor Auntie Siham used to tell us, "Laughter betrays either tranquility or insanity!" Her sister Hasnaa would snap back at her, "Let them laugh, they're still too young to have worries." We didn't know what worries Hasnaa was talking about, except that she was over forty and still not married...!

One evening, the neighborhood was quiet earlier than usual, and my grandmother went to bed early. She called out to me through the window to please lock the door to her house. Uncovered, her thick hair flowed down to her shoulders. She usually kept it tied back with a black elastic band, and she'd been dyeing it blonde for years. She was wearing a long-sleeved, white flannel nightdress with blue stars and a round opening at the chest, held together with three blue buttons. She had a collection of nightdresses just like this, which differed only in color and pattern, polka dots or flowers instead of stars, for example. She managed to avoid being overweight by not eating much to compensate for the lack of movement resulting from her joint pains, especially in her right knee. She also suffered from chronic stomach ulcers. Despite her old age, she always stood up straight and had enormous bosoms. Her long, pale legs flowed elegantly;

they betrayed no signs of old age, and neither did her neck or lower or upper arms. The only place you could detect she was ageing was in her face, more precisely her dentures, which she complained about constantly. They were poorly made and not the proper size for her jaw, as Doctor Nabih, our neighborhood dentist, once explained to her. No one but me ever saw them at night in the glass of water on her bedside table. I always wondered how we drank from that glass afterwards, even if we had washed and sterilized it. What if someone made a mistake and drank from it after she'd taken her dentures out of it? Ever since I'd had that thought, I stopped drinking water from the glasses at my grandmother's house. If I ever got thirsty, I'd just put my hand under the faucet and sip straight from it.

It was one of Abboud's disagreeable, crazy days—shouting, swearing, pushing, and shoving, just to swat at flies. All I could do was to go along with what he was doing and laugh about it. I loved him with all my heart and love very often makes us silly or even stupid. Back then I never took a firm position against someone I loved. I might criticize them inwardly, but I didn't announce my irritation so as not to anger them. I would tell myself, "As long as it's not hurting me, why am I criticizing them? I'll lose them." But this attitude wound up hurting me a great deal; I no longer had any standards. As long as I just accepted everything, I no longer knew the difference between what I did and didn't like.

Abboud asked me to bring him one of my mother's long, transparent, flesh-colored nylon stockings. "One new stocking that's never been worn."

"Just one?"

I ran home and got it. He pulled the stocking over his head

and it made him look like a terrifying monster. It flattened his nose, pulled his eyes down, and made his mouth crooked…He was funny and frightening at the same time. It was difficult to look at his face—it was like beggars who press their faces up against coffee shop windows or on cars stopped at traffic lights. He snuck up to my grandmother's window, leaned inside, and stuck his head in, roaring like a wild beast, his legs dangling out onto the street. Standing behind him, I laughed so quietly only he could hear, and then I left. I didn't like this at all and I was really afraid. Later I despised myself: How could I have let him do that to my grandmother? But actually, if it hadn't been my grandmother, I would have found it really funny. Not long after, his father's voice boomed out from the end of the street calling him angrily. He jumped down onto the sidewalk, quickly pulled the stocking off his head, and ran toward him.

I woke up late the following morning, around nine o'clock, and couldn't find my mother. I searched for her everywhere but she wasn't in the house. I opened the front door and saw an ambulance parked on the sidewalk across the street. People were gathered around it. My grandmother had died, and they were bringing her body back from the hospital. She had passed away overnight. I stood in our doorway helplessly, all strength sapped from my body. I was paralyzed by fear. I looked for Abboud, his father, or his grandmother in the crowd, but I found no one.

We had killed my grandmother. Abboud and I had killed my grandmother. The doctor said that she'd suffered a heart attack. No doubt from fear, I told myself. We are criminals. I'm a criminal. I'd killed my grandmother—my grandmother who'd raised me, my own flesh and blood. She had called me her darling, her soulmate, the apple of her eye! My mother was stricken by a deep, endless sorrow forever after. I never forgave myself and my regret didn't diminish with time. Throughout all the years after my grandmother's passing, whenever I found my mother silent and grief stricken, I would remember my crime and collapse in on myself. When all that regret made my life feel impossible, I spent a long time pondering how I could possibly live with myself. That was when I discovered denial, which really helped me a lot. I never spoke to anyone about this, or even acknowledged it to myself. Abboud and I never ever revisited what had happened on that night, and I forgot about it.

It's as if the sins we never talk about were never committed. Rather than bringing Abboud and me closer together, however, this grave secret drove us further apart. It made me afraid and I started avoiding him. Being around him felt threatening, and fear swallowed up any other feelings I had. Fear is stronger than love!

Summer vacation ended, school started, and we went back to being buried in homework and isolated within the walls of our houses. My mother was wallowing in a strange sort of grief. She didn't cry or talk, but she increasingly stuck close to me. She started taking care of me in a way she never had before, as if she'd started to fear a new loss. Or perhaps she really did see her mother in me, as she'd shouted at me once, "You've become my mother!" She dropped me off at school in the morning and picked me back up at noon. I applied myself to my studies and I didn't think at all about Abboud. He did try hard to get me to go out into the neighborhood with him or to come over and hang out at my house like before. But I would hide in my room using my schoolwork as an excuse. I was like a hedgehog slipping into its own body and showing its spines. Abboud then went to high school in another part of town. His father dropped him off at this school every day in their white Peugeot. All the children of our generation disbanded—we'd grown up and most of us left. We'd become young men and women, after having been children merely moments before.

THE FAMILY ALBUM

The day started normally in Cologne. It was July, but in Germany a summer day felt like spring in the Middle East. The humidity of a damp dawn still permeated the air, heavy with a luminous sun. The verdant, succulent smell of trees encouraged me to wake up quickly and have my first cup of coffee on the little wooden terrace, four steps above a well-tended garden, complete with potted red and yellow rose bushes, gardenias, grape vines, and planters overflowing with strawberries, asparagus, and mint seedlings.

I didn't want to wake up Carmen, as she'd suggested before slipping into sleep the night before. I was concerned about her after everything she'd done the day before. She had fetched me from the airport in Frankfurt in her new Toyota, which meant a two-hour drive in each direction. She suffered from a bad Achilles tendon, making her ankle hurt even under normal conditions. I also preferred that she not come with me on my travels around the city today, as I wanted to start out on my own. This would save me time, because I would learn the streets from day one. I wanted to make up for time that moves so slowly back in Syria. Scarily, it even goes backwards there, especially with Daesh ruling over Raqqa. The day before, I'd tried to memorize the map, familiarizing myself with certain places, like the tram stop two blocks from the house, which would take me to the center of Cologne in less than half an hour. I'm going to have to learn how to walk again, how to talk again. I'm going to ask questions, and memorize streets, places, and history. I will no doubt spend a long time here.

I went to Schildergasse Street in downtown Cologne. Vaulted archways hang above shop entrances in the cobblestone alleys there. Ancient cities all resemble each other. This place is just like Aleppo and the elegant sidewalk cafes of Azizieh, where people sit at small tables, reading newspapers and drinking coffee. Strangers are comforted by the familiar: it grants them a modicum of confidence and safety. It's like a child far from home looking at their auntie and seeing their mother's face. Difference engenders many regrets, how long will I keep making comparisons? Comparisons are exhausting and continually remind foreigners of their foreignness. I believe that we will begin to fit in when we stop making comparisons between our homeland and our place of refuge.

I followed the signs pointing east toward Cathedral Street, wandering between elegant houses and little modern buildings, inspired by a Gothic architectural spirit. The road winding through here doesn't feel very gothic, but it's been here since the end of the twelfth century, with its prominent arches and fan vaults. Some of these architectural features date back to their earliest appearance in Europe through Arab Abbasid influence, the most prominent example of which is the Baghdad

Gate in Raqqa! All along this road, planters overflowing with daffodils, white and yellow irises, and red Adonis flammeas fill the spaces between houses and buildings. Everyone talks about the beauty of long-stemmed Dutch flowers: swan-white and sparkling golden Calla lilies, colorful tulips, and roses. Holland isn't far away; Amsterdam is only a three-hour train ride to the north.

Few cars use the main street, some people move around by bicycle, their bags and umbrellas stowed in baskets attached to the front. I wonder when I'll stop fearlessly and unashamedly scrutinizing people. My stares take no heed of others' privacy. Perhaps this is less because of my character and more because I am a foreigner. I simply want to discover what people wear here, what they carry around with them, what they do—what their daily routines are. Are the things I've read about them accurate? Will I be able to integrate? Will I be able to start my life over again as I approach my forties? Or will I remain a temporary resident, stuck on eventually returning to my country no matter how long it takes?

The two great towers of the Cologne Cathedral, Kölner Dom, loomed ahead of me in the distance; the Rhine—one of the longest and most important rivers in Europe—on my right. It flows by silently, as if it has not borne witness to the screams of the Romans and the Germanic tribes who fought on its shores for four hundred years. I experienced less pleasure than I'd expected in encountering this river. But I'd come from the Euphrates, the holiest river in the world. It is more than two times longer than the Rhine. The Euphrates runs right in front of my house!

Travel is neither a privilege nor a pleasure in the world of refugees and asylum seekers, but rather a stigma and dishonor.

Germany is full of Syrians who arrived in a variety of ways—from First Class tickets to deadly sea-borne rafts, to crawling through forests and the bush. And there is intimidation, danger, and fear every step of the way; there is just walking out in the open with no guarantees. Everyone transforms into bandits and human traffickers, each in their own way—whether on the black market or claiming to be legitimate.

When I got off the airplane, I headed out of the gate, trying to concentrate so I could figure out where I was going. A large, red-faced policewoman wearing a navy blue short-sleeved uniform, accentuating her large breasts, and a gun in a white holster at her waist, called out to me, "Ma'am, ma'am." I didn't answer and kept walking. I assumed she was speaking to someone else, as I wasn't used to someone calling me "Ma'am." Someone speaking to me in a language other than Arabic was the furthest thing from my mind. She pounced on me and grabbed my wrist. I nearly died of fright! I suddenly shrunk before her enormous body. My heart stopped and I wanted nothing more than to shut down and run back.

I gathered my composure as she scolded me for not stopping. I told her that I hadn't heard her. She asked me my reason for coming to Germany and inspected my papers. I told her that I was a student. My body had contracted from fear and my face had turned yellow, suggesting that I was a mere middle schooler rather than a woman pursuing graduate studies.

My life experience had taught me to live in the moment and always make the most of things, because you never know what might happen next—not even those secure in their homelands know this. Why should I torture myself thinking about the future or about the past? I had to be kind to myself because I have suffered so much, and I deserved better days than the harsh ones I'd been living. I deserved to have just one day in which I could lose my memory, forget history, and be another woman whom I didn't know, and who would introduce herself to me for the first time. This woman wouldn't be overwhelmed by war and loss, and she wouldn't have anyone else to worry about. In fact, I didn't have anyone to worry about, and similarly, there isn't anyone worrying about me. This is a great blessing compared to those people who left their families behind or who crossed over illegally. As for the future, I think it depends on my ability to cope and to leave my nostalgia behind. The first step is to learn the language, so I won't betray my intelligence and the skills I've already developed. Perhaps if I hadn't followed my emotions all my life, today I would be in a different situation—a well-respected historian for example. But I never finished my graduate work, because I stayed with my mother. I don't regret it; we were together until her very last moment. Every day she would say, "God bless you." Her blessings paved the way for me. I'm proud that I never left her and I'm convinced that this is what allowed me to arrive here safely. I've used this knowledge as psychological support to fight against despair, sharpen my determination, and think less about what was and what should be. So I stopped on my way to the famous cathedral in Cologne, known in German as the Kölner Dom, which I'd read so much about in my research to orient myself before leaving the country, with its holy vaults dedicated to the Virgin Mary and Saint Peter.

Icy air seared my face but became milder as the sun rose. Large riverboats all along the Rhine transport goods, behind the river are buildings of pink stone next to little tunnels topped with elegant roofs, each one allowing fewer and fewer cars to pass. I was advised to visit the chocolate museum, and the lovers' bridge where people playfully hang metal locks, ensuring eternal love. I was not too thrilled about this idea. Love stories always passed me by, even though I must confess that a difficult love story brought me here. It allowed me this safe space, which was not mine by right. It belonged to someone else. I'll stop remembering now; I'll be decisive about my nostalgia for home and calmly manage my time and desires.

In order for a strange city not to swallow you up, you have to seize it by its soul. Cologne's soul is its cathedral. I visited a shopping area nearby, full of tourist items—tickets, cameras, mobile phones, suitcases, a currency exchange booth, cheap hotels with many international flags hanging off the balconies, hot-dog stands and shawarma shops that cater to the tastes of a diverse clientele, as well as all kinds of fast food…To my left in Cathedral Square, I found a lion-shaped fountain with water pouring from its mouth. Ten steps led up to it, surrounded by gates, then a wide expanse, and other stairs led to the main gate where many people were sitting, resting, and contemplating their surroundings. Surely all these visitors stop here to organize their thoughts, which fly in all directions when faced with such majestic beauty. The square itself was paved with large gray marble stones, matching the color of the cathedral's stones.

Above your head, which will seem small no matter how big it is, you can look up and see the cathedral's two towers, looming as if they might fall and crush you. This makes you feel dizzy. You hear the lilting sounds of chants and hymns as you near the gates. There is special iron scaffolding at the top for the restoration work that has been ongoing since 1880. This is the date the cathedral was finally completed, though its foundation stone was first laid in the middle of the thirteenth century. At the top of the staircase there are trestles that tourists use to climb up. You can take in a beautiful scene up there—the Rhine is like a robust artery running through a healthy body, the city and green forests surrounding it intersect elegantly, confirming the relationship of eternal harmony between humans and nature. Before visitors enter the cathedral, they often spend a moment in the square examining the exquisite buildings housing international shops, like Chopard, Hermès, and Lacoste, as well as luxury hotels, like the Hilton, Ernst, and Dom Hotel, which take pride in overlooking one of the most magnificent cathedrals in the world. It delights their guests, but I wonder if they realize how lucky they actually are!

I went to the famous shop that gave the city its name. Cologne: the perfumed water that became known in every household around the globe. I wanted to take a picture of the cologne fountain, which was an enlarged phial, representing the familiar, old shape of the bottles like the kind my grandfather Agha used to have. I went in and tried it. The pungent aroma took me straight back to the embrace of my grandparents who both used to wear it. I tried new types—mulberry, orange, and patchouli—all with elegant blue wrappings and the number 4711 printed on them.

The manufacturer's house number was 4711. They were the Italian Farina family who worked as traders in Cologne. The perfumer Johann Maria Farina conferred this scented water on the city, which welcomed this commercial activity. I decided to buy souvenirs but then remembered that I was not a tourist—souvenirs are for people going back home. The manager of the little shop, which was no more than five meters long and two meters wide, snapped at me and told me that photography was forbidden. I was surprised that this short, round, fifty-something woman was forbidding me to take a photo. It seemed to be simply an authoritarian desire rooted in that Germanic character I had read so much about. Photos of this place fill the Internet! I had not encountered a single friendly face here in Germany except for Carmen's. This confirmed my stereotypical ideas about the country, though I knew that our modern approaches to history demand we abandon stereotypes and understand them as colonial myths.

The Roman museum talks about the history of Roman civilization in the Rhineland, making it an essential part of my future life here. Bookshops surround the museum, selling works about the history of the cathedral and the country, reproductions of the icons inside the church, indexes of books with pictures of the two towers, refrigerator magnets with the pictures of the Virgin Mary, baby Jesus, and the Cologne Bridge on them, and CDs with recordings of medieval church music by famous European choirs and international composers.

The time came for me to go inside. I rested my hand on the heavy gate, inlaid with copper and bronze squares, edged with black rims. I was greeted by a statue of the Virgin Mary holding the infant Christ. Above this statue, winged arches called for reverent kneeling. Surrounding these figures were Christ's disciples, six on the left and six on the right. European churches are sublime and majestic compared to Eastern churches, which carry an eternal sadness within them and deliver it as a rite of communion to those who frequent them along with bread and wine.

I entered the great hall, an enormously long area with lengthy, wide arcades branching off of it, leading to chapels on the right and left. Each of these chapels contain an altar and statues of the Virgin Mary, holding her son as a man after he was taken down off the cross, or with him as a child in his cradle. I paused in front of two altars and lit candles. Their candles are small and round, not long and white like our candles back home. Our candles symbolize the extent of our suffering.

I prayed to God to have forgiveness and mercy on the souls of my parents and grandparents, to protect me, and provide light to guide me through darkness. Two tears slid down my face before I could turn and walk toward the large altar at the end of the hall. I moved away from the Gothic altar and icons on the sides of the arcades to reach one specific, larger altar at the center of the church. I then returned to the smaller altars. Things you notice because of their size are not necessarily the most beautiful; the little statues of the Virgin Mary displayed more tenderness. I stood at the ancient organ that was playing Bach and took a selfie. I took another photo in front of a huge model ship, called Noah's Ark, which announced a large project to support undocumented refugees coming to Europe by sea and commemorate those who had drowned. Wandering around landed me in front of the golden box that was the very reason for the existence of this cathedral, and lent it continuing importance. The Shrine of the Three Kings is meant to contain the bones of the Magi Balthazar, Melchior, and Caspar, whose remains have endured a long journey between truth and fantasy. The Bible says that they came from the East—one from India, one from Persia, and one from Chaldea in Iraq. They left their homelands searching for the infant who would be born to change the world. They met in Jerusalem, and traveled together to Bethlehem, where they witnessed the birth of Jesus Christ. Afterwards, they returned to India and built their church. They all died at the same time and were buried there.

Two hundred years later, Helena, the mother of King Constantine, who herself was later sainted, would visit India and carry their bodies in their splendid coffins to the jewel of her kingdom—the Hagia Sophia Church in Constantinople. Four centuries later, Emperor Mauricius would move them to Milan. When Milan rose up against Roman Emperor Frederick Barbarossa in the twelfth century, the Arch-Bishop of Cologne was called upon to take charge of the city. He helped and he got his reward. His prize was the remains, which are now called "relics." To honor these relics, the cathedral under whose vaults I am now standing, was built.

I used to go to the little church in Raqqa with Abboud and his mother. The Our Lady of the Annunciation Greek Catholic Church in the Thakana neighborhood was a ten-minute walk to the west of where we lived. All of the different communities prayed there because it was a small town. All the complications of differing sects and religions seemed unnatural for Muslims and Christians alike. Like everything and everyone in Raqqa, the church itself was humble, modest, and not prone to self-importance. Seeing it, you would not necessarily realize the wealth of Christian history rooted there, dating back to the first century AD, including Byzantine cathedrals and Arab monasteries. Another reason I prayed there was because I had studied in the Noubarian Free School, known as the Armenian Orthodox Private School, established in Raqqa in 1924, where we all performed the morning prayers in Armenian. I loved rituals, the enchanting scent of incense, the priests' beautiful robes, people dressed up in their best clothes, and the sounds of hymns and organ music. I also loved the idea of being close to God, of being near the prophets and the saints whom I couldn't see in the mosque where girls couldn't enter. I loved the narrow wooden pews with straight backs. I sat right next to Abboud until the end of the mass. When everyone got up, I would keep sitting, waiting to ask my questions. I asked my mother who'd sometimes go on a visit—to lay a wreath, attend a funeral, or celebrate a holiday—or I'd ask Abboud and his mother when I'd accompany them on visits: "When will the messiah come? Why doesn't he come out from behind the altar? Where are the people who attended his birth? Where are his disciples? Where are the saints whose faces we see illuminated in icons?"

They sometimes did and other times didn't respond to my questions. My mother teased me. Abboud would smile and say, "I don't know." His mother told me, "Jesus is coming, but not today." I'd try to sneak into the back rooms, behind the theater that was the altar, since I expected to find him there. But either the deacon wouldn't let me in or someone would tell me that we had to go because we were late. We were always late and we'd always have to go, even if there wasn't anything we had to do. Whenever I start getting close to getting what I desire, everyone around me makes me feel like this. Anna would say, "He'll come one day, we just have to be patient and wait."

At Christmastime, I would always go with them to see the tree and the crèche. The tree to the right of the altar would be large and beautiful, decorated with colorful hanging ornaments—each season had a color, red and gold, or blue and silver, with shiny silver and gold ribbons attached to the ornaments as well as strings of little colored lights. They used to make the crèche out of cardboard egg cartons, where they put baby Jesus in a cradle. He would lie there peacefully with his rosy face and golden hair. His mother would be sitting next to him in her sapphire blue dress, her enigmatic face somewhere between worry and joy, docile little sheep surrounding her. I always wished that I could touch her, but I was never allowed. I used to imagine that I could suddenly shrink like a cartoon character, jump in, and join her. Inside the crèche were figures made of plaster: a shepherd wearing a *kuffieh* and carrying a stick, three men kneeling in front of the cradle. These represent the three Magi who prophesied this birth. They place their gifts in this holy infant's hands: gold, which symbolizes royalty; frankincense, which symbolizes holiness; and myrrh, a priceless perfume, which symbolizes pain.

At that time, it never once occurred to me that I would someday stand in front of their remains in Cologne, where trembling memories beat against my body in a Gothic church inhabited by the spirit of the East, the spirit of Bethlehem, the city where my grandmother came from.

My grandmother danced with Badia Masabni's spectacular and famous troupe. We knew almost nothing about this part of her life. Most of what we did know was speculation on our part rather than stories she had told us. Her stories were always filled with captivating tales from ancient history. This meant that we would then forget later events, including those that marked her childhood, about her parents and small family. We listened attentively to these tales, begging her to retell them again and again in our evening conversations. We clamored for new details she had overlooked. Indeed, she would add something new every time—the color of a dress, a ship in the port, the name of a military officer, a prince's secret lover, the weave of a sofa's fabric, sumptuous dishes. She told us that the women in her family lived behind the cloistered harem walls at the Yildiz Palace, wearing veils and full-body coverings. Their wealthy men had financed the Ottoman Sultans when they went bankrupt. They used their wealth to establish Constantinople's mosques, markets, and palaces; they armed the Ottoman military and built the Galata Bridge, which connected the two sides of Istanbul. My grandmother insisted on calling this bridge the Tsarigrad, out of respect for its Bulgarian origins. We spoke a lot about this bridge, which brings everyone together—European aristocrats walked from new neighborhoods to come in contact with dervishes and mendicants emerging right from the heart of the old city. Whenever we would visit Istanbul, she insisted on strolling through both its old and new parts. She did this with the pride of a rightful heir to the city. It was as if her ancestors, who had come two centuries ago, had built the city yesterday! I told her, "Nana, this isn't the old wooden bridge that you meant." She would respond without a care, "This one wouldn't be here today, if that one hadn't been built!"

We gathered around her on winter evenings. She would sit on her big blue armchair, which she called "strand," to describe its woven bamboo. She would cross one leg over the other, wearing a knee-length skirt made of thick black or navy blue cloth, black chiffon stockings, and a blue or beige twin set. Before she dyed it blonde, her shoulder length hair was brown. She wore beige woolen slippers in the house, and a pearl necklace always hung around her neck. Her lipstick was red. She drank café au lait out of a crystal glass, saying, "When the English Fleet came from the Dardanelles to protect the minorities of Constantinople, Russia was furious because this was a violation of the new truce it has signed with the Ottoman Empire in 1878. The war reddened the sky over the Bosphorus. Although Sultan Abdul Majid announced that he'd rather die than see one Russian soul set foot on the land of his ancestors, the British ship, *Her Majesty the Antelope*, was anchored at Yildiz Palace, reminding him that salvation was available at any moment."

The Sultan held out because of a decline in Russian supplies, but the big financiers of the Bulgarian-origin Ottoman Bogoridi family boarded a ship to Paris taking their wealth with them. I might never have been born had the ship *The Caroline* not stopped in Thessaloniki, so that seventeen-year-old Carl—a clever young broker on the Galata stock exchange—decided to follow his heart and boarded another boat to the south towards Acre. He then went to chase his beloved Vera in Bethlehem.

Vera Dadian was an Armenian girl from an old, respected family, who Sultan Abdul Majid had granted many privileges. Members of the family made his gunpowder, worked as secretaries in his treasury, and were his doctors, photographers, and decorators. He lodged with them in their luxurious villas in the coastal town of Yeshilköy, their high standing attested to by the silver font and chalice which he used to wash his hands on his visits, both of which are now preserved in the Armenian Saint Stepanos Church in Yeshilköy.

Vera had spent her previous summer in Pera, the fashionable Istanbul suburb inhabited by diplomats. Carl met her there at a dinner hosted by the British ambassador. She was petite and well proportioned, with jet-black hair twisted into a chignon at the nape of her neck and held in place with an emerald-inlaid pin in the shape of an olive branch. She was wrapped in an elegant gown, different from the heavy Victorian dresses of the area, made by the British fashion designer Charles Frederic Worth, who had opened a new high-end ladies' tailor shop in Paris in 1858. The dress was cut from black velvet cloth and edged with gold brocade, it had slightly puffy sleeves and a low-cut décolleté. It was somewhat scandalous since it was the first time a woman had dared to show the natural shape of her backside to polite Istanbul society!

From that first encounter, Carl knew that this girl, as graceful as the swans of Lake Van, would be his eternal beloved. He thought that his evenings on the Bosphorus would afford him the long trysts he was hoping for. But Vera was compelled to return quickly to Bethlehem with her brother. The Grand Vizier had sent him back with the people who would be responsible for arranging the division of the Church of the Nativity between the Catholics and the Orthodox after problems had arisen from the theft of the silver star that marked the place of Christ's birth. This is the same star inscribed with the words, "Here of the Virgin Mary, Jesus Christ was born," which was the cause of the notorious Crimean war. Marriage between the Orthodox Vera Dadian, who fell under the protection of the Russians, and Catholic Carl Voghoridi, supporter of the British-French alliance loyalists, seemed impossible. But nothing can stand in the way of youth and love. This is all the truer because war changes peoples' perceptions and attitudes, and makes everything else easier.

My grandmother became domineering when she found us hanging on to every word of her stories—Abboud, me, my aunties Safia and Maria…She'd then make us wait, while she

49

took a phone call, or asked one of us to make her a cup of coffee, or went into the kitchen to check on what she was cooking, to turn down the heat on the stove, or add an ingredient to the pot. We'd simply wait to hear what came next. Even my mother would listen closely as if she were hearing the story for the very first time.

When Carl arrived in Bethlehem, he found Vera preparing to leave once again. Her brother had died and she had no family left there. So Carl settled down with her in that little town and found work carving olive wood. He made curios out of carved wooden sculptures, selling them to the many tourists and pilgrims who flocked to the holy sites in large groups. With his business acumen developed in the burgeoning souqs of Istanbul and its stock market, Carl was able to further his trade prospects. He started exporting his holy goods to neighboring countries like Egypt. Then he found a way to send them further, to American markets. His children took over his business and expanded it after he passed away. They became known as the Olive Tree Emperors. The youngest of them, Stephen, was my grandmother's father, who married his cousin Lucy. They all lived in peace and harmony until the English came and the sparks of the revolution set the country on fire.

This is where the tales of my grandmother, who was presumably born in the early 1920s, end. My mother later learned from someone in Raqqa, who'd fought with the Arab Salvation Army in Palestine, more about Karma's untold history. She discovered that her grandmother's father Stephen, who had inherited his family's historical friendship with the British and was their soldiers' catering contractor, was shot dead by a Palestinian revolutionary fighter in 1936 at the Edison cinema in Jerusalem.

Her mother Lucy was enamored with a British officer who was a friend of the family, and one evening, she returned from his place, when the old city had been set on fire by Palestinian revolutionaries, only to find the houses in her neighborhood burned to the ground, hers with her six-year-old son still inside. She then entrusted her two daughters—my grandmother and her sister, my great-aunt—to the Cremisan monastery, and killed herself. My grandmother Karma was prone to being moody in adolescence. She was unable to imprison her nubile, statuesque body and aristocratic demeanor within the thick, limestone walls of the monastery, so she ran away. She later resurfaced on the stage at the Bannour café in Yafa, as one of the new dancers in Badia Masabni's troupe. She later traveled with them on their tours to Alexandria, Cairo, and Beirut.

Damascus-born, Lebanese-Syrian Badia Masabni breathed new life into the creative arts of the Arab word. She brought together traditional Eastern songs with the music of the tango, which she'd brought with her from Buenos Aires, where she lived for some time with her impoverished family. Earning a livelihood was difficult for Levantine families like theirs. She used to sing, dance, and act in famous Egyptian troupes like those run by George Abyad and Fouad Selim. Her most famous association was with the troupe of Najeeb Rihani; he later became her husband. When she left him, she established her own troupe, which rapidly became popular throughout the Arab East, performing widely in places like Aleppo, Damascus, Haifa, Yafa, and Nablus.

As for my grandmother's sister who stayed behind in the monastery, we know that she became a well-known translator, fluent in Turkish, English, and French, as well as Arabic. She settled in Cairo where she married a Muslim who carried a certain amount of weight in the royal palace, and one of her daughters married a relative of King Farouq.

My grandmother didn't go off in search of these lofty family ties, the cost of which would have meant reopening the pages of a book she hoped to destroy. The story of her glorious history began to fade whenever we dug deeply into the story in the East. Riding the wave of the Second World War suidted her. This war attempted to completely cleanse humanity with bloodshed, preparing new ground to sow the seeds of the future. My grandmother preserved anything from her family's ancient past that would make her world different than her surroundings. Her aristocratic nature made everything she did seem noble. Whatever did not fit this image disappeared, even her real name changed. Perhaps it was Evelyne, Eugenie, or Raymonda! But my grandfather named her Karma, because like Dalia it means grapevine, and because like a fine wine, he found her intoxicating.

Similarly, I never knew my grandfather had a name other than "the Agha." I only found out late in life that his name was Ibrahim. He owned extensive lands and orchards along the river, unparalleled by any others, except two families in the Euphrates Valley. When the wheat or cotton harvest came, the Agha collected his money in a suitcase. He added this sum to his capital. He'd use it first to renew whatever he needed to and then he would travel to Aleppo, Damascus, Beirut, and Alexandria, perhaps even Paris and Rome. He stayed in the finest hotels and had new clothes made by the most famous tailors. He and his friends would enjoy evenings in clubs, accompanied by soft, refined young women who'd come from the ends of the earth looking for work to alleviate the hunger caused by the damned war. It seemed this war wouldn't stop until humans had destroyed everything their ancestors had left them.

After my grandfather sold his season's seeds, he got in his sky blue Pontiac with the white roof, and headed for Beirut. He usually stayed in the Saint-George hotel in Ain Mreisseh where King Farouq stayed, as did King Hussein, Brigitte Bardot, and Umm Kulthum. He would spend his evenings in the Kaokab al-Sharq café in Martyr's Square. That's where he met my grandmother.

Karma was third from the right, dancing to the music of the song: "Oh Kawini, your passion melts and burns me/ and there is bad blood between you and me." This was before Badia appeared on stage to perform her dance with castanets, riffing, "Oh Kawini, why are you listening to people who are just jealous?"

Karma gracefully extended a youthful, feminine leg, and her alabaster thigh peeked out from under transparent, billowing white layers, draped over another layer of brightly colored satin covering her breasts, attached to the muslin sleeves of her dress. She wore a small white turban with silver chains hanging from it, undulating against her jet-black hair. She could have seduced even a monk with her gray eyes and wide smile, which effortlessly revealed her straight white natural teeth, which had no veneers or laser treatments.

She shone in this splendor like an Eid decoration. She was so vibrant that the Agha couldn't turn his gaze away from her, even when Badia appeared. She danced flirtatiously and confidently. When she sang along with the tune, her soul was suspended somewhere far from the stage at Kaokab al-Sharq, no one could guess exactly where. When the dancers swapped places, Karma approached the table where my progenitor and his friends were sitting. The Agha then took a white rose out of the lapel of the jacket of his evening companion, Joseph Chamoun, the largest wheat exporter in Beirut. He threw it at her. His throw however was so strong and unexpected that the rose's short green stem poked right into her eye. She stopped dancing to deal with her traumatic injury, and withdrew into the stage curtains. The Agha quickly followed her; no one could prevent him. Complex destinies can arise from a simple smile, skirmish, or even tossing a rose.

My grandmother left that noisy, colorful world of her own free will, getting into the sky blue Pontiac and driving toward Raqqa—a far-away little town shrouded in pitch-black obscurity. Nana Karma said, "You can own a house anywhere in the world, but it's rare for a person to possess a bit of an eternal river." She would close her eyes and revel in the intensely blissful feeling that she'd achieved—something equal to her teacher and icon, Badia Masabni, who owned property on the Nile. Karma found in that enigmatic bachelor, Agha Ibrahim, the characteristics that she had not found since the loss of her father: wealth, noble origins, good looks, kindness, and affection.

He had a certain scent that could never be erased from her memory—the scent of tobacco mixed with a woody perfume, sandalwood or pine. It carried the aroma of unpretentious masculinity. It worked on Karma, who had run away from the monastery searching for freedom. She fell deeply in love. She lived with him happily because she'd found everything she wanted—culture, wealth, confidence, and to be the lady of the house who could reclaim her missing aristocratic side. My grandfather protected her from the shame that disgraces dancers and circulates in small towns like Raqqa, told as a series of amusing, entertaining tales. He believed in her passion for her art, and didn't hesitate to travel with her wherever there were seasonal dance and musical festivals. They spent their time living a joyful life of leisure, distant from stagnant Raqqa and its limited pleasures. He took her with him to roam the parks and cafeterias of the cities of the East. He lavished her with costly gifts including a mink coat and pearl necklace, which remain in my closet to this day.

Karma spent a long time in Aleppo, where the Agha owned a luxury apartment in the Al-Jamaliya district, which was modern at the time. They stayed out late at the Montana, the Aleppo Club, and Luna Park. They watched first-run films at the Ramita, Amir, and Zahraa Cinemas. Then she went back to Raqqa with her new skirts and dresses, which she'd had made at Madame Atta's shop in Azizieh or at Zadik's workshop on Al-Telel Street, and gourmet foods like sujouk, salami, basterma, cheeses, and cured fish from Sirop's, Automatic, and Victoria Kalbaks. It is true that she left art world behind. But she lived a life of pleasure and riches with my grandfather that rivaled that of movie stars. I loved that I really resembled her and that my story was like hers—not my mother's. No one wants to repeat her own mother's story!

Karma never opened up about her past to anyone. It was as if she'd never belonged to the world of the stage, she hadn't walked the corridors of passion and pleasure, she'd never ever worn shiny dance costumes that increased the delicious temptation of her body, and she hadn't balanced candlesticks on her head. But this ancient memory no doubt will one day overflow. Many secrets become permissible to tell under the weight of time. When I was around the age of thirteen, and Karma felt that my features had begun to mature and my countenance had changed, she started telling me the reasons for my mother's failure to attract my father's masculine energy. She used to try in good faith to help me avoid falling into the same trap with my future husband. I disliked this kind of talk, which offended my spiritual sanctity, and crushed my feeling of youthfulness. But she healed me in her own way when she gestured at her history in which she played the role of a seductress who captivated many men before settling down with the Agha, becoming the lady of his well-preserved house. I took her photos out of their oxidized silver box with its blue velvet lining, and though she got bored retelling the story of every photo, I never ever did.

Tiny triangles of thin white plastic attached these black-and-white photos to the detached pages of the photo album. My grandmother looked like Carol Lombard, Viviane Leigh, Asmahan, Leila Mourad, or Madiha Yousri. For me they were all so beautiful, it was difficult to distinguish between them. Their bodies were perfectly symmetrical—their femininity marked with tight-waisted décolleté dresses, which showed off their ample hips narrowing once again under the knees. Or the ball gown might remain flared with a tulle skirt, so as to increase its length and make a barrier between them and the audience, so they could remain in the realm of fairy tale princesses. I asked her what colors the dresses in these black-and-white pictures were, and she responded, "Burgundy, black, purple…"

Karma always wore a pearl necklace or a diamond brooch. Her hair was pressed into a retro style or a chignon and she sometimes wore a black lace veil over half her face, attached to the bottom of a tiny hat with a feather or roses on it. She drew lines of kohl atop her eyelids and used dark lipstick. I couldn't be precise about the color, when I asked her she said, "Usually burgundy, it's my favorite color." I said, "To hell with black and white! They blur the memory of colors and standardize every-one's faces, though they do make them beautiful."

Generally I convinced myself that this woman before me—with her crooked teeth, veins bulging out on the back of her hands, wrinkled face, and lumpy body—was the same one in the picture. She was solid, tight, and compact. It was only her bosom that remained the same against the ravages of time. It was well preserved, demanding attention. She used to tell her girlfriends that this was because of the nightly massages that the Agha gave her. My grandfather faced a daily challenge with his own imagination, which would tease him, reminding him of the worlds of pleasure his wife must have enjoyed with other men. He asked about where he stood in relation to these other, possibly imaginary, relationships and the relative amount of pleasure Karma derived from them compared to what she had with him. This used to get him into a terribly excruciating state of arousal on the one hand, and on the other, sink him into feelings of inadequacy and a deep depression. He managed to cope by reminding himself that, in the end, he never came down with syphilis, a disease known to be transmitted by women who'd had multiple relationships. It is perhaps this lack of a clear truth that tethered the Agha to Karma up to the very last day of his life. She used to say, "A woman must always keep a secret chamber in her heart that is never opened to anyone. The darker this chamber remains, the more mysterious and difficult to attain she becomes."

Karma began to tell the stories of the Casino after my uncle Najeeb died. She made sure that my mother couldn't hear her. If my mother ever heard fragments of this kind of conversation from me, she would scold me into silence, saying my grandmother had gone senile after losing her son, and we had to deal with her like a small child with an overactive imagination! Karma talked about beautiful women—everyone was beautiful in her stories—and the wealthy, elegant men who fell in love with them. It was all burning passion, scented envelopes, lavish gifts, furtive meetings at the edges of rooms furnished in red velvet with gold-framed pictures, and bouquets of roses proffered by pleading, groveling suitors. She spoke to me of caustic jealousies, feminine tableaux, long, thin cigarettes held between bejeweled fingers with bright red manicures, and the private VIP room that Katy frequented. Katy's real name was Zahra. She would always be naked except for her bikini and black satin, high-heeled shoes, with laces halfway up her calves, and a black bib tied by a ribbon around her neck. Katy served champagne at the Casino to lucky, wealthy men. She had an ample, full-figured body, and cleverly concealed her smallpox scars by tying pieces of black velvet around her leg, studded with shiny crystal beads. Katy sometimes followed along with Badia's monologues and found herself even more beautiful and stunning! Nana Karma would then sometimes sing funny songs in a low voice that only she and I could hear:

Jealousy, the flames of jealousy
        they burn everything around them
When you feed jealousy
        you plant confusion among women

I interrupted because she had captivated me with the scene she'd just described, "A black bib Nana?"

"Yes, yes, a black bib."

With every session, Karma would bring me closer and closer to her memories. We even managed to arrive at the fact that the pictures hanging on the walls weren't actually of the pashas in her family, but fictional ones done by a Damascene painter—the kind who sold history to people for a few dozen liras. It turns out my grandfather bought them to show the people of Raqqa, who are obsessed with stories of old-stock, noble origins, that his in-laws had an ancient dignity. It was actually true in reality, but the evidence had been lost through wars and migration. I didn't notice the signs of dementia in Karma's mind or her behavior, which my mother had, until the very end of her life. She simply became more irritable and impassive than before, and also more silent. She engaged less in things around her, the opposite of the women who increase their busybody ways as they age. She wore the same clothes until she died: a black maxi skirt, a black blouse with silver and gold threading, and a big black rose-shaped pin at her chest. She also wore a ring with a large rectangular garnet, held in a platinum casing. I later discovered that the stone itself was made of plastic and the ring of cheap metal; she'd bought it from a street vendor in front of Zechariah's tomb in Aleppo's Al-Madina Souq, where she'd gone to tie two green ribbons at his shrine and had given some money to one of his followers as part of a pilgrimage.

Often her clothes smelled of mothballs and lemon cologne, or an old perfume that had been around so long it fermented and no longer smelled of anything, though no doubt it was once very posh. What mattered was that this mix of aromas was the scent of my grandmother: a mix of pleasure and ancient pride, alienation and concealment, as well as profound sadness. Her black clothes were an expression of the theory she used to espouse that no matter how cheap, a very dark black can conceal any imperfection. Despite the conflicting feelings I had about her—compassion, admiration, and resentment about her past, which made my mother a victim of depression and shame—she was the only person who showed me how to feel life's beauty. She was able to take me beyond the prison bars of this small town, with its harsh customs that everyone secretly violates, but only the unlucky get caught.

When he went to Palestine as a volunteer fighter, our neighbor Issa inquired into my grandmother's origins in Bethlehem, in the way people from Raqqa often do, searching for relatives, acquaintances, and people they know in faraway places. He told some of his family members what he'd learned about her family's history when he was there. Drops of what he said trickled down, leaving us between certainty and doubt. When Issa was martyred, the issue of Karma's origins went away. But when my mother was growing up and going to school, she constantly heard people defaming and insulting her mother. She started wondering about that story of the lake, but no one could answer her questions. She was haunted her entire life by the bitter truth that she was trapped forever in a society that celebrates tradition, reputation, manners, and morals.

My grandmother gave birth to my mother and called her Najwa. Then about twelve years later she gave birth to my uncle Najeeb. She named him after Najeeb Rihani, who was a difficult figure for her because he was the husband of her teacher, who had been her protector and benefactor. Neither talent nor time could help her become what she wanted to be, and perhaps she also feared this. She had achieved what she desired and lost—a secure life with a respected man who was able to provide her with family stability.

My grandmother didn't care about customs or rituals since no rites were able to make her feel attached to her surroundings or allowed her to belong. Only her husband and children did that. Despite this, she raised her children in a way that contradicted the relationship she herself had with the place. She was very conservative and serious with them, like any traditional woman who had grown up in this area, including the few women who we might consider the exceptions. These include my grandmother, and her companions Maria and Safia, both of whom I'd wait for with Karma impatiently, so I could hear about their adventures. I found life with them simpler and freer than the way in which my mother had planned out mine.

We could say that Auntie Maria was the bad apple that would spoil the whole barrel! She used to sit on the low mattress on the ground next to the heater, her large body taking up all the space in the room. My grandmother would sit next to her on the green velvet sofa, embroidered with big beige flowers. Soon after, Auntie Safia always used to join the gathering. They would take their shoes off at the door before walking on the Persian carpets. Maria's black leather shoes were so stretched out that they were flat. Safia always wore new black plastic shoes. Karma made her friends an Arabic style seating arrangement on the floor, because that is what they were used to—they didn't like sitting on chairs. She refused for years to let them sit on the floor, saying that whoever came into a house had to follow its traditions. They used to say they were uncomfortable, and when they stopped coming my grandmother gave in and designed them a traditional seating area. With the passing of time, Karma gave up on her radical theories and she discovered many things were not important at all.

Auntie Maria's pale skin was saturated with red freckles, and no one could believe that her copper colored hair, parted down the middle, showed no signs of white roots as she aged, even into her late fifties. She wore one thick long braid down her back, tied back with a black elastic band. She stood about five feet-nine inches tall and weighed over two hundred pounds. She used to sit cross-legged like the Buddha. She was able to get into this position easily, undisturbed by her fat, and sit straight-backed, her large breasts braless. At the height of winter she used to dress simply in a long navy blue cotton gown with white polka dots with a brown woolen shawl draped around her shoulders. Her cleavage would poke through the opening of her dress, a dark labyrinth against white skin, resembling a valley leading to some distant paradise. She cleaned the spinach, sorted the beans, or peeled the onions. When she prepared onions, she put the peels on her head, before chopping the onion into small pieces. Once I asked her, "Why do you put onion peels on your head Auntie?"

"So I won't cry. They say that if a woman cries when she chops onions it means she's afraid of her in-laws!"

Auntie Maria was free both in how she spoke and how she moved. Nothing impeded her; she wasn't embarrassed to speak about anything. Whenever people asked her how old she was, she'd look in their face defiantly and say that she was still menstruating. She'd balance her long, Kent cigarettes on the edges of her lips when she was using her hands to do something else, taking calm drags—one eye open, the other closed—even when very excited. She stretched her long, full legs out in front of her, showing a bit of pink flesh that peeked out above her short, brown, nylon stockings. Everyone, old or young, was surprised by her daring way of speaking. She spoke about her memories, her intimate relations with her husband, and she called things by their names: penises, sexual desire, positions for intercourse…

She was married at sixteen after falling in love with one of her cousins and gave birth to ten children, seven boys and three girls. She used to meet her husband, Amo Hadi, under the bridge. At that time he had a white GMC pickup truck. They drank tea together on a damp stone bench alongside the Euphrates. He caressed her body, drowning in her soft skin. She said that they were friends, and they lived together a long time—more than forty years. She grew up more at his house than she did with her own parents. He owned agricultural lands in Raqqa and took road construction projects in Latakia with an important contractor there, so he spent most of his time traveling.

She took the children to the seaside at Latakia, but rarely, as it meant more work and more responsibilities; it was a big job to move around with such a large family. She told me, "In Latakia, he met a girl who was singing in a restaurant where he used to spend evenings with his business partners. She was a rising star and later became quite well known. She would always sing during the breaks in football matches that were televised live on the state TV channel. He started having an affair with her and showering her with money."

"What did you do?"

"Nothing. I let him tell me about it and laughed with him about it."

"How could you?"

"It's normal. Men do this. It was a long time ago, the children were little. I was busy with things other than him. When he returned, nothing had changed. He enjoyed her body a little and that was the end of it."

My mouth gaped with an affected smile, as I asked her to go into more detail. But she stopped, drying her onion tears with the edge of her shawl.

Auntie Maria accepted her husband's relationship with another woman's body as simply as that. She never used any dramatic words, like betrayal or cheating, to describe it. I thought that she must be much more beautiful than that tiresome singer. She sat like a goddess, there was nothing more luscious than her substantial breasts, and she was good-humored, dragging on her cigarettes. Despite all this, she accepted what was happening to her and mocked him.

So then why couldn't my mother accept what my father did? Why couldn't she let things simply pass, and we all could have avoided the incomplete life we've been living? In short, it's because she couldn't truly love and so she couldn't truly forgive, whereas Maria loved Hadi so she could forgive him. She could use her personal philosophy to transform his sins into something exciting. She said that it aroused her when he was with other women, and that she felt triumphant when he returned to her.

Auntie Safia laughed calmly, taking her turn in sharing memories of being in love. This was her love for her husband Hassan, of course, who was also her cousin. He was around fifteen years older than her though. Auntie Safia was low on both beauty and charm. She was tall and thin, with a long hooked nose and pale skin. When she uncovered her legs to show my grandmother her newly protruding varicose veins or to complain about some kind of redness or swelling because of fluid retention, her translucent skin would stun us into silence. We all looked at her flowing legs expertly, even Auntie Maria wouldn't hesitate from making a forgiving comment every time she glimpsed them: "Her legs distracted her husband from the hideous state of her face."

Auntie Safia wore traditional Arab clothes in two layers. The first layer, called a "qasira," was usually red or navy blue, with circles, flowers, or polka dots. She wore a second layer over it, a loose black cloak in a lacy fabric so the color of the dress underneath showed through. She cinched her dresses at the waist with a man's leather belt and combed her hair into two thin braids hanging down at the sides of her face, topped with a scarf and a headband. She was pleased that her husband hadn't traded her in for another wife and that she was the lady of the house. Her daughters were unhappy with their marriages, and she encouraged her sons to take more than one wife, showing some of the devil in her! As she used to tell it, she had panicked and refused her husband on her wedding night. She said that his penis was frightening and hung down to his knees, so she slipped out from between his arms. He grabbed the cane he used to carry and beat her with it. Then he left to go out with his friends, leaving her all alone sobbing out of confusion, contradictory feelings, and how strange everything seemed.

Just before the wedding, her sisters had made her clean the large courtyard of the house she was leaving. It was a big area with many rooms around it. She cleaned it, bathed, then put on her clothes and went to the wedding at the groom's place, just across from their house. She walked over alone without anyone accompanying her or singing for her, and without any member of the groom's family coming to get her. And then she was beaten like this without any warning? When her husband came back from his evening out, he cornered her and penetrated her. She stifled her cries and tried to ignore her unjust suffering. She was proud that she had finished fifth grade, since that was the highest grade in her primary school—if someone wanted to continue studying they had to transfer to the school in Deir ez-Zor. She had repeated the fifth grade three times, and stood in front of the French High Commissioner General Catroux, making his acquaintance at a reception in his honor and delivering a short speech in French demanding Syrian independence.

We used to fear Uncle Hassan. He would point his bamboo cane at us, while walking along the road, and we knew that he carried a pistol under the vest he wore over his galabiya. After hearing about this incident, I could no longer resist looking at Uncle Hassan's body whenever he passed through the neighborhood. I tried to spot the scary thing that had so panicked Auntie Safia. I wanted to talk to Abboud about all that strangeness, but of course I couldn't broach such a taboo topic. Only kids living on the streets could talk about such things. In fact, the idea of what this meant was not at all clear to me, perhaps it wouldn't have been to any girl of my age. I would never have even encountered such a conversation to this day had my grandmother and her girlfriends been more conservative in what they used to say in front of me.

My grandmother called Auntie Safia, Sophie. Once Auntie Safia turned to me and said, using a sarcastic tone, somewhere between my grandmother's European-style coquettishness and her own true Bedouin personality, "Do you see Lulu? At the end of the day, I became Sophie!" Laughing at my grandmother's insistence on acting European, "Sophie? If Hajj Hassan could hear you, he'd get a real kick out of it!" She'd laugh and we'd all laugh with her.

My grandmother listened to her girlfriends' stories thankful that she was the happiest, most beloved, and best taken care of. Her husband had never fallen in love with another woman, he never spoke a word of anger to her, and he never laid his hands on her except to caress or stroke her body.

Karma knew that to keep a man a woman should act like a lady by day and respond to him like a concubine by night. She really did this, and she tried to transmit her expertise in the arts of femininity to us however she could. She failed with my mother of course, and to this day, my grandmother's teachings have yet to succeed in influencing the external factors beyond my control that have left me unmarried.

This is how the conversations in my grandmother Karma's living room went, as the teapot, which rested on the big black stove, burbled and bubbled with its eternally boiling water.

I learned to walk late. I'd reached almost two years of age and God still hadn't granted my feet this ability. I could stand unsteadily, holding onto the edge of a low table or chair, but I didn't trust holding anyone's hand. This is why one day they bound my feet with a rope and, with all the neighborhood children trailing behind, my uncle Najeeb picked me up and put me in front of the door to the big mosque during Friday prayers. The first person who left the prayers lifted me up and started quietly reciting Qur'anic verses, while everyone looked on anxiously. He then loosened my shackle with his right hand and I started taking jubilant steps—one step, two steps, and then three. Afterwards I kept on walking, waving my arms cheerfully, laughing in the way I still do when I manage to free myself from whatever is restraining me.

Soon after I started taking people by surprise. I would exit through any open door I found myself behind. Passersby would find me on the sidewalk, or in the middle of the street where cars or vegetable sellers' donkey-drawn carts had come to a complete stop. Someone from one of the shops would have to run out to get me and take me back home. Or a bicycle rider would stop and ask the people nearby what family this baby belonged to. As I grew a little older, the neighborhood women started watching out for me while they were sweeping the sidewalks. Whenever they'd gathered dirt and leaves from the trees and swept them in little piles with their soft hay brooms, I would run over as quick as a rocket and mess them all up with my little feet before they could catch up to me and threaten to whack me.

Despite all this, my mother discovered when I was about seven years old that I still didn't know how to walk properly. I ran and jumped very well, but I walked "crooked" as they used to say. Sometimes I walked like a thug, other times a barbarian. My gait had no feminine sway. My grandmother agreed with my mother's observations. I was really puzzled about how to choose an appropriate way to walk. I was like someone who couldn't decide on a style of dress, or a signature look. As soon as I left the house I would begin preparing how I wanted my walk to appear—after having spent hours choosing my clothes, which always used to result in a solid-colored t-shirt and jeans. Once I relaxed my whole body, I began moving, swinging my hand at my side. When I'd reach the end of the street, I'd have to return along the same sidewalk. That's when I would straighten up and hold my hands together in front of my body. Another day I might pull my torso upright and push my bum out behind me. This is how one of my uncle's friend's girlfriend walked.

I was jealous of her and liked imitating her. I fell into a great confusion because of my anxious walk, which became a major issue in my life. What made it worse was the audience of people sitting in front of their houses along the street—Abu Abdullah, Umm Riad, Umm Farhan, and Hajjeh Aamina…From the time of evening prayers at around six PM, after the neighborhood streets were doused with water, the old folks would begin their daily ritual of coming outside and sitting in front of their houses. They would put down their little mats that were specially designed for the area in front of the door or take out their small, low straw or plastic chairs. In reality, they were using the road to escape the walls of their houses, which had stored up the heat of the scorching summer sun. They left all their windows and doors open to catch some overnight moisture so that they might perhaps sleep better.

When I passed in front of Umm Riad's house, I found her sitting on the raised threshold of her doorway watching me in her long Arab-style dress, head covered, passing her tongue over the little but prominent mole which rested atop her left upper lip. She narrowed her small, brown eyes to be able to see me better. I smiled at her and confidently said, "Hello!" She responded, "Hello to you!" inspecting me from top to bottom, with intense seriousness. It was as if she were seeing me for the first time. I went back two minutes later and passed in front of her, heading the other way. I thought about whether or not I should greet her again. I decided to do it, but with less confidence, and she responded the same way. I went to play with the other children, and forgot about how I was walking. When my mother called out to me to come back home or sent someone to get me because it had gotten late, I would once again think about my gait and stance and whether or not I should say hello or not for the third or fourth time. Umm Riad used to sit in front of her house every day questioning my social and physical movements—to this day I'm still searching for their final version.

My awkwardness lasted for many months, so I sought out a radical solution and asked my grandmother, "Do I say hello every time or no?" She told me, "Do as you like, it's not that important. Greeting people never hurt anyone." My mother said, "Saying hello too many times is like saying it too few times— once a day is enough." My mother gave me a useful and efficient solution that relaxed me. My grandmother's indulgence on the other hand increased my confusion. She made me think about all of my responsibilities. My mother, who herself had a supple, elegant gait and was easily able to adapt her psychological state, decided to teach me how to walk again. She had to get me "into the rhythm" as she put it. I believed that she wanted to busy herself by taking care of me so as not to take on the fact that her constant problems with my father might be the cause of me lagging behind. I was supposed to be as free and happy as she had been in her childhood.

She started waking me up at five in the morning to put on my exercise clothes. My mother's outfit was hanging behind the door of the bedroom where we'd been sleeping together since my father had started sleeping in another room. It was dark blue with an orange stripe across the chest. I would wear a blue cotton t-shirt and black leggings that showed off my short, stubby legs. My mother drank her coffee and a glass of water, and told me to drink water as well. Then we'd leave the house quietly as if not to awake anyone as we were sneaking out. We closed the iron door carefully, to avoid its usual clicking sound, and exited joyfully—emerging from bad dreams into a place where morning had begun to illuminate the sleeping city. A few minutes later, we had left behind our crowded neighborhood for a large, wide street, which led us to the old bridge. On Euphrates Club Street, everything changed.

The air became moist and the horizon a deep, endless blue. All signs of buildings or architecture disappeared and we could see the water. We would leave behind the statue of Ishtar, which seemed to have been crafted by a blind sculptor, on our left at the entrance to the bridge. We would walk steadily down the narrow sidewalk where it met another sidewalk, with a walkway of about sixteen feet between them. No one was there but my mother and me. One or two half-full trucks would pass by, carrying vegetables from farms near the bridge, but they didn't interrupt our privacy even when I'd wave at the driver. With Mama I always used to feel that there was no world beyond our interlocked hands, but then I would often experience a sudden anxiety about our future. I feared that my father might have died while we were away, leaving us there together on the bridge. But I would quickly banish the idea from my mind, and lose myself in the scene that we were walking toward.

It took ten minutes to cross the bridge. I would touch the permanent iron barrels installed all along the bridge's embankment to pull the water. She would sigh with a mottled voice, "Nooooo Luluuuuu." We'd turn right and walked down to the river that is at its purest and calmest when the first sunbeams hit its surface. When the birds wake there is a quiet bliss, and that's when we'd begin our rhythm exercises. We had to walk and that was it. We could leave our thoughts someplace else.

I can see it as if I'm there now: Mama says, "Look ahead,

pull your shoulders back, and invite your body to choose its position freely. Imagine we are walking towards the future!"

"How?"

"In our thoughts, we are walking towards whatever is behind the hill. There's beautiful land beyond there."

"I know there are Roma people who hang swings on tree branches," I quickly confess to her that I'd been there with Farhan and she ignores me.

"There is a university, an airport, Aleppo, Damascus, America, France…"

"And Monte Carlo?"

I meant the radio station that I loved to listen to, but its frequency unfortunately didn't reach Raqqa. For me it was a way to travel to amazing places.

"Yes, and Monte Carlo too"

The duck begins its morning swim, the pump station monitors breathe in their tin rooms, dew drops still glimmering on their roofs. Green pierces the surface of the water creating little grassy islands. After crossing the bridge we enter the Kasra region, where peasants now own their own homes and lands to cultivate fruit trees. Their inviting, spacious homes, some of which are surrounded by high stone walls, are located right in the middle of the orchards. There are other houses walled in by rose bushes: orange, yellow, red, white, and damask roses look like jewels hanging above a carpet of green plants concealing any evidence of manufactured building materials—as if people were living in houses made of flowers and trees. I'm enchanted and walk over to pick a rose or two. Mama doesn't stop me like she would have if we were in the city. Perhaps it is because there is so much abundance here! Little crab apples hang from the tree outside the walls. We don't need much effort to pick them, and there are peaches and apricots too. We take them with no guilt, as if this abundance allows us to feel collective ownership. When we pass by fields of sunflowers, Mama says, "Look Lulu, how they turn toward the sun and follow its movements from sunrise to sunset."

"Every day?"

"Every day, forever."

"Could they decide one day not to turn?"

"No."

"Don't they get tired?"

"This is where we get the sunflower seeds you like so much, as well as our cooking oil."

"From here?"

"Yes, from here."

She takes me by the hand and we walk through the sunflower field together. She grabs the nearest one and puts the palm of her hand on the flower, stroking it two or three times. Touching the fresh, tooth-like seeds excites me, "Mama, why does the water look blue from a distance but becomes green when you get closer?"

"Because of the reflection."

Sometimes I avoid hearing the answer, because it is enough simply to pose the questions, demonstrating my interest and maturity.

She always tried to push me towards the things around me, just like she wanted to break free of the rigid framework that she'd imposed on herself. She'd ask me to touch blades of grass and distinguish how they felt different from each other, to observe the colors of the sky and phases of the moon. She wanted me to observe a hesitant bee trying to approach a flower. She wanted to introduce me to everything before someone else beat her to it. She would explain a Qur'anic verse that we'd heard on the radio to me, or would say, "Lulu, come here so we can race against our shadows…" She listened to Umm Kulthum every evening, keeping my grandmother company. Whenever she heard the song "Al-Atlal" she'd call out to me, "Lulu, listen, listen to this beautiful image, 'and we ran, appearing ahead of our own shadows'! How can a person appear ahead of their own shadow, Lulu? Shadows follow us and that's it."

I knew what she meant; she wanted to say that only love could make us appear ahead of our shadows.

My mother went back to work feeling active after these summer morning excursions of ours. I went to the library with her and headed for the large children's section, while she would remain behind her desk in the adult section. Sometimes I would stay with my grandmother and run around the neighborhood or sit in front of the door of her house waiting for someone to pass by who I could play with. Or else I would help her sort and clean the okra and beans, or pick through the lentils for stones, while she sat in the garden getting ready to cook, with both the street and me within her range of vision.

My father used to wake up at around eight AM and drink his coffee. Then he would eat a light breakfast, which my mother had put on the table for him before she'd left the house: a cup of tea, rose petal jam, and white cheese. Sometimes she would make him two hardboiled eggs, served with a tomato slice, which he sprinkled liberally with freshly ground black pepper. He would take his daily shower and put on his clothes. He passed by my grandmother's house next. She'd have put a big coffee pot, red or green with white polka dots, on the stove, with a bottle of Bukkin mineral water in front of her. Then she would begin her morning. She would pick a sprig of jasmine or gardenia from her little bushes, and put it in a tiny tea glass. She'd be wearing house clothes: a sky blue cotton dress, cinched together at the waist by a belt, revealing her shiny yellow legs, with a few reddish hairs poking out. Her toenails were always painted orange or red, her house slippers white like a bride's. Her hair would be pulled back in a bun, and she wore her pearl solitaire necklace, light lipstick, and Nina Ricci perfume every day. She would light a cigarette and listen to Nour El-Houda on the gramophone, crying out, "Neighbor in the valley, I feel joy and memories of you come back like dreams!" She used to talk about how this song gave rise to a relationship between the Arabic teacher in Bethlehem and one of her colleagues. My grandfather the Agha guessed it was her and not her colleague who had a love story with the teacher. He used to sit and take his coffee in his dark red robe wearing his midnight blue striped pajamas under it. My grandfather brought everything he needed back from Beirut with him, even his underwear. After this he would take a tour around his flowers, and eat some cheese and honey on whole wheat bread, and perhaps a piece of fruit. Then he would put on his suit jacket without a tie. His driver would come and he'd ride in the back seat so he could pass by his tenants and his shops, including the petrol station that he owned on the main road leading to Aleppo. I went with him sometimes and hung out with the workers there. They would buy me sodas and Derby potato chips, and pick me plums from the tree next to the gas station. My grandfather came back at midday to sit in a café and all the people who brought him news of what was going on would gather around his table, drinking tea and coffee on his tab. They would reminisce about the good old days. They agreed with him about everything, so long as he paid their bills, fed them, and cared for their families.

I loved my grandmother's stories about Jerusalem and Bethlehem. She talked about the German Emperor, William the Second's, visit to Jerusalem coming back from Istanbul. She said, "One of the city's notables received him and prepared a great feast. The villa was filled with lit candles so that anyone looking would have thought it was daytime in the depth of night. This man had a young daughter who was very beautiful and intelligent and her father wrote a little poem for her to recite as a welcome to the Emperor. The little girl looked like an angel and stood in her splendid silk gown with her long blond hair, captivating everyone with her recitation. The Emperor approached her and gifted her a valuable necklace. Then she withdrew and walked among the still blazing candles. Her hair and dress brushed against one of them and it immediately engulfed her in flames. She died a few days later. Her father didn't tell the emperor about the tragedy caused by his hospitality."

My father would leave Raqqa to work on establishing connections in state-run offices. Every season there was a helper he would give some money to, or a secretary he bought gifts for that were equivalent to her favors to him: leather purses, gold rings, perfumes…Or even organizing for her to travel to Aleppo or Damascus in his Cadillac, where he'd take her out to dinner at the Siyahi Hotel's restaurant, or at the Pasha or Strand. This is how he solved dilemmas at work and enjoyed his life, leaving my mother to wander around among her books, jewelry, and fancy lingerie, him being the only thing missing.

It took three months of daily trips with my mother for me

to learn how to walk properly. I'd become graceful, my gait confident. I did not choose a particular way of walking—it chose my body. I'd been liberated from the evil forces that had been constraining me and I felt I could take on the entire world with my toned, athletic legs.

My mother and I kept on walking across the bridge every morning, while everyone else was asleep. No one ever did this before the afternoon prayer time. But by then the duck would have left, and the birds would have grown weary of looking for fish. I totally stopped thinking about how I walked. I greeted everyone I passed or at least exchanged smiles, sometimes looking beyond them straight ahead at a place that existed only in my own mind. That's when I discovered that we sometimes survive things by ignoring them. Our daily exercise stopped at the beginning of September when the seasons began to change. We had to start getting in the mood for school, the colder weather to come, and the seasonal rains that would pour down upon us.

THE SCENT OF ABANDONMENT

For a long time I believed that my mother was one of the ten most beautiful women in the entire world. This made me feel even more confused about the fissures between her and my father that seemed to deepen each day. Neither of them succeeded in repairing them or even plastering over their cracks. Mama was always as elegant as if she'd just stepped out of one of her fashion magazines. When she went out in the evening, she would wear dresses made of muslin, a fabric that Anna recommended she buy in Czechoslovakia, adorned with her three-strand pearl necklace. Otherwise she might wear her diamond choker, which she'd received as an engagement gift. In any case, she would drape her shoulders with her brown fur stole and I would always wonder at how it never fell off even when she moved her arms. When Mama put on her pajamas I would study that alabaster space between her neck and the top of her breasts. It mesmerized me. I loved to bury my head there, wondering about what dark things obscured this dazzling beauty from my father. When she went to work, her demeanor prompted even her relatives and acquaintances who also worked there to treat her as seriously and formally as they would a stranger. She would wear her suede coat, black or brown winter boots, and put her rings with precious stones on her fingers and thumb, finishing off with Yardely lotion and Chanel or Ungaro perfume. She strongly believed that she wasn't meant to live in this country. Thus, as soon as summer vacation started, we'd travel with my grandfather by car or bus to Istanbul, and from there on to Belgrade or Romania. My father would stay and pursue his amorous adventures at home, after providing us with sufficient travel funds.

My mother stayed married to my father. But she succeeded in taking her revenge on him and punishing us all. She and my uncle had a secret love affair that everyone tried to ignore, but whose poisonous ramifications shook up all of our lives and we could do nothing about it.

I never once met my uncle Faris. It was rare to even find a picture of him. I'd heard that he was like a storybook hero—no woman could resist him because of his generosity, affable character, and kind smile. Women used to come looking for him at his father's shops, where he was a manager. My paternal grandfather sold replacement parts for agricultural machinery. He never seemed to notice any woman, but then Najwa was able to finally catch his attention. She was the daughter of his maternal uncle and was practically raised alongside him. Though his younger brother, my father Amer, was always there, she'd always been closer to him in their childhood. After Mama completed her studies at the Teacher's College in Aleppo, she waited for them to be together. She fully expected to get married to my uncle. But when he felt the space separating them beginning to melt away, he rejected her. This enervated her, and she turned her back on him. Only my grandmother heard him admit that he was scared to approach her. He was afraid that his body might not respond and he'd lose all his strength on the very first attempt. He traveled to Aleppo, Damascus, and Beirut to find a cure, and the definitive opinion was that he didn't have a physical problem. Karma advised him to go to a brothel in Aleppo and have sex with one of the women there, so he could verify his sexual prowess. After this, nothing would then be able to keep him and Najwa apart. Faris was ready to do anything to reignite his dormant masculinity. So he went to a brothel and chose a woman who was able to turn him on. He then married her, ran off to Greece, and never returned.

Najwa went crazy. Her dignity had been damaged and she never could get over what had happened, despite her complete knowledge of the details of the disease and its cure. My father, Amer, was the best person to help her exact her revenge. He was an ally and an enemy both, the savior who could rescue her from a psychological crisis and acute embarrassment in front of her family and friends. My father always came in second after his brother Faris. But he'd be able to make up for this by possessing the legacy that its rightful owner would no longer be suitable for and thus able to enjoy. Inside herself my mother knew that she'd have left Faris had she continued to have to coerce him to be with her. But she enjoyed playing the victim and blamed my grandmother whose foolish advice is said to have ruined her only daughter's life.

Najwa and Karma's relationship worsened. It transformed into silent, seething, taboo rancor. Their interactions were so blemished by profanity, impurity, and disloyalty that once Najwa even told Karma that she'd never be anything more than a product of seedy nightclubs. But my grandmother acted as though nothing had happened. She never tried to ask her daughter about the source of her information or to squabble with her about what she had heard. She didn't remain in her family's house long afterwards. She married my father who embodied the memories and bloodline of her lost love. But he was not her true love. It later became clear that my father would not enjoy his legacy either. He received a great deal of blame and criticism for this. Their wedding shut everyone up and they simply watched them from behind the closed doors of our new house. I came along nine months later, to confirm everything that needed confirming. My mother named me Lamees. The neighborhood troublemakers made fun of my name rhyming it with simple words—like "kees" for bag or "bees" for kitty, "Lamees, we will put you in a kees, and call you bees bees."

Everyday life was not able to erase this legacy of tortured mutual hatred. Instead it breathed new life into it, like yeast makes a loaf of bread rise. My father soon moved out of my mother's bedroom into the room next door, on the pretext that my nighttime crying disturbed his sleep. Against my will, I was stuck right in the middle of their problem. My father put a complete set of bedroom furniture in his room and stretched the phone line there, cutting it off from its original spot. My mother and I started sleeping together in the big bed, and we did this until the day she died.

We all went through life with the two of them avoiding each other. Only necessary words were spoken. His long absences from home, shouting about trivial things like laundry, cooking, or things not being put back in their usual place, and the rare nightly visits between the two bedrooms, quickly transformed me from observer to referee. By the age of eight, I could announce the end of a battle, reconciliation, or a transgression. I would sometimes cry and throw myself on the ground between them. Or I would threaten to run away from home. When I was all alone I often thought that the only solution to get them to finally reconcile was that I die so that they would then be able to share their grief over my passing. Thus, I started imagining my own funeral, seeing my body carried in a coffin on people's shoulders, the two of them locked together in a sorrowful embrace. I imagined how each member of my family would deal with my passing, and the regret that would solve everyone's problems. I was really ready to be that person, in exchange for peace.

My grandmother was well-versed in the details of this struggle. She would annoy me when she described my father as bad, even though I sometimes detested him myself. And the issue of how I would get rid of him was no tragedy. I tried to flee whenever she brought up the topic of my parents' arguments. I left her talking to herself and made up any excuse—I had to leave and return home, or go into the kitchen, or finish my homework, or water the plants…I felt sorry for my mother and despised her at the same time. This used to torture me a lot, and made me cry in bed at night, until there was a truce with my father. But when she got back up after the battle, gathering her strength, refusing to speak or do her work around the house, all in a dignified silence, I would once again really admire her.

When we went to Aleppo or Damascus in my father's Cadillac, the three of us would sit silently listening to cassette tapes of Fayza Ahmed, Warda, and Fairuz. My mother would be thinking about my father and my father would be thinking about another woman. The two of them would turn and make comments or tell me to look at something out the window. My mother would say, "Look Lulu, at the sheep grazing." My father would say, "Lulu, that Mercedes truck is taking beets to the sugar factory." When they'd talk to each other the conversation was mostly general, or a criticism of someone we knew. He complained to her about work, the lack of resources, corruption, bribes, and taxes on machinery. She'd shake her head saying, "Yes, the city should be burned to the ground, by the deeds of its people and the corruption in their souls," her words an arrow shot straight at him.

She would then repeat previous conversations in which she kept her more rebellious feelings under control. She would recall the story of when my grandfather and his friends visited Farid Al-Atrash's house in Cairo. They had taken a boat from Latakia to Alexandria and from there on to Cairo. They eventually arrived at his villa in Helwan and knocked on his door. His maid named Khudra answered. They asked her to tell Farid that they were his relatives from Raqqa in Syria. They heard his voice from inside the house telling her, "Throw them out, I don't have any relatives in Raqqa." She then shooed them away with her dustpan. Mama talked about her happy life at her father's house and how she used to study by the streetlights in the middle of the night, before people had electricity inside their houses. She talked about the beauty of the pine nut trees on the road between Timişçoara and Bucharest. Then she would grow silent waiting for him to say what he never did about the woman he was seeing at that time. My mother sometimes tried to heal the rifts between them, but she always failed. My grandmother told her that she had no confidence and still had no idea how women got men into bed. She told her to buy a negligee to sleep in instead of her pajamas that were basically a chastity belt!

My mother had a set of theories, which no one could alter because they were the product of her lived experience. She believed that she could see things better than anyone else because she could look down from the heights of her life's major disappointments. She would say things like, "Just as offering holy sacraments won't bring you a child, you can't find a husband through magic and sorcery." My grandmother would be speechless when she said such things. She also often announced, "Damn this life of always giving in," by which she meant being deceived and denying it. Mama was always stubborn, she never conceded and she never broke. She hovered over her disappointments—she could tell from the way a woman greeted her or by looking out our window at someone passing by if she'd had a relationship with my father.

Not one of them ever thought to steer this ship away from the obvious danger of the dark and narrow straits. Had my mother married into another family, or my father married someone other than his brother's girlfriend, or had my grandmother conspired with my grandfather and challenged them getting together, we would not be the protagonists of this horror story today.

One day, Najwa went to get her hair done at Ahlam's Salon, two neighborhoods away. This was unusual, because she didn't entrust her hair to anyone except Harout, a coiffeur who she traveled to in Aleppo about once a month. The salon consisted of one room dedicated to working with clients within Ahlam's family house. My mother didn't know that I used to go there regularly with our neighbor Afaf so she could get her eyebrows threaded. They put thick powder on her face so that she looked like a clown. Everyone said that the girls who worked there had bad reputations. That's what Auntie Maria and Auntie Safia said anyway. But I loved exploring this questionable milieu. Every time I went there, they welcomed me, pampered me, gave me manicures, and braided my hair. One of them would ask me how mom and dad were doing, and if they slept in the same bed. Honestly, being with them was fun. They always teased me, saying I was naughty and assured me that I was beautiful.

When my mother went they celebrated her as if she were an angel descended from heaven. They brought her coffee and cigarettes, treated her with excessive respect, while she laughed and listened to their stories about what was happening in the city. My mother asked Ahlam to give her a nice hairdo. She did it and Mama looked gorgeous. Afterwards, she went into the next room, with the excuse that she needed to pray. What she found looked like a bridal chamber, filled with expensive perfume, a lavish box of cosmetics and jewelry, lingerie hanging on a peg, and my father's pajamas that had been "lost in the wash." She walked back out and sat down to get her hair finished. She went back and engaged Ahlam in random conversation like a hostage outmaneuvering his captor. She went back home, clutching a book with all her might. She didn't say anything to anyone. A few days later she exploded hysterically. She told my grandmother everything she'd seen and heard, threatening to set my father on fire and kick him out. "Go be with your whore!" He said he would leave. A little while later, he came back to calm her down.

I asked my grandmother: "Why do people live together when they don't love each other?" She replied: "There are things that keep people together other than love." My mother retorted: "No, once love is gone, it's over."

A month of silence passed. My mother withered. I took her side. I avoided my father. I acted with antipathy towards him. I brought her news of the salon. I pondered a way to get revenge for her. But all I could do was cry and want to be with Abboud, without listening to any complaining about it. I went back to the salon with Afaf. They treated me as kindly as they did before. I invented stories of love and harmony about my parents. At the end of my ramble I asked, "Are you all whores?"

They laughed heartily and said, "No."

Our house reeked of repressed desires: to scream, to get divorced, to murder, to have sex. Sometimes this transformed into violent confrontations, attacks that battered my small body when I inserted myself between them. When my mother hugged me and cried, every bit of my sympathy and feeling was with her. When I sat with my father and he carried me in his arms to buy newspapers and sweets from the corner shop, I cried and clung to him, then found excuses for him.

My mother took a phone call. I heard her say, "Ahlam's house," Then she left in the car. Why did she go by car, if it was only two neighborhoods away? My mother was one of the few women in the area who knew how to drive back then. There wasn't really a need for cars when nothing was more than an hour's walk away. The streets were quiet when people go home to nap in the afternoon heat. My father hadn't come back home yet. When my mother returned that evening, I learned that he'd had a heart attack and was in the hospital. She was tense, pale, and glum, but she didn't feel sorry for him. I asked her why she didn't stay with him because I was afraid for him; I missed him and started crying. "No visitors are allowed," she answered. I knew that everybody sleeps over with their sick relatives at the city's only hospital. Why did she leave him alone? Families sit on the sidewalk outside, drinking tea and coffee, and eating. There are entire families there—including the neighbors —who stay until morning waiting for visiting hours to start. There's always at least one person inside to keep the sick person company. So who was staying with my father?

Later, I learned that my mother had to take him out of Ahlam's room because he'd had a heart attack while they were having sex. She took him to the hospital and told the doctors that he was with her. She kept this totally secret until one day I heard her shouting the truth in my grandmother's face. My mother didn't come back home after my father got better. Our lives could only be described as hell. After more than a year, my father joined my uncle Faris in Greece. He hugged me before he left. I saw the glimmer of a tear in his eyes, when he promised me he would come back soon. But as usual, he didn't keep his promise.

Mama never let this story travel beyond the walls of our house, so it transformed into a popular folk tale. She showed a unique ability to be rock solid, not easy for a woman who'd been left by two brothers. But her body began to wither away and decay; it gave off a strange scent. I no longer needed a sound or image to know if she was in a certain place, since I could immediately detect her pungent odor. If I walked in the street somewhere she'd walked first, or she had been in our bathroom at home ahead of me, or in my grandmother's bathroom, I would know she had been there because of the strong odor of her excretions. In a certain way it resembled the scent of Abboud's mom Anna's body in her final days. I believe that this is the scent of abandonment. A woman produces it when a man replaces her with another woman. I started to know abandoned women by their scent. My friends Abeer and Shazza used to bet on this, analyzing our neighborhood women's intimate relationships with their husbands. I won the bet every time. They trusted my vision, the power of my intuition, and I transformed into an emotional counselor and spiritual trainer. I didn't care about anything when Mama was with me, steadfast and healthy. Whenever she fell asleep I'd worry, and hover around her bed like a moth above a flame. I tried to check that she was breathing, watching her chest rise and fall. I would take her hand to feel her pulse and she would pull it away grouchily, raising her voice at me, "Go away and leave me alone!" I would calm down and leave her room relieved. I would reassure myself that she was strong, since she ate well, exercised, and didn't go to the doctor all the time or complain about her ailments. She would stay with me until that undetermined day in future that I never wanted to think about.

Only a few pictures and letters from my father arrived. At first he sent money, but then he stopped. In his letters he used to say that he would send me an airline ticket to spend the summer with him in Thessaloniki but this never happened either. His trip had turned into an eight-year-long sojourn when we got the news that he had died. I went in for my final high school examinations soon after. Though at that point he was merely a two-dimensional character to me, I felt lost. The first time I left the house after hearing the news was to take my exams. I felt that I was walking naked down the street and that everyone was staring at me. I shrank to manage my body and this shrinkage has left a mark on me to this day, in the simple curvature of my back. It always flares up when I am sad. My mother was silent on that day. She invited me to sleep on her lap, with the excuse that it would help ease my exam stress. But she was sad too. At that time the truth was that we were alone in the world. In the past, my father had been far away, but he was somewhere out there. We could retrieve him somehow at any moment—to get his support, his repentance, or to take revenge on him. I could threaten my mother that I would join him as well. When he died the heavens were emptied of both angels and devils.

OLD TRAIN CAR NIGHTS

We breathed a deep sigh of relief when my father left. There were fewer conflicts and our regimented life eased, with less strict commitments to dinnertime, bedtime, when we woke up, and social engagements. Before he left, he dissolved his partnership in the shop and gave my mother a sum of money for us to live off of. To this amount, she added the money that she had inherited from my grandfather and she became a partner in the shop, which provided us with a very good income. My mother, grandmother, and I lived in singular harmony until Nicholas came along and everything changed. It was as if the world turned us into a chapter in a book, or a spaceship took us to a new galaxy.

Nicholas was staying at the Huriyah Hotel. It was a miserable place frequented by third-rate "artistes." It had a small door on the street, which you entered by walking up stairs covered in an unraveling red carpet and giving off a urine-soaked smell, as if emanating from a busy, nearby toilet. Rusted bronze candlesticks hung on the wall next to a portrait of the President of the Republic. Most of the rooms had multiple beds and a shared bathroom, with the exception of the VIP rooms. An employee sat on a stool behind a wooden counter in the lobby holding a large ledger. Behind him, room keys hung on a wooden board. Next to the wall sat a black leather sofa that had been sliced open by a knife, its yellow foam filling spilling out of the gash as if trying to complete its own evisceration. The three hotels in the city were more or less the same. Nicholas had no a better choice.

Whenever the door leading from the hallway to the kitchen opened, the smell of beer and salted pistachios filtered through. This odor mixed with the smell of the used clothing shops under the hotel. Next door was a vegetable market. This mix of smells made up the character of Quwatli Street, which most people simply knew as Souq al-Sharqi. People who passed through never forgot its sumptuous aroma, no matter how refined their sense of smell became.

Nicholas worked as Professor of the Public Understanding of Science at the University of Munich. One day he passed in front of my grandmother's house. I was sitting on the doorstep with Abboud, watching the passersby and having conversations leading everywhere except where I hoped they'd lead. He wore beige cotton trousers and a red shirt with a hat. He was tall and stood with a dignified stoop. He had chestnut hair and a mustache growing all the way into a thick red beard. His toes were lined up like soldiers in a military parade inside his brown sandals. He asked us about the road to Tell Bi'a in classical Arabic spoken with an accent. We gladly gave him directions and even drew a map on some papers he had in his canvas backpack. My grandmother called out and invited him in for a cup of coffee. He accepted this invitation without a fuss or hesitation, as if he'd known us for a long time!

When he entered the garden, Mama didn't get up from where she was sitting. She was leafing through the news about high society and movie stars in Maw'id magazine. She glanced at him, peered into his eyes, and smiled in a friendly way. When she learned what he'd wanted, she changed her posture and asked us to accompany him. He offered to give us 100 liras for the tour, and to do the same whenever we took him somewhere. Mama refused disapprovingly, saying that this is our duty toward guests and we do it for the sake of our country and our history. To be honest, I loved her serious, moralistic discourse about respecting our heritage! We offered to take him by bike, but he wanted to walk. Walking is how you really solve the puzzle of a place, he claimed.

We headed east and went into the old souq. He asked us about where we were and we replied, "We are in Rafiqa, built in the Abbasid era." When we got to the old city walls, he asked about Raqqa al-Samra', Raqqa Wasit, and Raqqa al-Rashid. It seemed that he knew a lot about us! He took many pictures of the arches and engravings at Baghdad Gate with a camera with a zoom lens. He approached the area slowly as if afraid to disturb it, bending or stretching his slender body as needed, and then closing it back up quickly. We grew tired and sat at the workers' café near the industrial district and drank tea. Abboud and I were happy to be together and doing something shared and useful that had my mother's approval. We got to Tell Bi'a and walked among the ruins and excavations, and also inside the areas blocked off for ongoing archeological expeditions.

By the time he was sure he was in the spot he wanted, the afternoon was fading fast and the sun had begun to set behind the hills in west Raqqa. The Euphrates was to our north and we began to feel its cool breeze. Suddenly Nicholas asked us to give him space to be alone. So we moved away, sat on two boulders facing each other and watched him. The spirits of the sons of the ancient city of Tuttal—a gift to Nikephoros the Victor—crept into our bodies. We saw him bend down on his knees, leaving the world—and us—behind him. He clasped his hands as if in prayer, bent his head, and began to cry. Afterwards, he stood up, took a paper out of his bag, and started reading from it. Later we learned from my mother that he had been reading out a poem by his mother, who was a famous German poet. She dedicated it to the Arab astronomer Al-Battani who lived in Raqqa. He had built a grand observatory on this hill on which Nicholas now stood. He also later told my mother that the University of Munich Symphony Orchestra had performed a piece dedicated to the memory of al-Battani on the occasion of a meteoric crater on the moon being named after him by the International Union of Astronomers.

We returned filled with a strange feeling. I was so tired that I fell asleep early. Nicholas's voice reading his mother's poem rang in my ears as if it were a holy proclamation coming from an unknown planet, or hymns of people lying beneath us, buried in ancient tombs for thousands of years:

Oh Sultan of the Galaxies!
I left my lover on the road
Because it is wrapped in shadows
My heart is fire burning his tender flesh,
A desert ravaging his tender body
Oh you whom his majesty sees with the light of my eye!
Draw him as an eternal orbit for me
As an amulet in the Raqqa sky

As a cross in the cold nights on the Rhine
Blessed are the eternal ones forever!

My mother took him to the Barakat family's house. They were our neighbors who owned two small, furnished apartments in the basement of their house that they rented out. The apartments were nice. Nicholas liked them, and chose the one whose window opened out onto a little alley connected to my grandmother's back garden. It was if he were in our house. Mama told him that Miss Zuhur, her colleague at the cultural center, had been assigned by the Antiquities Office to assist him in his research. But a week later, he reassigned my mother to take her place, because she was more fluent in English, so she would be able to communicate with him better, despite the fact that he knew Arabic very well because he had studied it in Germany and then pursued an intensive course in Damascus with his sister who had majored in it. I was worried about my mother's assignment, taking her colleague's place. It gave me a whole new psychological complex. I struggled between my appreciation for Nicholas whom I found to be a replacement for the missing male unit in our family, and my fear that he would steal my mother from me. My heart pounded with love, jealousy, and hatred. Nicholas became our shared man, and because of him my mother and I became co-wives. He was very friendly with me, he cared about me. He acted as though Abboud and I were members of his crew. He assigned us tasks, like organizing the train car that he'd rented at the site, equipping it with writing materials, a table, and chairs. He asked us to give him information about the language and people of the region, asking us to read him some books which Mama brought him from the cultural center library: Ptolemy's *Almagest*, Al-Qashiri's *History of Raqqa*, and Ibn Kalikan's *Wafiyat al-Ayan*. He was also able to speak Czech with Abboud. To thank us for our services he brought us gifts: chocolates and Roamer watches that he'd bought at Aqqad's shop in Souq al-Sharqi. He gave me a white Walkman that he'd brought with him from Munich. I really loved it and it kept working until I no longer wanted it. It became my only friend, especially after I broke up with Abboud. I listened to Rachmaninoff alone, the Walkman spinning a cocoon around me. I started to enjoy drawing Nicholas' attention to my perseverance, my initiatives to help him, and finding solutions when his plans went wrong. When his glasses lenses detached from their frame, I took them to the optician's shop on Mansour Street to have them fixed. I developed the film from his camera, and bought him new canisters. I brought him Pasperan from the pharmacy when he caught a gastro infection and was vomiting.

I wanted to be the one he had a crush on, not my mother. Once his presence between us had become a reality that I could not change, I had to deal with it the best I could. All the things happening in our life made me feel overtired; I couldn't open a new battlefront with anyone. But this didn't mean that I agreed, or consented, to what was happening. The more he drew her closer to him, the more I avoided him. I knew very well that however firm and strong my sense of self, that to him I would only ever be a compassionate and clever girl. I also knew that if he and my mother grew more intimate it could lead to a dangerous secret between the two of them that would make me want to kill myself if I found out it was true.

At Tell Al-Bi'a, near the main road, there was an old train car that had been taken out of service long ago. Some rioters had dragged it far from the station toward a residential area. Drunks and homeless people slept there, children used to hide in it and use it for their more and less innocent games. It was immobile, had missing seats, and smashed-in windows; a little platform at the end separated it from the next car. Nicholas decided that this would be his observatory for the six months he was working here. He rented it from an important man in the area and paid a good amount for it. He then took it to the best shop in the industrial district. He had the interior completely emptied and fixed up. He put in new windows, painted it, and installed a toilet. Nicholas also added a red velvet sofa, a desk, chairs, and a table lamp. He hung lights from the ceiling. Some local guys connected electricity they had taken from a line on the road. He also borrowed some potted plants from my grandmother—basil, jasmine, and purple evening flowers. He put them on the platform at the back and hung a string of Christmas lights on them. This is how the neglected train car became a nice, elegant place to relax, sparkling with light amidst the ruins and scrap shops.

In the afternoon, I joined my mother when she was supposedly working with Nicholas. She normally worked only mornings, but Nicolas spent his mornings at home doing research or walking around the city. My mother stayed home. He sometimes asked her to read some Arabic references and summarize what was in them for him. My mother started reading all the time, and she changed from her usual novels and biographies of famous people to histories and books about scientific phenomena. She would stay with him at the site until late, and then come back home while he remained and proceeded with his actual work, which was to observe the sky. He'd start when the sun began to set and could stay up all night until sunrise. He would also sleep in that train car. Sometimes he'd come back at midnight. Sometimes he'd stay up outside the door, with people who he'd met. They'd put out iron chairs and sit with him contemplating the sky, talking about the region, its archeological ruins, and teaching him local Arabic words. Plates of food would come and go, along with glasses of tea, cups of coffee, sweets like mchabbek, kleicha, and Turkish delight, as well as grilled liver sandwiches, gifted by people living nearby or bought from little local shops. He installed an easel and gave me fancy oil paints that he'd brought with him from Munich, asking me to paint the sky and the fields all around us. While I looked at the sky with him, he urged me to record my observations in a red notebook with blue flowers. Abboud also joined us, and he was brilliant at drawing. The train car was near the hill where Al-Battani's observatory had been 1,100 years before and Nicholas was trying to reproduce the geographical and astronomical conditions of the time as closely as he could, to be as credible as possible.

While my mother and I were preparing to leave the train car one night, they were discussing a visit to the site for some summer camp students so they could learn the principles of astronomical observation. During this discussion, he gently rested his hand on her shoulder and patted it, as if he wanted to pull her to his chest. Her facial expression changed. She smiled at him sweetly, and she leaned over toward him ever so slightly. She looked gorgeous. But she immediately caught my eye, as if she'd just remembered I was there. At that moment, I felt something inside me collapse. I hated them both and decided that they had teamed up against me. They'd become the enemy.

I no longer wanted to play the role of my mother's chaperone or bodyguard. As soon as we'd arrive at the train car, I'd go out to the nearby pastures and simply walk, walk, walk with no path or set destination. I never reproached my mother or asked her about this provocative moment. Some questions are proof of what we want to deny. There were little prefabricated huts scattered in the fields to the east of the train car as well as a big stone house with a tin roof. I saw some young men there who I figured were workers for some NGO.

I walked all around, the smell of organic fertilizer and animal dung filling my nose. There were horses grazing and many little haystacks. Behind the stone house, which turned out to be a stable, there were fields of clover, horse tracks, and metal bars but no one was riding and training. I came across a thin, tanned man of medium build; he was in his forties with jet-black hair and a thin mustache hanging down around his lips pointing toward his clean-shaven chin. He had a big mole just below his cheek.

His cigarette hung from the corner of his mouth as he picked up the brown horse's front hoof. He put its hoof between his narrow thighs and flicked his cigarette far away. He started fixing a metal horseshoe to the bottom of its hoof. The horse submitted to him, letting out a quiet sound, not a snort or a whinny. He picked up his hammer, and started nailing the horseshoe in place. He asked me to hand him another nail confidently, as if he knew me. Without even turning, he asked me who I was and what I was doing there. I told him that I loved horses but I was afraid of getting too close to animals. I watched equestrian show jumping competitions on television and liked the way the announcers said, "Last call for the jockey so-and-so, on horse such-and-such." I knew the errors, the timing, and the competition rules. He told me that he trained some young men who wanted to establish an equestrian center here. He said I could join them if I wanted to, for free, though they didn't have any other young women there. He would teach me the basics of what one needed to train horses.

He asked how old I was and I told him I was thirteen. He also asked me if I could commit to coming every day. I told him yes, without thinking about asking for my mother's consent. It occurred to me that she had forfeited the right to interfere in my business, so long as she had begun to spin a cocoon for herself that had no room for me.

The brown horse was restless. I asked one of the young guys who seemed only a little older than me the horse's name, he replied, "Ibn Furat, Son of the Euphrates." He was skinny compared to the horses I saw in show jumping competitions on television. Abu Layla said, "Usually foreign or crossbred horses are taller and better suited for show jumping, they can lift their legs almost to the fences. They are very expensive. Ibn Furat is an Arabian, agile and nimble. Arabians are better for racing, they are light, quick, and they need a lot of training to jump. The skill of a jockey is to adjust his rhythm to the horse's and understand his moods above all else. Lamees, it's the jockey who makes the Arabian jump, whereas a trained non-Arabian can jump on its own."

No one had called me Lamees for a long time. I realized that Abu Layla was sending me a message that the name Lulu wasn't appropriate for a real horseback rider. To demonstrate my true desire to overcome my old fear of animals, I went right up to Ibn Furat. One of the men standing there told me, "Don't approach him from behind and don't let him feel your hesitation. Walk right over to him, take the halter under his neck, and put your hand confidently on his forelock, or stroke your open palm along his head." This is how I began to develop my own original world in which no one could imagine that a lone, insignificant person like myself could excel in.

Abu Layla taught me to build the fences, or "wooden beams" as he called them—the parts that made up the fences. He gave me all kinds of hard work that I didn't tell my mother about—cutting clover from the little field with a sharp scythe, washing the horses, organizing, cleaning, and rubbing the saddles down with Vaseline. I treated the horses' sore gums and teeth with a mix of garlic and yogurt, washed them, and bathed them in a rubber bath we made from damaged car tires. We walked the horses down a slope to a flat place about sixteen feet deep, filled with water to bathe the horses. Then there was a little rise about the same length as the slope down. I would go down to the water with the horses—such a unique feeling of joy filled me, riding on a horse's back while it was floating was like being on an amusement park ride.

I stuffed my jeans into the tops of my plastic boots and didn't care—they wouldn't need long to be dried by the sun and wind. Not all horses liked swimming. For example, Maymouna was afraid and didn't go down into the water. She would stand on the edge observing like a hostile bride dictating her orders to everyone else. But Ibn Furat, Najmeh, and Abla were passionate swimmers.

I learned to care for the horses. I put on and removed horseshoes from hooves. I learned to feed, walk, groom, and clean them. My grandmother's driver would drop me off or Mama would drive me in my late grandfather's car after my father sold his and left for

Greece. I stopped beet trucks on the road, which transported them through the fields towards the sugar factory, and would take a few beetroots for the horses. I usually split them in half and fed them to Najmeh, or I held sugar lumps out on my open palms and she licked them up, sending a tingling feeling down to my toes. It's a delicious feeling to make an animal happy. Horses feel happiness, longing, and even sometimes cry. I've seen tears in Najmeh's eyes, and Ghazwa always had dust in hers. Flies circled around them both, and I wiped them away with a damp rag. Ghazwa used to thank me by rubbing her head against my chest. Sometimes she did this so violently, she almost broke my ribs.

I washed Najmeh and Ibn Furat daily, the scent of the shampoo mixing with their natural scent and mine, which had become horse-like—a mixture of sweat, grass, and manure. I sometimes brought my hairdryer from home. Abu Layla laughed, saying that his horses weren't used to being spoiled in this way and had never felt a woman's touch before. When my grandmother's driver left us at the end of the dirt road, my mother headed for the train car, and I for the club. She called out to me, "Take care." I didn't reply. Inwardly I thought, "You're the one who should take care." I no longer asked her many questions about Nicholas or her work, so that she would leave me for as long as possible in the world of horses.

I asked Abu Layla, "Why are you married to four women?"

"In order to satisfy my four uncles."

"They're all your cousins? How do your co-wives pass their days together?"

"I leave them to figure it out and they live happily together."

He's easy going and laughs stoically. But whenever we talk, I feel like he has a bigger secret than he lets on. He always keeps a bit apart from the rest of us. What does Abu Layla want from the world?

Layla is the name of an old horse he used to ride in his youth. He left his four wives and his children, as well his parents, to spend time with the horses. Sometimes he slept in a room at the stable or in the caravans, as he called them. He made them into a sort of office for himself. He laid out mattresses in front of the door and slept there. When I asked him about this he said, "Horses choose their lovers, and there is no cure for this passion." Yes, I know. I've tasted this passion. It helped me avoid feeling my father's absence, and Abboud's rapidly impending absence. The most important thing is that it distracted me from paying attention to my mother, and the likelihood of her leaving me too. Who would my mother leave me with if she ran away with Nicholas? Would she really be able to do that? Would I go with her? Would I go live with my father? I was afraid to ask her. Auntie Maria told me once that if we voice a bad idea, it will materialize, and if we voice a good idea, it won't. My mother couldn't leave me. This seemed as well established as sunrise and sunset. But considering that everyone else had left—my uncle, my grandfather, and my father—perhaps she would too.

I strolled up to Abu Layla when I saw him calmly contemplating his horses grazing in the distance. He was in his element, smoking a cigarette and drinking a cup of tea. He called out to me, "Come on over and sit down." I longed with all my heart to tell him about my hardships and troubles—to admit to him that I was afraid my mother would leave with the German man and that I missed my father who had tortured us. Without looking at my face he said, "You are brave Lamees, you have a good heart—that's why the horses love you. Don't let anything break you. Life is scary because there are so many hurdles to clear. But if we are afraid of the hurdle itself, we've lost. If we mount the horse confidently and jump but fall, it's not important, but we have to know how to fall—not on the head, not on the back. We try to fall on the arm or the shoulder—to lessen the damage. Remember your thrill when you cleared your first hurdle? Think about how afraid you were beforehand, your heart pounding! Remember how you jumped over it and left it behind you."

He was saying exactly what I needed to hear; it was his way of mentoring me. He taught me how to renounce everything so I no longer had needs. I spent one whole year wearing the same pair of jeans and blue long-sleeved shirt, knotted at the waist. I wore plastic shoes, like farmers and cleaners. I'd bought them at Souq al-Sharqi for twenty-five liras. I no longer wanted to go back home, especially in the winter when training hours were reduced. It meant I had to spend time face to face with my mother—with Nicholas's ghost hovering over us—and I fell into a depression. I slacked off in my schoolwork. Abu Layla was the Shaman who helped me see the truth, the horses taught me wisdom: when to go forward, when to stop, when to loosen the halter, when to pull it tight, when to give up. When a horse takes off with you atop it, out of control, your heart leaves your body for maybe a half hour and then it returns. You simply accept this. You don't pull tighter, you don't panic—you just surrender to it. Stay calm atop your horse. The horse will be faster than the wind, stretch its legs as far as possible, its belly gliding over the earth. After three or four turns it will expend its energy, then it will calm down and you'll be back in control.

Abu Layla didn't burden me with his theories about the world, but rather asked me to look at things and question them when needed. He made me face up to my experiences. He forbade me to ride only one horse. In his point of view, we should always be familiar with alternative scenarios. The horse could get sick on the day of the race, could give birth, could die…We have to be ready to accept alternatives. I tried to model my life after his, but I loved dapple-gray Najmeh the most. Love is a choice from God. I spoke to her about everything. I complained and I cried, and she responded with a sad look, and a quiet whinny. Sometimes we looked into each other's eyes for fifteen minutes and we simply enjoyed the unquestioning silence. Najmeh alone could absorb all my turmoil with love. She made me feel her love, by rubbing her strong bones powerfully against my chest, so much that it hurt. We shared mutual protectiveness, good humor, and friendship, like sisters or friends who've committed themselves to eternal loyalty.

When Abu Layla was worried about my excessive attachment to her, he didn't let me near her and forced me to ride Ghazwa. She was bug-eyed; the blacks and whites of her eyes were reversed. When I asked him what was wrong with them, he replied, "Her mother is a cow!" I laughed. My fear of her and how difficult she was dissipated. I no longer hesitated to share my concerns with him. I had listened to the guys' gossip about a groom called Antar. They said that he got drunk every night and slept with the horses. Antar was a thirty-something-year-old man, but he looked like a skinny little boy, with dark hair and a gold tooth in place of one of his canines. He wore dark blue jeans, a yellow or red t-shirt, and boots like mine. I called Antar Mr. Boots, because he resembled the character of a cat called Mr. Boots in a story my mother used to read me as a small child.

"I'm worried that Antar will treat Najmeh badly." Abu Layla understood what I was suggesting and addressed my discomfort with absolute seriousness: "I will castrate him if he does that. Don't worry, he sleeps with mules down by the river, not the purebreds." Abu Layla surprised me by his frank answer to my question.

"Why does Antar cry when night falls?"

"Because he shot and killed his brother when he was young."

A light comes on in the train car, dancing against the night. Bitterness rises and falls in my heart. What are the two of them doing? Is he holding her hand? Kissing her? Can he smell the scent of the dish soap she uses? Can he detect the smell of garlic, which she peeled to prepare lunch, mixed with the aroma of the orange she peeled for me just a little while ago? Before, Mama used to ask me, "Should I peel your orange whole, or in slices?" Usually I would say, "Whole," and she would peel the orange in a spiral, not stopping until the entire orange had come out in one whole piece. Then she would cut the whole peeled orange in half. It is delicious when I taste it and the juice runs down my lips and chin, burning any cut or dry spot on my face that it touches. Since being all preoccupied with Nicolas, Mama has stopped asking me our usual questions. She just gives me sliced oranges in pieces, lost in her own thoughts.

What frightens me the most is that the scent of abandonment seems to have left her. But how? Perhaps Nicholas knows! What could this man, who somehow manages to move stars, possibly see in my poor mother? Every evening he tells me, "Come here, we will move the heavens." And truly I would observe one of the stars in a certain location and an hour later see it somewhere else.

I asked him, "Is it the stars that move or the sky?"

"Actually it's the earth. The earth moves clockwise in a rotation from East to West."

"If the stars are there night and day, and their locations don't change, why don't I see them in the morning?"

"Because of the light of the sun, and the earth's atmosphere."

I finished the initial stages of training with Abu Layla—walking and trotting—in less than a month. I trained for an hour and a half or two hours every day, until my body got used to the proper posture and position to sit atop the horse and my leg muscles began to grow stronger. I didn't use spurs or a whip. I held a small bamboo stick with the halter, hanging down parallel to the belly of the horse so he couldn't even see it. I used it to hit him lightly, tapping his haunches, simply to tell the horse—I'm here. A light gallop became my expertise; my body rose and fell in synch with the horse's motion. I discovered with experience that female horses are kinder and tamer than male horses. I suffered a lot of falls, bites, and even abductions, when the horse would kidnap me, whisking me away outside the racetrack. I suffered one violent incident, which left a scar on my head just under my hairline, and I had to have ten stiches, which are no longer visible. After that, I became someone whom people called the horsewoman upon whom dust can't settle. Abu Layla said, "A rider can't become a rider without falling at least one hundred times."

The horses took me to a parallel universe completely separate from the human world. When a horse ran away with me or I ran away with her, I heard myself saying, "Surrender to me now!" She'd go with me as if she was taking care of me, or showing me the world in a new, wonderful way. I became stronger than Abboud and forgot him. I preceded him and exceeded him. While on horseback, I threw aside images of reality, one after another, finished with them. I was certain that I'd left the world behind me and was close enough to touch the future. I left the world behind me—I'd transcended it and everything belonging to it.

I was unable to move from a trot to a gallop, which is a horse's fastest movement, like running. The horses' front legs reach far behind then dart to the front, devouring space. This changes the rider's rhythm too, since you fix your body without getting up and sitting back down by squeezing your thighs hard against the saddle. You hold your back up straight, and you relax your core into the rhythm of the horse under you. The horse takes off like a flying carpet. As soon as the first trot transforms into a gallop I pull on the reins to stop. I try and fail. Abu Layla scolds me, "You're going to mess up the horse's training." I feel paralyzed, there is a beautiful world waiting for me that others don't know about, and a paradise I have withheld from myself because of a fear that prevents me from pursuing adventure. This is the same fear that prevents people from going skydiving, relaxing in the water when we learn how to swim, or leaving an abusive relationship. As Abu Layla also said, "God gives those he loves the ability to rip aside this curtain of fear." This was a trick he used to help me; he took pity on me when I felt overcome by despair and he could see my tears of defiance.

I was fed up with trying to reclaim my father, to keep my mother honest with me, and to prevent Abboud from turning away from me. I traded them all for a single desire at that time—innocently galloping away. Abu Layla and I each got up onto a horse. We attached a harness and a bridle. My horse walked ahead and I followed, it pulling me along. Then his horse began galloping and my horse followed. I kept my body supple. I tried to relax and not be tense and rigid, trusting Abu Layla. He went a bit ahead of me, keeping me at a distance, but a safe distance. He held a rope connected to my horse. If I felt danger, he could pull on my horse and I would come up next to him. He held the halter under the horse's chin and could stop him at any moment and rescue me, like a knight rescues a princess. I began to gallop and entered another level of existence. I noticed nothing but the kuffieh tied around his thin, taut waist, cutting him in two. There we were together—teacher and student—two people riding on a holy chariot crossing into another world. One image after another flashed before my eyes: trees, fields, houses, people. When I dismounted I was so completely satisfied with the world, I even forgave my mother. If I ever fell back, Abu Layla would tie us together and we would return once again to the prairie.

When the sun had completely set into the river and I had washed my horse, walked him around a little, fed him, and closed the door of the stable on him, the world around me became gloomy again. My mother still hadn't finished her work; the light in Nicholas's room flickered in synch with the anxiety I felt inside. I went into the dark saddle room, to fill myself with the scent of leather, redolent with the sweat of horses. The saddles were lined up on metal bars arranged one atop the other. I sat on the ground, hiding my head among them, and burst into tears. The iron door opened and when my tears dried up, I said to Abu Layla, "I'm tired of training." He didn't ignore my sadness, and didn't leave me alone and close the door on me.

Rather, he pulled me by the hand to sit me in front of his office in the moonlight. He poured me tea in a glass someone else had already drunk from, after rinsing it with water. The tea was delicious, though it was weak and had a lot of sugar in it.

The young people at the club say that after we all leave, Abu Layla drinks araq, listens to sad, traditional Iraqi music, and weeps. They say that the horses respond to him and echo him.

"Why do you seem so sad?"

"Because I love horses!"

"I love them too, like you do. Why are you so attached to them?"

"Because they don't stay with us long."

"What do you mean?"

"They die after only a few years, if they aren't properly cared for, and this care costs a lot. If they get sick, we may be forced to give them up or give them away to other people. The fact they are temporary makes them so precious."

Later I learned that Abu Layla had not married the woman he loved because her family were carriers of an inherited, sudden-onset mental illness. It caused the person suffering from it to harm others and sometimes even kill them. There was no cure. People said that this illness could be traced back to a saint's tomb at her grandfather's house. They destroyed it and built a new house, but then they were cursed. His beloved then married someone else from outside Raqqa. She left with him, had children, and none showed any sign of madness. When she left, Abu Layla married four other women and abandoned them all, weeping every evening.

I was anxious and excited, ready for the tournament. Abu Layla told me, "You don't need to win today; it's your first tournament. I just want you to participate." Just before my turn came, Najmeh fell ill; she had bad colic and was no longer safe to ride. Abu Layla didn't say anything. Before they called my name, he came to me and told me he'd prepared Ghazwa to ride. I crumbled inside and told him I wouldn't participate. The announcer called my name again with Ghazwa's name. I felt Abu Layla's whip on my thigh. He said, "Go on, get up on her." I was surprised by the blow; tears gathered in the corner of my eyes and almost burst out of them. But I gathered up all my strength, jumped up on the back of the horse, and completed the circuit without any errors, in the shortest amount of time. I won. I was the winner!

When I left the ring, Abu Layla held my horse and helped me dismount. He wanted to hug me, but I stopped him. I went into the saddle room and burst into tears. I felt that I deserved to own the whole world, but the world was evil and didn't deserve me. What was I doing here? My mother and Nicholas were in the crowd. I was aware I'd won, but I felt sad, lonely, and defeated. Abu Layla's blow had wounded me. All the pain in my short life up until now had collected within me. It was the source of my confidence and strength. And it was what protected me and freed me from fear. It took me to another level of beauty and freedom. My pain taught me how to be free of hesitation, how to make my fragile defeated heart feel strong and successful again.

My soul remained heavy. I could still feel the fiery lash of his whip against my thigh. It turned blue after a week, still hot and painful. But I went to practice the next day, and didn't reproach him. I asked him how long it would take me to learn to jump a meter and thirty centimeters. He said, "We still have measles and smallpox." This is an expression we use in Raqqa to mean that we have to persevere in the face of harsh experiences in order to survive, like how children suffered before vaccines were widely available against fatal diseases like measles, smallpox, polio, and diphtheria. That is how I remained grounded with Abu Layla, while my mother was floating towards the heavens with Nicholas.

I watched the lights in the train car and saw images that exhausted me. I didn't know if they were real or a figment of my imagination: he's holding her in his arms and telling her how much he loves her. He tells her he will make up for her difficult past and she laughs in a way I certainly have never heard. It is the laugh of women in love—the same laugh as when my uncle Najeeb used to talk to her about his relationship with his girlfriend Uruba, or with her only friend Muntaha when they smoked in the back garden. It's the laugh she had when reacting to Auntie Maria's dirty jokes. I had to shake off these negative images. I banished them from my mind so nothing could happen between them. As a daughter I said, No, no, no and No. But as a woman I thought, Yes, yes, yes, and Yes. I went in the saddle room to cry. When Nicholas cut off the electricity, with the excuse of cutting down on light pollution, the whole area was covered in a terrible darkness. I cried bitter tears.

I didn't so much care that Nicholas was attracted to my mother or even that he loved her. But I knew better than that. I knew that a man couldn't see her and not be captivated by her hazel eyes, shoulder-length curly brown hair, which was always well cared for, and the perfumed fragrance of olive oil-scented Alseve serum, which moisturized the tender skin of her rosy cheeks, wafting off of her. Though she wasn't tall, in the way that height signifies beauty to us here, her body had no defects at all—breasts, hips, or thighs. She maintained a narrow waistline as my grandmother always had her on a diet of one kind or another and encouraged her to dance. My mother, however, prefered to exercise by walking. I never aspired to be more beautiful than her by any means, but what really devastated me was that I never expected her to have these kinds of feelings towards him. Our mothers are supposed to have romantic feelings only for our fathers. We can't imagine them loving anybody else.

I was now definitively sure that she really was in love with him, because she simply gave him hearts of romaine. She did this for him with exaggerated generosity—I knew that the hearts of romaine were special to her. She didn't give these to just anyone, she usually kept them for herself. If I asked her for one, she would complain. A heart lodged among wrinkled leaves like the different sized fingers of a baby just emerging into the world from its mother's womb. Sweet, ending in a hard root that you peel carefully, opening its green leaves slowly to clean between them with water and vinegar, taking time to prepare it. This is why it is only offered to dear people. She also would prepare a little table for him when he happened to pass by my grandmother's house at lunch or dinnertime. She would make her famous dishes—mutabbal, hommos, French fries, chicken cooked in yogurt and garlic and roasted on the grill by hand, decorated with carrots, tomatoes, and sprigs of parsley. She never showed any desire to prepare food and decorate the table until she met Nicholas.

My mother found her lost beauty with this strange German. She went back to how she looked in her crazed adolescence, a child spoiled by her coquettishness. I aged and the melancholy of the world weighed on my heart. Whenever I tried to forget my suffering, some sign of their deceitful love would appear before me. For example, once I enthusiastically left my grandmother's house to go meet Abboud. We had decided to go to the Granada Cinema on Kuwatli Street only a couple of neighborhoods away to see Duraid Lahham's film, *The Report*. Auntie Maria's daughter Zeina, who studied pharmacy in Damascus, was coming with us. I changed my clothes ten times until I settled on a bright yellow dress with layers of orange ruffles and a black broach shaped like sunglasses on my chest. I wore my hair in a ponytail, and had on navy blue cloth espadrilles, which were in fashion that season.

I passed by my grandmother's house to look for her and my mother to tell them I was going out. My mother was swinging on the swing she'd made like the ones the Nawar people had used out in the country. She tied a thick hemp rope around the top of the bars adorning the big black iron door. She had put a pillow where the seat would be and was swinging; Nicholas was pushing her from behind. He gave her a gentle nudge on the back and she laughed in that way that turned my blood to poison. I walked through, shoving them as if the swing were blocking my way. Blood rushed to my head. I was overcome by a crying fit. I sat on the neighbor's doorstep, my body folded over my knees, my face buried in my arms. I surrendered to my hatred for everything around me. They were lovers! She was in love with this repulsive man with his stupid accent. He couldn't even pronounce the heavy "q" sound in Arabic needed to say the word for moon, "qamar," and so he sounded ridiculous talking about the "kamar." In our dialect, "kamar" means belt. I wished I had a kamar right then to strangle him with. Then I'd strangle her with the rope of her silly swing, and finish the two of them off forever. How did he fall in love with her? What was the first spark and what did he do about it? What did he say to her? What happens when he's angry with her? How do they make up after they fight? What do they do when they are alone together…?

I didn't have answers. I had very difficult images, images that weighed on my still-forming heart. From that time on, these images have filled me with a painful curiosity about love stories, without ever being party to one myself. With any lover, I would try to inquire into his journey, his lexicon, the fingerprints he might leave on my heart, and the traces that would remain on my body. With more knowledge, I have come to realize that they all are alike. There is no alternative map for love that can save you from suffering. Just like there is no alternative map for Raqqa that can make it a bridge between east and west without crossing the river.

I found Ibn Furat lying on his back one day with his feet up in the air. His body was stiff. It was the first time I'd seen a dead horse, and before I could lift my hands to cover my mouth and stifle my screams, asking what happened, the other equestrians told me that Abu Layla had been compelled to kill him because he'd been shot in the leg and was no longer useful.

"Why did he kill him, he doesn't have to be useful, he could be free in nature?"

"He would have suffered a lot and been attacked by hyenas, death is better."

Abu Layla didn't seem sad. But he was silent. Perhaps he didn't hear what was being said. He pulled his checkered scarf tight around his waist so his back would stay straight as he always claimed it was. He took a shovel and dug powerfully, cigarette hanging from his mouth. He removed a lot of soil each time he struck the ground, and piled it up next to the hole where he would put the body when he was finished. He paused, took a drag from his cigarette, and looked into the hole he'd made. The sun was orange, about to set, and the air around us was hot and sticky. Flies were hovering over Ibn Furat's corpse, landing on the inner corners of his open eyes and then on Abu Layla's hands, which were gripping the handle of the shovel. He batted them away involuntarily, his concentration focused on his coming battle now that he had located his enemy.

They dug a big grave for him, and covered it with soil. I cried. We recited the fatiha for him, as though we were sending a human being and dear friend off to his final resting place. I was afraid of Abu Layla. I had the sense that I did not know him well enough to be this close to him. I liked the distance that he had maintained between us; he never allowed me to grow overly attached. It made me feel safe. Now this space had been transformed into a wall. Abu Layla didn't simply leave me to my fears and didn't ignore my feelings of anger. He never said, "Let her figure things out alone, if she isn't happy that's her business." He simply showed an interest in me. He taught me to respect the truth no matter what it was, to find the spirit of it and deal with it on that basis.

"Lamees! Come here. Death was the best solution this time. He would have suffered for a long time and then died anyway."

"You are too cruel."

"Mercy sometimes springs from cruelty."

"Then nature is cruel."

"Nature is neither cruel nor merciful. It is simply indifferent. We can't worry about it. It will solve its own problems. You should get riding, when's the last time you jumped without a saddle?"

I withdrew, and went to train but with less enthusiasm. Everything good in the world began seeping out of a wound somewhere inside of me. How is killing a horse different than killing a human?

I knew that Ibn Furat had been wounded after being shot by a government agent from Raqqa. It was a threat and warning to Abu Layla. Abu Layla's program, which he had started from scratch, had succeeded. Some officials started to notice how important it was, and the profits that it would soon make. They gave him state land adjoining the club's land, which he owned, so that he could invest in the expansion of the track and stables. Then his project transformed into a government sports project. If he didn't accept this partnership, the least they would do is to close down the club. They bought horses and equipment, then established a board of directors. To express their good will towards him, they appointed him director. After the club consolidated its power, how everything worked became clear. He started generating money from training sessions and his horses started winning championships. Then they removed him and accused him of embezzlement. When he stood up to them, defending himself and his life's work, they shot the horse.

I stood by Abu Layla in his battle, and I dropped out of it with him later. This light that emanated from the horses was like everything that shone bright in Raqqa. When the battle concluded in favor of the opponent who can never lose, Abu Layla left Raqqa. He left his four wives and children in the care of his parents. He left me too, to wallow in my sorrows. He took a few of the horses, including Najmeh and Ghazwa, with him and went to Damascus where he trained the children of an important army officer to ride. He searched for someone more powerful to take revenge on. Once again I became simply a speck of dust in a battle no one paid attention to.

When the revolution broke out, three of Abu Layla's sons were active participants. They were imprisoned after demonstrations that called for the fall of the regime in Damascus, where he had finally settled down as a special trainer for army officers in a club of theirs. His sons refused to speak to him, accusing him of serving power. He accused them of sabotage and treachery. Two of them left and sought asylum in Europe. His connections to the military elite couldn't help him get his third son released. He died under torture.

I loved Nicholas except for that stinging feeling he left in my heart. I was always conscious of this feeling that made me steal and rip up papers related to his research, or bang my head against the wall. No doubt he would explain his love to Najwa with the same confidence with which he talked about scientific facts. He'd tell her those same stories that enchanted me before they impressed her—about the signs of the zodiac, stars and planets, dark and light. She listened to him while running her hand through her hair and leaning back on the low red sofa. She'd spent a long time on her hair, instead of taking care of me. She crossed her legs, not aware of how the edges of her blue dress had lifted so far up and aroused the curiosity of anyone who could see that deep, dark opening between her creamy white thighs. His speaking voice nauseated me; the scent of his mint shaving cream mixed with his skin made me feel like I had to vomit.

After getting up to organize some papers, Najwa asked about crystal balls, the signs of the zodiac, and birthstones, reporting that hers was the garnet!

He smiled and walked over to her, putting his arms around her shoulders in an ugly, louche move that tore at my heart. I announced loudly, "Baba said that he would call today!" My mother looked at me, unfocused and unaware of me, as if I weren't her tormented daughter. At the same time, he tried to butter me up with his silly smile, going back to his stupid conversation, "The real world has profound and inexhaustible beauty, which we must understand scientifically to be able to genuinely appreciate it. We don't need artificial marvels; we need look no further than what we already have. It's worth it to expend sincere effort on such beauty."

"Yellah," I say, "Let's go home, Mama. I'm tired and I want to go to sleep." He carried me with affected playfulness to a chair at the entrance of the train car, with me kicking my legs in the air the whole time. He settled me into the chair and wrapped a blanket around me, saying, "Sleep…" I don't feel very clever, but rather that my heart is splitting apart like parched ground in a drought. I look up and find myself besieged by the sky—the sky of the enemy who comes from the North. What does he have and what do we have? He wants to steal our sky, our stars, our Al-Battani. And along with his claims to love and appreciate all these things, he also wants to steal my mother.

I journey into the sky and find it very frightening! I'm able now to distinguish the constellations as Nicholas taught me. There, near our neighborhood, is the North Star, Polaris. I count five spaces to find it and use it as a guide to find Ursa Major and Ursa Minor. I can find these two constellations all year long. I also can easily spot the Cassiopeia constellation, which looks like the letter W when I draw a line between its three bright stars. Behind it is the Andromeda constellation, where the Andromeda Galaxy—also called the Chained Maiden—is found. It's a spiral galaxy that isn't part of the Milky Way, to which Earth belongs. Nicholas told me that if he stayed until April, I would be able to see the winter constellations with him—like Orion, which is one of the most beautiful, and in front of it the Scorpius constellation, with the bright red star Antares right in its center. Behind Orion there is the Taurus constellation, with its distinctive star called Aldebaran. Its name comes from the Arabic, because it seems to follow the Pleiades, a cluster of three thousand stars. Behind the Taurus lies the Gemini constellation. But I don't want to wait for the winter stars, since it won't be good for me if Nicholas stays with us here that long. Perhaps before this a meteor will hit the earth, or a black hole will swallow him up and we'll be done with him! Unlike most years, I just want this summer to end as quickly as possible.

Perhaps the worst thing that could happen to a person is to spend a summer with the enemy!

Nicholas told me that the larger the diameter of the telescope's lens, the more clearly we will be able to see things. It's difficult for him to bring his telescopes from Germany. He will have to present himself to the security officers at the airport and these telescopes that he had with him, he borrowed from a professor who was a friend of his at Damascus University. He said that at the Observatory at the University of Hamburg they use giant telescopes and that he worked with telescopes with five-foot-diameter lenses at the La Silla Observatory, in the Atacama Desert in Chile. The European Organization for

Astronomical Research in the Southern Hemisphere sent him to work for a full year at the observatory there, where the sky is very dark and the air is very dry.

There were four telescopes, two stands, lenses of various sizes, and a number of filters in Nicholas's train car. He used to let me use his telescopes to look at the sky. Sometimes he would fix one on the stand to determine a location and then call out to me, "Hey, come now, so we can catch it!" I'd stand behind the telescope and see a huge number of shining spots, thick in the center, and thinner around the edges. He said, "This is called a globular star cluster." I grabbed the biggest telescope but he took it from me and gave me the smallest one, whose lens has a diameter of only five inches. I could hold it easily. Through it I could see the moon's craters, Jupiter and its four moons, Saturn and its rings. He had a collection of strange maps on the table. He said they were an atlas of the sky that indicated the positions of the stars, constellations, nebulae, and galaxies.

Often we went out when people were asleep. The lights of Tell Bi'a are turned out, making the people above the ground equal to those below it. Nicholas would cut the electricity to his train car, take out the black metal stand and affix the big telescope to it—the one with a lens fourteen inches in diameter. Then he'd give himself over to contemplating the stars.

"Does the larger lens magnify the stars and planets?"

"It seems to bring them closer, but the telescope doesn't magnify them. It works to gather the light of distant stars and galaxies. Therefore, when the telescope's lens diameter is larger, the amount of light it can gather also increases. So the number of objects you can see through it also increases. The further away these celestial bodies are, the more dim they appear and the more light we need to see them."

"Why don't we know a lot about space?"

"We do know a lot. People have been thinking about space for a long time, since the ancient Greeks. The sky has always been an enigma to us. The Greeks concluded that observable phenomena could be described and interpreted, and this could be articulated scientifically, not simply through anthropomorphism. Then we began observing; observation is the basis of all science. Now we have a huge accumulation of knowledge—it brought us to the moon. Astronomers plan to reach Mars using robots or human crews. Perhaps we will also reach the edge of the universe, if we manage to make a vehicle that exceeds the speed of light hundreds of thousands of times. It will take approximately sixteen million light years to reach the furthest distance we have known up until now. Our problem therefore is that space is so big and time is so short. Ptolemy the Roman wrote *Almagest* in the second century. The book describes celestial movement but doesn't explain it. Astronomers remained dependent on that book until our friend came along. And who was that, Lulu?"

Abboud answers sarcastically, "Alexander the Great."

He doesn't know so I reply, "Al-Battani."

"Super! Yes, Al-Battani"

Whenever Abboud came with us to the train car, he got completely absorbed in everything. Actually, his desire to learn surprised me, as did his patience, his calm in working on intellectual subjects, and the wide-ranging knowledge he had, which far exceeded mine. Any time he was introduced to a new phenomenon, he'd immediately isolate himself from the world around him, his blank, brown hazelnut eyes scanning it thoroughly. He would bite his orange lips, thinking about how reasonable what he had seen or heard was.

He monopolized the small telescope. Then he tried another, changing the lens. My mother warned him that he might break something that belonged to Nicholas, and I thought to myself, I hope he does. My mother started asking me not to bring Abboud with me. She said that she was at work and not on a field trip. Once I was immersed in the world of horses, I started to detach myself from what they were doing. Abboud, too, got busy with the apiary his father built on a farm he'd bought in the Al-Sahel area west of the city. He stared spending a lot of time there and finding his way into making and harvesting honey.

My mother had studied just about everything written about Al-Battani. She prepared for this as if she were about to take a crucial examination. Being in love motivated her. She was always someone who worked on improving herself. Now she wanted to bridge the gap in knowledge between the two of them in any way that she could, though it was impossible. She exhausted herself researching and studying; this exhaustion somehow made her more beautiful, youthful, and anxious.

She read a lot. She used to spend the night reading so she could impress him. Meanwhile we couldn't tell what he was thinking. He was an unknown figure, who cried over speculations whose validity were in doubt, over graves that had been erased, and the illusions derived from so-called scientific facts that people use as they find convenient, jumping from one to another as they see fit. We also didn't know if Nicholas was spending time with her because she was helping him, because she was friendly with him, or because he was really as enamored with her as he was with this place, Al-Battani, and his stars. I heard him tell my grandmother, "Al-Battani never knew Najwa's star sign, but Nicholas does!" My grandmother laughed and her eyes shone, remembering what it was like to be in love. The way foreigners flirt is always understood as well intentioned, indeed as love and appreciation.

Najwa brought many books home from the cultural center—hardcover, brown, leather-bound books, which were all the same, with the center's stamp embossed on them, and volume numbers printed at the base of the spine. She opened them up on our dining room table, and started collecting information to prepare a summary to give to Nicholas. This included the translated works of Al-Battani. He would compare what she produced to the knowledge he had been collecting his whole life. He found a text to base his book on, accompanied by his photographs of the location of the observatory in Tell Bi'ah. A picture of him with all of us in the train car would appear in his book as well:

> Al-Battani lived in the ninth century AD. He was born in Battan in the province of Harran, between Raqqa and al-Raha. He was Sabian and then became a Muslim. The Sabian houses of worship were located along the banks of the Euphrates—their holy river—and they used to heed the movement of the skies and stars in their worship rituals. Al-Battani was also the nephew of the Arab scholar Thabit ibn Qurra, who was interested in astronomy. Al-Battani carried a copy of Ptolemy's *Almagest* with him at all times. He built an observatory in Antakia, then settled down in Raqqa, building the observatory whose ruins were are standing on today in the

year 878 AD /264 AH. He began this work when he was twenty four years old and spent forty years observing the stars.

Ptolemy and others proved the stable inclination of the sun's altitude and its movement. They also showed that the altitude of the sun's movement meant the movement of the spring and autumn equinoxes. But Al-Battani explained that this inclination changes with time. He made his astronomical instruments himself, like his device for measuring the angular diameter of the sun. He is the author of many works including: *A Commentary on Ptolemy's Tetrabiblos*, *Letters on Geography*, and *The Alignment of the Planets*. His most famous book of all is the *Kitab al-Zij* or *Book of Astronomical Tables*, also known as the *al-Zij al-Sabi* or *Zij al-Battani*. It came out in 900 AD /287 AH. It has an introduction and 57 chapters. Alfonso X of the Kingdom of Castile ordered it brought to Spain and in the twelfth century it was translated into Latin more than once. Copernicus studied it in the sixteenth century and relied on it to prove that the earth was not the center of the cosmic system. *Al-Zij* was printed in Rome in 1899, edited by Carlo Alfonso Nallino based on the manuscript preserved at the Escorial Library in Spain.

Al-Battani corrected many of Ptolemy's errors. For example, he proved that planets move around the sun in an elliptical, not a curved, orbit. The eighteenth century astronomer Richard Dunthorne relied on his research to prove the acceleration of the moon and the annular solar eclipse. He used tangent lines of arches to help calculate the solar quadrants. He also used sines and cosines, instead of just the hypotenuse, in astronomical calculations and trigonometry.

Mama sat on my grandmother's Strand chair and read out this information in a quiet voice, transfused with a beautiful huskiness that amazed me when she used to tell me stories. This was not so long ago, only four years ago or a bit more. I used to think that her husky voice came from having something stuck in her throat. I sometimes put my fingers on her warm, tender neck, to try to pull it out. She recited this information as if it were a love poem, "What is a Zij?"

"The term Zij comes originally from the Persian word for cord, to signify the cord a builder stretches along a wall to know its variants and to ensure it is level. Here it means the tables Al-Battani compiled to indicate the movement of the planets and their variations—he collected them all in tables. These are the computational rules pertaining to the motion of each planet when it is fast, slow, aligned, and retrograde. All of this helps to determine its exact position."

"Do hedgehogs eat strawberries?"

I ask her questions, which confuse her thought process and make her stop and think. In reality, Mama takes every scientific question I ask seriously. She never remains ignorant about any information that she might present to me. She didn't know the answer to this one and there was no Google back then. A few days later, she told me, "Hedgehogs do indeed eat strawberries, they are herbivores that eat fruits and plants. They awake in the strawberry season after hibernating all winter long."

"What about the astro...astrobabe?"

"Astrolabe. No Lulu, it's not acceptable that you are thirteen and you don't know how to say astrolabe properly. If it had been one of those naughty words you would have memorized it like it was your own name. The astrolabe is a domed astronomical instrument in the shape of the sky, which shows how the sky looks at a specific place and time. It also can measure the sunrise and is how we can tell time." When my mother said this, it ruined my day and I had no more desire to learn anything. I left her and sat out on the stoop in front of our house.

Nicholas memorized al-Battani's full name, just as we all say our own names, repeating it before us, like a challenge, chanting: Abu Abdullah Muhammad ibn Jabir ibn Sinan al-Battani al-Harrani al-Raqqi al-Saba'i.

Mama said that his unfortunate death happened for political reasons. He had accompanied a delegation from Raqqa to Baghdad to bring the people's grievances to the Sultan. He died near Samarra. Ignorance kills in all eras of great genius.

In the year 1651, an Italian scientist, Giovanni Riccioli, named a crater on the moon's near side after him: Albategnius. The International Astronomical Union officially confirmed this name for the ancient meteorite crater, located in a central place on the surface of the moon's near side in 1935, in recognition of his major scientific achievements. In 2013, one of the armed militant groups, which occupied the city of Raqqa and tampered with our destinies, brought down Al-Battani's statue. Most likely because he felt that our relationship had to improve, Nicholas asked me with a contrived seriousness, which I had my doubts about: "Have you studied deep space objects yet?"

"No," I replied, really longing to know more about them. I swapped some of my anger and jealousy for talking a little bit about this subject that I loved perhaps even more than my mother did. She loved it because she loved Nicholas. I loved it though I hated Nicholas.

"Deep-sky objects are all celestial bodies except the sun,

moon, planets, and stars."

"What is left in the sky then?"

"Comets, for example, which change locations every night."

"You mean like Haley's comet?"

At that time, we had heard that Haley's comet would appear in the sky and that we would be able to see it from Earth with the naked eye. It appears only every seventy-five years or so.

Children who thought they knew a lot were saying that it would fall on us and kill us. We were all really worried about it.

"Yes, Haley's comet is the most famous. It was named after the English astronomer Edmond Haley, who confirmed its existence but never got to see it."

"My grandmother says that the Star of Bethlehem was Haley's Comet."

"Exactly. Giotto's famous painting *Adoration of the Magi* was inspired by it in 1301. But Lulu, the nebula remains the most beautiful thing in space. It is a star whose center has collapsed and has begun to die."

"Ya Salaam! The idea of a dying star is sad, but also beautiful. A star can get tired and die, just like everything else."

"Bits of helium gather and extinguish the flaming center of the star so that its heart collapses."

Nicholas showed me pictures that NASA had taken of nebulae, dying stars.

"This is the Carina Nebula, it's made of dust and gasses."

"What a beautiful death…"

"You are going to be a poet, Lulu!"

I looked at his atlas, and pointed at a distant star: "What's the name of that star?"

"Maybe we could name it Lamees."

"I'm asking for real…"

"Not all stars have names. Our knowledge about the numbers of stars has developed with new observation methods and now they have numbers."

Najwa asked him, "Why isn't there a star sign for Orion, like there is Capricorn, Aquarius, and Pisces?"

"Orion is one of the constellations the sun, moon, and other planets do not pass by, though they do pass by other constellations, which make up the better-known signs of the Zodiac."

"My grandmother says that stars are the pure guardians of the heavens, the souls of those people who survived the atrocities of the earthly world, and are at different distances from the earth depending on the good works they did in their life on Earth. Those who are farther away are happier because they are closer to the heavens and therefore to God!"

My mother gazed at me lovingly, "Remember Lulu, how Anna used to always say that each of us was born of a star shining in the sky, protecting us throughout our life, and when we die, our star goes out."

"In reality, collapsing stars are what produced us. We are created of their remains, they are made of the matter of which everything is created: the calcium that makes our bones and teeth is what makes stars, so is the iron in our blood, the nitrogen in our DNA, the carbon in a piece of cake we eat. Not every star in the sky has a human body on Earth connected to it—as Anna would have said—but perhaps each atom in us comes from a different star."

My faith in Nicholas was renewed after these conversations. I lied to myself about his relationship with my mother: He's a foreigner, not an Arab…It's normal that he touches her shoulders and hugs her. He thinks of her as an assistant, a friend, or even as a sister. He hugs everyone in that same way—my grandmother, Auntie Maria, Auntie Safia…He's a scientist; he doesn't even really have time to think about such trivial things as love or women.

I would have preferred to stop worrying. I went out to sit in front of the train car, fatigued and exhausted. I brought a light blanket with me, the one Nicholas used so as not to be caught out in a breeze in the middle of the night, and stretched out to fall sleep. I heard whispering and muffled voices and I didn't want to understand what was being said, or have it clarified, so long as there was nothing I could do but cry or kill myself.

"No doubt you are made of most noble stars, loved by God," she laughed flirtatiously, the light of lost love shining in her hazel eyes. She leaned into his chest, and he held her shoulders hugging her. He rested his chin on her head, his fingers running through the thick waves of her hair:

"I can't give you a Zij or a crater on the moon—I'm not that great, Najwa. But I will write a book dedicated to you and it should be done soon!"

I was sure she wasn't thinking about these kinds of things. Such words didn't mean a lot to her. All she was thinking about was being in his arms, and how she could stay there for the longest possible time. She would rather have had that than a galaxy. But did my mother like to take refuge in Nicholas's lap the same way that I liked to in Abboud's? Or do grownups have different desires that transcend these kinds of feelings? I believed that God was punishing me for thinking about Abboud, by making my mother think about Nicholas.

Being so busy in her new job calmed my mother down a great deal. She no longer spoke badly about my father. Indeed, she stopped mentioning him at all, as if he'd ceased to exist. She was more concerned about herself—exercising, cooking, reading magazines. She started passing by the car parts shop to check up on business, and also visited my grandfather's properties. She went back to spending a lot of money on our clothes, and taking care of our house, which we'd more or less abandoned except as a place to sleep. We'd started spending most of our time at my grandmother's house across the street. Because of both her own grandiosity and Nicholas's help, Najwa managed to forget how two brothers had both left her. Her self-esteem increased exponentially, to the point even of megalomania, after the German astronomer compared her to one of the planets above:

"Now I know the reason Al-Battani was so attached to this place and spent his life observing the sky from here—not for celestial bodies but because of those walking on the earth! He must have fallen in love with one of your ancestors, who had your eyes and your ginger hair."

His long fingers played with locks of her hair. He parted it into two bits while she was sitting on the edge of the wooden chair which had become a sofa—its back to the train car's wall, a new green mattress laid down across it.

"Why don't you have black hair like most Arab women?"

"My mother is Turkish."

"Perhaps from one of your father's relatives?"

"Maybe. This would have happened hundreds of years ago and that's a long time! I don't believe that those tribes lived here, where you and I are sitting."

"But I believe in rules of existence that say, What happens once can happen again!"

"A few months and you will go, leave me, and forget all about me."

"You can come with me."

"We belong to two different worlds, that are like two parallel lines."

"You and I are both space. In space, everything changes. It is possible for parallel lines to intersect."

Nicholas used to engage with scientific truth as he pleased. He didn't distort it but he changed the way he presented it. Abboud and I were exposed to a different level than the one he used to lecture Najwa about. He played with ideas like a circus clown juggles colorful balls. I believe that this is the very meaning of his title—Professor of the Public Understanding of Science.

Najwa asked him, "Why did al-Battani come to Raqqa? Is the sky here clearer or closer? Or are the stars here closer together? Are there more of them?"

He replied neutrally, while organizing a stack of his fifty-page notebooks, the kind with a cardboard cover and a photograph of the president on the front: "He came because of the earth, not because of the sky."

"What do you mean?"

"Come, come here, you and Lulu too!"

He opened the notebook and sketched out a little map. He drew lines between three points, forming a triangle. "He came for this triangle—Raqqa, Harran, and Raha. There were universities dedicated to science and translation here. Many Syriac people, who were the preeminent figures in astronomy, medicine, and translation, had settled in the area."

We stayed late that night. We sat in front of the train car—door open, meager light cast off from the lamps hanging from the ceiling, limping out from inside it.

Najwa said, "The sky tonight is crazy—it's chaos. I've never seen more stars and can't distinguish between them."

"An astronomical system is hidden within this apparent chaos."

He took a pencil and started drawing lines between the points, to give shape to the constellations. Leo appeared, and then the twins, which make up Gemini. Then there were four consecutive broken lines, Aries. I make a dramatic statement to provoke them, "Stars are like pimples dotting the face of the sky—they are ugly and need popping!"

The two of them ignored me, and my mother continued on, "What about al-Battani's private life? His family?"

"We don't know too many details about his private life. But at the time, when scientists fell in love they surrendered to it innocently. They lived it and didn't talk much about it. They chased love like a secret of existence. Like everything they do, scientists approach love little by little, study it in detail, and then master it. Words are for poets!"

"And you? Why did you come here? Don't you have a sky where you are from?"

He replied with exaggerated seriousness that he came to hear the sound of the stars, which captured al-Battani, to walk in his blessed footsteps, to dream his dewy dreams on the shores of the Euphrates.

Without looking at anyone's face, I said quietly, but so that they could hear, "You came to destroy our family!"

My mother snapped back at me, "Get out of here and go play, Lulu, now."

I wished I could have gotten out of there forever so she would never see me again. I hoped for God to punish her by taking me away, so that she regretted it and repented for her wrongdoing!

She told me to get out? She thought I didn't understand. She wanted to be alone with him to talk to him secretly, to cry on his shoulder, and badmouth my father, lost time, her abandonment, her betrayal. She wanted to play house with him: she'd be the queen of the castle and he'd be the king.

Shortly before we left the train car, Stephanie and her assistant Rudolph arrived. Stephanie was the director of the German archeological expedition, which had been excavating Tell Bi'a for the three years prior to Nicholas' arrival. Everyone here listened to her, not only Nicholas. We started considering her a sort of messenger of Tuttal, the Roman City that was established here in 3000 BC. We asked her about people in the past—their customs, their houses, as if she were one of them, who had snuck out from one of those graves and joined us. She always gave us answers that satisfied our questions about our roots and made us proud of the place we grew up in.

Stephanie became friends with my mother and grandmother, and the neighbors too. She spent her Fridays in our neighborhood accepting everyone's invitations to lunch and dinner. She exuberantly devoured their food, no matter how basic, with pleasure and never refused an invitation. Everyone called her the old lady and Rudolph the old man. She was somewhat advanced in years, but the way she looked made her seem even older. Her gray hair hung to her shoulders, her skin was wrinkly, and Raqqa's harsh sun had quietly left its mark on her and toasted her brown. She was tall and big boned, but not at all fat. She'd perhaps added six or eight pounds from all the liver, kebabs, and kishk she consumed.

She wore a colorful scarf around her neck, one of those silk ones with traditional patterns that the women of Raqqa tied around their heads. She was always well dressed in cotton trousers and a white or blue blouse. Her watch had a brown leather strap and large black Roman numerals set against a white enamel background. Her prescription glasses had tinted lenses that could be clipped over them. She had learned a lot of local vocabulary and said things like, "yawal" for child, *jayyif, shain*, and pronounced the word for coffee with a light "k" sound instead of "g." Instead of calling someone a thug she would use our local expression, *Baba Hassan*. Everyone loved her and when children ran into her in the street they would teasingly call out, Heil Hitler, giving her the Nazi salute.

In the evenings she sat with Nicholas and spoke to him in German. When there were local young men, women, and girls—sometimes people my age—from the area, they would switch and speak in Arabic, mispronouncing words and laughing: "Give me a glass of shanyana yogurt."

Stephanie's authority was not only derived from the fact she was the messenger of Tattul, or lived with her team in the government guesthouse. But we saw her as the person who was in charge of deciding which of us got to enter the past, represented by the yellow tape marking the restricted area. This is where a big square hole had been dug for the excavation of the ancient city. Large metal signs warned that it was forbidden to approach it or take photos.

Stephanie pointed east toward the Baghdad gate saying, "This is the official gate leading to the overland road to Baghdad, through which the Caliph would enter and leave. Its distinctive architectural design and decorative motifs all indicate this. I found writing on it that stated, 'This door is commissioned by Prince of Believers, Harun al-Rashid—may God grant him a long life—supervised by his chamberlain Fadl ibn al-Rabi.' To the north there is Raha Gate, which leads to Raha and Harran, now in Turkey. To the west is the Gate of Paradise, which leads to Raqqa's famous orchards, with their greenery, beauty, and fine wines. As for the south, that's the Euphrates—no friend or foe could approach the city unless they crossed it." Stephanie continued, "We also found a cup belonging to the Roman Emperor Charlemagne here. He was a friend of Rashid and exchanged gifts with him. He is buried in my city, Aachen, in Germany, in the well-known Emperor's cathedral there."

She also said, "Rashid was attracted to the two rivers of Raqqa, Al-Hani' and Al-Mari', and his brother Hadi, who wanted to grant the state to his son Jaafar, encouraged him to do it. Rashid said, 'If I could possess the Al-Hani' and Al-Mari' rivers, and be alone with my cousin Zubeida, I wouldn't want anything else.' But his adviser Yahya Khalid al-Baramki said, 'Surely you can't compare this to the Caliphate?' Later Hadi was convinced and stuck to what was his by right."

I walked with Stephanie and Rudolph toward our neighborhood. I loved to accompany the two of them on walks and listen to them talk. My mother stayed an hour or two later than me to finish her work, or so she said. She gave Nicholas a lift after he'd enjoyed his fill of Stephanie's stories about Caliphs and Empires, cups, plates, and chalices...He looked out towards the tombs and the lights of the Euphrates glimmering in front of him where the ferries that Rashid once loved, locally called *harrakat*, passed back and forth. Their lights reflected in the water. He filled his lungs with air and whispered, "The fresh scent of life, the scent of immortality, we will not allow such beauty to fade. How do we just go and leave it?" Then he wept…and Najwa wept in his arms. Had she become so sensitive toward beauty and history? Does love infect us, teach, and make us conform to our lovers and reconstitute ourselves? Or does she weep for time that she has poured into the wrong vessel, leaving her destitute and broken?

He hugged her to his chest saying, "This universe will gradually fade away and die, like a rubber ball loses its bounce and begins to rise and fall more slowly. Let's delay that, Najwa, let's delay things." Najwa shared her warm kisses in a process of delaying the slow depletion of the universe, caressing his hair back gently, running her fingers through his fine mustache and long beard. His hairs were twisted in her carefully filed, shiny white painted fingernails. These were the same nails she used to scratch my head in the bathroom until they nearly scraped my scalp off. Then she pulled his head right onto her chest to plant his lips between her breasts that she had infused with the scent of amber, sandalwood, and plums—from Yves Saint Laurent's Opium. I had become the dying star whose center had collapsed and transformed into a nebula.

With the beginning of September, the northern breeze creeps in to occupy the city. The sun's tyranny is broken; white clouds gather and rise over our heads. Little ripples curl the surface of the water and those people with sensitive noses can begin to detect the scent of the earth, which announces the coming of the rains. School children know well the feeling of gloom that September brings. It's not the yellow leaves on the trees or the sun withdrawing, but rather returning to the prison of being at home, at school, and asleep on a schedule. The neighborhood grows sad; even the birds are silent as if they've forgotten their summer songs.

One timid morning Nicholas sat down to drink coffee in my grandmother's garden. He was wearing a navy blue cotton jacket over a white t-shirt and gray trousers, leaning his head back and stroking his hair. He slid his body onto his seat and intoned words like a poem. Najwa was sitting on a chair across from him, reluctant to look at his face, gazing instead at the lemon tree, which had started to lose its pale leaves. Her eyes glowed with tears, lending them a singular innocence. He was also gloomy. I'd never seen him in this state before. He followed her movements, eyes brimming with heavy tears. His features caught me off guard. I find tears in a man's eyes so beautiful! He started translating lines of his mother's poem about September for her. Then he massaged his temple with his long fingers, burned by the summer heat, as if trying to get his blood circulating.

Summer's train rushes to September

I walk, and do not meet it

Alone I sweep the station's sidewalk

And wave at the passersby with a broken hand.

Stop a minute and hold me with half exhilaration

And half extinction

If September doesn't teach you love,

Let the old women gather up the plates of figs from the rooftops.

If September doesn't teach you love,

Let us have a majestic funeral for this tale tonight!

Nicholas began gathering up his things, preparing to go back to Germany. The train car was returned to its owners. He left copies of the pictures we were all in, and gifted me the small telescope after asking permission to do so from his friend in Damascus. I wasn't as happy with his decision to go back as I'd expected to be. What had happened, happened, and it couldn't be erased by his leaving.

He hugged me when it was time to leave and I felt a big lump replacing a certain warmth that had left my heart. I didn't know what he and my mother had agreed on, but she couldn't suppress her sobs. My grandmother didn't ask anything or console her. In Nicholas, my mother had found her eternally absent brother, as well as the two men who'd left her. Like Auntie Maria, Auntie Safia, and the rest of the neighborhood, my grandmother was sad too, since he brought the familiarity of a bygone masculinity back into her home.

They all bade him farewell at the Karnak bus station in the square. Karnak was the only transportation company operating in Raqqa. Abboud insisted on helping them carry his things. Nicholas would go first to Damascus and then travel on to Frankfurt.

Mama went back to being indifferent. She no longer read or dyed her hair. She gained a little weight. We became two empty, wounded beings. Our sadness once again equalized us. Almost two weeks later, Abboud and I committed our sinful act, killing my grandmother and her pure soul. I entered a phase where I struggled with my own sins that cast a shadow over me. I wished at the time that my mother could have brought Nicholas back.

He would ease her sadness, and liberate me from some of my guilty conscience. But he never came back. She in turn quickly fell into a menopausal mood, and then biology caught up with her. Parting from Nicholas meant she was bidding farewell to the joys of the spirit and body forever.

THE DAY OF THE APPLE

The world basked in the celebration of fabulous films at the cinema that year: Fellini's *La Dolce Vita*, Kubrick's *Spartacus*, Henry Hathaway's *North to Alaska*, and Fatin Abdel Wahab's *A Rumour of Love*. The performances left my grandmother Karma empty, weeping and full of grief. But this was shattered on the winter night when my uncle Najeeb was born, with the help of Terfanda, the only Armenian midwife inside the city walls.

Terfanda had gotten pleasantly drunk with Doctor George. It was Christmas Eve and they were alone. A single, unattractive, fifty-something-year-old woman, and a sixty-something-year-old man, a dentist who spent his life inside his patients' mouths, fixing bridges, inserting cheap metal fillings, and popping out decayed molars for villagers who never thought to visit him until after they'd exhausted all their traditional remedies and were walking around in pain. Doctor George gave off the smell of anesthesia at all times, even on holidays. His wife had traveled with their two children to America so they could continue their studies. He'd stayed behind alone to work and send them money for their endless expenses. His tiny clinic's waiting room was flooded with more clients than chairs, so they spread out on the floor. Those who couldn't find a space inside sat outside on the rickety old steps of the building to wait their turn. Terfanda would call them in using her commanding public voice like someone announcing a Sultanic decree.

Terfanda worked as a nurse between two clinics—those of Doctor George and Doctor Khalil, who was a gynecologist. My grandfather the Agha was very nervous when my grandmother's water broke. He pulled tipsy Terfanda by the hair and held her under the faucet to wake her up. She cursed at him in turn, wishing him and his wife ill in the three minutes it took them to walk together from her house to his. But when my uncle's head popped out into the world, she was so happy she cried tears of joy. She told my grandmother that a new messiah had been born and they should call him Issa, Arabic for Jesus. My grandmother had long ago chosen a name and she hung around his neck a golden chain with a pendant of Saint George on his horse, holding the sword that he used to slay the dragon. She said, "He is my intercessor, the intercessor of Bethlehem, and your intercessor on heaven and earth, my baby Najeeb." The chain never left my uncle Najeeb's neck and everyone who saw him thought he was Christian, especially as Terfanda called him Issa until the day she died. My uncle always used to pamper her, making her liver and kebab sandwiches served with araq. They would chat into the evening over a glass or two…or three. He was basically her only companion after Doctor George went to America and never returned. My uncle Najeeb truly fulfilled Terfanda's prophecy—he was granted both Christ's suffering and His redemption.

My uncle Najeeb grew up good-natured, loveable, and earnest all at the same time. The first image I remember of him was as a university student. I didn't hear much about his early life from my mother or grandmother. I believed that he'd begun life as a young man with no childhood. Even the black and white photo under the glass on my grandmother's vanity in her room didn't make me think of him. In it you see a child wearing hand-knitted woolen overalls and a Saint George pendant hanging on a gold chain around his neck.

There is another picture of him with my mother under the glass of her own vanity. They are on the beach by the Turkish seaside at Alanya, playing with pails and shovels. He is dressed in shorts and Mama is wearing a swimsuit: two small bodies with delicate features, topped by thick hair. But I can't connect these two people in the photo with the two of them. In pictures people seem happier and more relaxed—surreptitious snapshots of fun suggest that people were always happier in their past.

Everything said about Najeeb indicated he possessed an unusual intelligence. He achieved his goals quietly, with studied wantonness, like an arrow that never misses but whose path is unknown. People in the neighborhood felt that Najeeb supported them and would never let them down. He read a lot. He had a rich library and followed the news live, on many stations, from London, Cairo, and Damascus. He sat with his five or six friends on the large balcony overlooking the neighborhood's central courtyard. They would talk about politics, and my grandmother and her friends would join in. The magical power of youth assailed these women, and they all stayed up together until dawn, while my uncle and his friends would prepare a home-style dinner for everyone: cheese, labneh, fried eggs, and makdous. Other times they would buy grilled meats or roasted chicken from the nearby market to honor these elderly women in their seventies, reclining on summer sofas like lonely sultanas. In return they would hear these ladies' outrageously ribald nightly tales, with the ladies prepared to simply order the sultan, "Get up" and he would get up…

My grandmother always insisted on offering everyone her famous juices: plum, peach, apricot, or lemon. My grandmother would squeeze anything she had on hand at home, and chill it in the icebox until it was frozen. Then she would present it in her precious Bohemian glasses, putting a mint or basil leaf on the top of the cup, so you would feel like you were having a drink at a five-star hotel. She would offer everyone juice in her crystal glasses, even the garbage collectors. As she always used to say, "When we die, we leave everything behind."

When there were lengthy electricity cuts in the eighties, my uncle would go with his friend Majdi to his family's factory in the Chevrolet Camino convertible. They would prepare blocks of ice there, two roads away from our house. They would break them on the bathroom floor, wash them, and distribute them in buckets. The water was always very cold. They would put pieces of ice down each other's backs and my grandmother would smack them because they'd gotten the floor wet. My uncle and his friend cleaned my grandmother's house and insulated the ceilings and the walls during their summer holidays. They washed her carpets after the winter was over. They also painted the rooms that she wanted to renovate.

In the winter she used to put rugs down in the sitting room and they would play Barjees for some kind of a bet, usually they'd play for a lunch of grilled meats. They would divide into two teams and start throwing the shells: dast, banj, do. They would repeat the traditional taunts of the game: "bara wara'ha khsara" and "shikka wara'ha fikka." They would shout over each other and accuse the other team of cheating. When defeated, my grandmother would fold up the black velvet playing board with her copper pieces, as well those of her opponents, inside it. The sound of metal would ring out along with the protests of the players. Part of the board would remain open, so you could just see the words of "Inta Omri" and Khayyam's *Rubiyat* embroidered on it in green thread.

My image of winter in the neighborhood includes Barjees and café au lait. That's before the rains and the bountiful wheat seasons, when the pothole-filled streets would overflow with pools of muddy water. Because of this, there would be lines of shoes in front of every house—to walk on the carpet with shoes on was the one unforgiveable sin! Despite the warmth and familiarity of our winters, Raqqa remains a summer city. And jolly Uncle Najeeb remained a man of joy not only inside the house but out in the neighborhood and in its interwoven alleys, which are a maze that only locals can weave their way through.

My uncle Najeeb loved swimming in the Euphrates. Because of the state's neglect of public facilities and its disregard for the simple recreational aspirations of its citizens, he and his friends made a beach especially for themselves. They chose a sidewalk under the bridge, directly on the water, and set up some reclining beach chairs they'd bought in Aleppo. Each of them had a different color cushion for his chair. They used to bring towels, sunscreen, and fruits with them. They brought cherries, apricots, and figs with cheese in straw baskets. They drove the Chevy Camino down to the mobile wooden shack that they'd constructed. It was a bit larger than the guard's stations outside important people's houses.

They spent the summer there, going daily, sometimes even sleeping down on the banks of the river. My mother, grandmother, and I, and sometimes even my father, would join them at night. We often went on an unbearable afternoon when we couldn't stand the heat. The kind of day when the air is still and you feel that all the troubles of people have been gathered up together and weigh heavily on the city's chest so it can't breathe. But down at the shore of the river, only three miles from our neighborhood, space opens up and there are generous breezes. All together they used to shout: Allah! We imagined that the door of paradise had opened up just a crack.

My uncle always had that permanent tan of light-skinned people who stay out in the sun all the time. His tan never faded. He would invite us to eat grilled mullet or catfish he'd bought from the fisherman standing on the bridge. He would show me the fish, which were still flopping around in the water of the metal buckets and I would touch their sharp, wet scales with my fingertips. The grill came from a nearby café. My uncle would take the bucket, followed by his friend Kamal, who would supervise the washing of the fish and spice it with cumin and coriander, olive oil and salt. Then he would grill it over the coals, and serve it with French fries, baba ghanoush, and a green salad. The scent of beer would waft through the air, mixing with the smell of water, reeds, and manure, as the sun beat down on the gravel, inflaming the lust of women and men and making them effervescent: their breath hot, their words enigmatic, their bodies sticky. They created the city's scent, which was a mix of all of this. My grandfather raised his glass high, and drank a toast to summer and the Euphrates. He allowed me more than one bottle of Sinalco Cola, while my grandmother and mother preferred Seven-Up.

My uncle called out to me, "Come on and let's fish a watermelon out of the water!" I actually believed for a moment that we caught watermelons in the Euphrates. My uncle always put melons in the river to keep them cool. He held my hand and helped me roll it to the shore. "Be careful the current doesn't take you!" he warned me. At night, the tide would begin to come in because the dam's turbines would open, making the water level rise. It would suddenly sink the chair legs, which we had put on the gravel road, several centimeters down, and they would shake. I hurried to sit on a little straw chair and plunge my foot in the cold water which would reach half way up my leg. This was the purest and cleanest water, redolent with the smell of the sun and greenery that it had stored up all day long. That is how it made this nighttime perfume, which only existed in Raqqa.

We went back to the neighborhood and left the young men sleeping under a roof of twigs and reeds. My grandmother warned them about the water's power. She also told them that she knew that they brought girls down to their little straw shack and that this could cause a big scandal. I loved to listen to this particular part. I would put my ear as close as possible to their hidden world and discover the secrets of their attractive and powerful young manhood: their strong brown bodies, their mature, naked chests, the gentle folds of their bellies, the gold chains laced around their necks, their taut, well-defined leg muscles wrapped in white shorts, and the powerful, fragrant perfumes they wore.

Najeeb and his friends used to throw themselves into the water from off of the top of the bridge. Cars driving down the main road would stop so the passengers could watch them. Tourists who happened to be passing through would gather and encourage them, along with the screaming children. There was a photograph of Najeeb diving into the water headfirst, that someone had taken with Mama's Japanese Nikon camera. I used to stare, my mother would put her fingers in her ears, my grandfather would cover his face with his hands, and my grandmother followed along, clapping enthusiastically. Every time the boys threw themselves off the bridge, my grandmother would repeat the same refrain: "The boys used to jump into the sea from the walls in Acre, just like this!"

I used to like Kamal's hands, as he had fascinating fingers. His pinky was retractable, and the bottom joint was separated from the rest of the finger. I held it and asked about why his fingers were crooked. He said that it was an old break, which was never splinted. He could fold the first joint of his index finger over like an umbrella, but keeping it straight. He would wiggle it in my face and make me laugh. I put my hand in his whenever I got the chance. My uncle's friends would always joke around with me. Majdi said, "Would you be my fiancée, Lulu?" I grimaced at him, turned my head, and smiled to myself. I thought all night long about becoming his fiancée. We would go out together, and kiss each other, and go on long vacations and hold hands on the plane and in the boat…I thought about how we would get rid of Hala, who we all knew he was in a relationship with. I imagined that she would cheat on him and he would leave her, or perhaps she would die. Then we could be a family and have children…In the morning, I would go back to my world, knock on Abboud's door, and we would sit together like we did every day. But I had matured a little so Abboud seemed younger than me. The stages we pass through in our imagination have an impact on our reality.

When Majdi proposed to Hala, the bride-to-be's family insisted on inviting him to lunch at their house. Before they put the food down in front of him, her sister came to wipe the table with a rag made from an old pair of women's cotton underpants. When Majdi saw this, he refused to eat lunch and left their house in disgust. He renounced their engagement. Hala took her case to my grandmother, who tried to change his mind. She told him that many people use such rags because the cotton used in underwear is purer and better quality than actual cleaning products. We told him, "Of course they washed it very well before using it!" but he shook his head and refused. Hala never married.

Kamal never married either. I didn't see him for a long time after that. When I was in my third year of university in Aleppo, he surprised me after one of my lectures when I found him standing at the door of the hall. He was elegant with a neat beard and wearing a casual shirt, trying to efface the many years' difference between himself and the students he found himself surrounded by. We sat in the garden at the university; I had no doubt about the reason he had come. He talked quickly, clearly, and it seemed he was aware of the marriage train that he wanted to catch before it left the last station. He said that he would ask my mother for my hand in marriage. I loved this idea; I loved being with him! We had a history that would provide the backdrop for both our sweet and our bitter times. I would relive my childish flirtation with him, and he would be able to understand how this stemmed from my old suppressed desires for him in his youth, which had now begun to fade.

Kamal was the branch manager of the People's Credit Bank. He carried the sadness of the sixties generation, which you could see seeping into the folds of the delicate skin around his eyes. He also agreed to grant quick loans, or high value accounts, and in return received a percentage in his personal account. I didn't see this in his eyes or on his hands, since they were very clean and his features were obviously the same ones I knew. I asked him to move his finger like he always used to do and to fold his index finger at the joint like an umbrella. I burst into tears, and encircled his finger in my hand. He wiped my tears away with his other hand. Then we strolled arm in arm and ordered burgers at a sidewalk restaurant in the Muhafiza neighborhood, near the university. I told him, "Mama would slaughter me if she knew that we were together." He replied, "I'll talk to her, let's go, stand up, Lulu, make me a promise." So I did. It was as if he were asking me to feed him a sandwich with my own hand or to give him a sweet out of a confectioner's bag. I spoke to my mother when I returned, and she started shouting and cursing at me. She accused me of being badly raised, which was her favorite insult for me, and which always backfired. She said that Kamal was a corrupt old man. She threatened to skin me alive if I met up with him again. She told me, "You are going to travel far away, your prince charming is not in this country." After she calmed down, she asked me to assure her that this matter finished here. I promised her and I lived up to my promise. When we left Raqqa for the final time, because of clashes between Daesh and SDF, Kamal accompanied us. He helped elderly people deal with their daily chores, moved his Auntie Umm Riyadh by motorcycle, and brought water for me and my mother. He stayed with us until all of us left to scatter ourselves throughout God's wide world.

Nahil, my uncle's other friend, was married. He was one of those friends who has more experience with life and its struggles than others even though he is younger. He has a daughter called Hind a few years younger than me. He fed her and looked after her more than her mother did, encouraging her to eat all of the food on her plate, since she liked to giggle, play around, and never finish her food. I used to love stories, always finished my plate, and would even ask for more. Nahil told Hind the same story every day, but she ate different dishes each day at dinner. When she was eating okra, he would tell the story, "When the Persian Khosrow visited the Roman Hercules he asked him for okra. So Hercules's cooks would mobilize, put on festivals, sing out with cheer, and receive a cart pulled by forty horses, loaded with pots of gold, emeralds, and diamonds. The soldiers and dancing girls would shout: ok-ra, ok-ra, ok-ra."

If the dish she was eating on another day was mulukhiya, the chant at the end of Nahil's story would change, while feeding Hind he would say, "mulukhiya, mulukhiya, mulukhiya." Nahil had fallen in love with a distant relative and married her when they were still in high school. He was the only child of a wealthy family, who owned bathroom supply shops. Everyone in the area was surprised at the couple's early marriage. They used to say, "Married so young, they are most certainly going to devour each other with lust."

I went to their wedding party at his family's house. The bride wore a frilly, white, off-the-shoulder dress. I stood and gathered up her dress and rubbed it between my fingers. I tried to touch her body, raised up on the bridal platform. She was very happy, dancing calmly, and waiting. He was in the room next to the courtyard where the party was. I looked for him, and found him cutting his nails. I told my grandmother that I'd seen the groom, still clipping his nails. Auntie Maria winked, "So he doesn't scratch her!" I held onto her expression, and I kept mulling it over it in my mind, while listening to everyone clapping for the bride and groom in the zaffeh procession. When Hind was in first grade, Nahil was put in prison because he belonged to an opposition movement in the communist party.

Hind had long black hair that she plaited in two rows. She was brown-skinned, with small, strikingly attractive eyes. Her laugh was pure as were the tears that rolled down her cheeks when someone cheated in a game. Her features were as soft as a newborn bunny rabbit's. Every morning, she got to the place where we would all meet up to walk to school on the back roads before her classmates did. She sat on the sidewalk and waited for them in her beige waistcoat, scarf, and peaked cap, with its two red or white ribbons. She stood as a prefect for one of the groups lined up, getting them ready for action. After the comrades had gathered, she would ask them, "Why are you late?" without waiting for an answer, of course. The wave of national anthems would begin, all in praise of the homeland, the Baath Party and its founding, the leader, and the pioneers:

"We are for the Baath, oh Pioneers, we are for Victory, oh Pioneers! The fields are before us, our path is to the factories…"

No one who saw her enthusiasm and pride while singing the national anthem so correctly would ever have thought that her father was a political prisoner. Her father had been detained for three years and she was singing for the people who had disappeared him. I found her to be a tough girl, carrying around the sorrow of being a temporary orphan and maybe even a permanent one. Sadness choked this little girl's heart. No doubt it would transform into bitter hatred when she discovered the truth—that she'd been singing for a state that stole her from her father's lap, as her little throat repeated the state's slogan: "One Arab Nation, carrying an eternal message!"

There's also no doubt that her mother was exhausted by trying to find a way to frame the accusations against him in a way that wouldn't harm her daughter or make her bear her father's burden. She wanted her to be allowed to live in peace, without the grudges or feelings of vengeance that coalesce into a bitter truth. This bitter truth pointed to her father's betrayal, or his falling prey to an injustice, which would make her a fresh young palm tree with no roots anchoring her in the soil. How could she not speak to any of us about the pain caused by his absence, and to not broadcast her longing for her father? Hind's immense suffering, and the exquisite pain of glorifying those who had made her a girl without a father by praising his executioners, and singing for their heroes, was a grave injustice. How could her mother defend this human holocaust to her? How could she bear to hear her singing to the enemy? Those who oppress us, and take our fathers from us, are no doubt our enemies.

The rest of the groups lined up in three rows. My group's line was complete as well. The shouts began. The sounds of rhythmic clapping rang out, as did chants. This all happened under my leadership as my group's prefect. I led them like a conductor, guiding the movement of the musicians and taking charge of their disorder. I was the officer who controlled the momentum of the troops, and moved them like pieces on a chessboard. Our group was the most active, had the loudest voices, was the most harmonious, and had the best rhythm. All of this excited my grandmother under whose window we were all gathered and cheering. She stretched her head out and shouted at us, destroying the rhythm I'd built up.

The worst part of this is that she ruined the solemn and authoritative image that I'd created for myself in the eyes of my colleagues through a great deal of diplomacy and perseverance. "Get out of here, take your friends and get out from under my window…go!" This is how Karma lost her cool. The only alternative to me bursting into embarrassing tears was to resort to a security threat, "I'll turn you in to the mukhabarat and they'll put you in prison!"

"Put me in prison, bravo…bravo, well done. Put me in prison, but get the hell out from under my window!"

I carried on with my responsibilities with great anxiety, after keeping calm in front of my classmates. I strove to seem unflappable as I suggested that we walk back to school because it was time, when in reality it wasn't actually time yet.

I went back to my grandmother's house in the afternoon. She welcomed me and gave me my lunch as if nothing at all had happened.

The ancient walls surrounding the old city of Raqqa contain endless stories. The houses support each other. One house is built atop another, and little rooms are built randomly on rooftops, making you feel that they're about to fall. They're often unlicensed and unsafe, but standing. You can find a house with a ceiling propped up by perpendicular tree trunks next to a brick house and another of reinforced concrete. There are formations that the finest architects couldn't design, resembling a medieval Italian neighborhood in Rome. The balconies and doors are encircled by mimosa trees, purple and red roses, white jasmine, and honeycomb which we squeeze little drops of nectar out of and lick up while listening to the conversations of the ladies standing in the doorways. These plants are often grown in old rusted barrels that used to contain cooking oil or ghee. Most of the houses aren't fancy but they overflow with familiarity. You feel that every house is your own, and every person you see is someone related to you.

Perhaps an abysmal sorrow created this familiarity! A sadness of unknown origins molded the people of Raqqa and transformed inherited emotions into a climate. You find this climactic state in our air and water, as well as on the city sidewalks. Even the ducks swimming in the Euphrates—you'll find them staring at the city along the shoreline apathetically, their thoughts elsewhere. Despite the fact that the river stretches along the southern edge of the city and doesn't penetrate its center, we interact with it as if it is a fact of daily life like yogurt, tomatoes, cucumbers, or the cooking oil every household needs. As long as it exists, we can tolerate anything: desert storms, the neglect and corruption of local officials, the sounds of strangers controlling our wealth. The Euphrates is the source of our calm and our fear at the same time. We know that we would not exist without it, but we know that there is danger that comes from it as well. This is especially true when we recall the Zionist slogan, "Israel's borders will stretch from the Euphrates to the Nile." These words always make us feel our importance, but also that we are targeted, that the Euphrates is the reason for our existence and our destruction all at once. Perhaps this is the reason for the sadness that is nestled in each and every one of us.

When you approach the city from the North, lights greet you like bright, colorful planets, swarms of stars projected on the ground. You will choose to cross one of the two parallel bridges over the Euphrates, which connect the countryside and the city. There is the old bridge, which the British built in 1942 to facilitate their soldiers crossing from Iraq to Syria during their battles with de Gaulle's troops against the Vichy forces. Then there is also the new bridge, which the Syrian government built in 1966 and remained the most used up until the most recent conflicts.

Fisherpeople and itinerants will greet you after parking their bicycles next to their buckets filled with bounty such as you might see at a wedding reception. Children swim under the bridge and families gather to drink their evening coffee. Perhaps some women will have gathered together the woolen stuffing from their mattresses and washed it in the river, preparing to return home where they will dry it out for a few days. They beat it with sticks and then re-stuff the mattresses, so it's like sleeping on a brand new bed—the kind of sleep God promises his most loyal servants awaits them in heaven! Then it is the turn of the drunks, downtrodden, and fugitive lovers. They leave bottles of Batta-brand araq and Sharq beer discarded on the gravel road, along with the tissues used to wipe their tears that either were swept away by the wind or got stuck on the stalks of the reeds standing on guard like an army protecting the waterbed.

When we left Raqqa not one bridge was left. Skirmishes between Alliance and Daesh airplanes burned the bridges leading to the city, which took us back to the boats of the 1940s. From now on, until further notice, pilgrims will not stand at the bridge, waving their farewells to their relatives. There will be no place for lovers' trysts on or under the bridge. Even brides will be deprived of the tradition that their mothers and grandmothers experienced before moving to their marital homes—every girl had to cross the bridge in order to truly become a woman. Moreover, as the tales go, a person is freed from any magic curse as soon as they cross the bridge out of the city!

You inch closer slowly and catch a glimpse of the lights of the city glittering like an undersea treasure, which the sea pushed onto the shore. But when you enter you find a terrible darkness. Darkness comes from inside, from an unknown location. Whenever you come near it, it escapes to somewhere else. Darkness returns to the many ruins scattered throughout the city, which transform into landmarks. If you wanted to direct someone to a house, shop, or even a government department, you would say, "Next to this or that ruined building." Every house is next to some kind of ruin, where we might sit or get stones read to play krinji, or fill the holes in the drainage pipes. Some may throw things they don't need into a ruin, and we will perhaps find some waste in there. There are always pieces of destroyed buildings in these ruins or the remains of walls with windows still in them. They could even be mistaken for pieces of Roman ruins in the city. There is also some kind of a wall that has an antique wooden door. If you push open the door it leads to another part of the ruin. You will find broken iron beds and empty whiskey bottles smashed in a drunken rage. There might be sheep grazing on the grass, which has sprouted up between the plants and pools of rainwater.

In one of the ruins of the city there is a scrapped car that has been there for thirty years. Children sit in the driver's seat and play driving, putting their hands in the empty space where the steering wheel should be. All houses also overlook ruins, on one side or another. The ruins have been around so long that they have become a part of the people's memory. The owners of the properties died before they found the money to invest in reconstruction. This is all despite the water, the green trees, and the clear blue sky. The color of ruins dominates in Raqqa, and brings it to our consciousness. The ruins are in our consciousness; this is what makes us us. Despite our laughter and joy, we end our stories with a lump in our throats and our conversations with sighs and hope.

Houses made of concrete are in ruins too. One large house that was demolished stayed that way for thirty years. The original owner's son works in Greece. He financed the building and completed the structure, but then fought with his siblings who were co-owners of the land. They wanted him to build them houses without having to pay for them, and without him increasing his share in the building. This is the case with so many of the ruins in the country, disputes over buildings and grudges about inheritance. The concrete building remained intact for twenty more years until being bombed by coalition planes. Before that, everyone in the neighborhood considered that building their property. We'd all invested in it; we'd had our weddings and funerals in it. We hid inside it and played hide and seek in its unfinished rooms and apartments. It witnessed so many of our tears, furtive kisses, and our bodies' secret stories.

There are concrete buildings in every neighborhood. Most of the city's houses are unfinished. People live in them before they're furnished and perhaps even before they've installed tiles or inside doors. They live as if in a shelter, completing their dwellings slowly. As soon as a house is finished, concrete appears on the roof for one of the family's sons, who is ready to marry and make his home there. Construction is ongoing and always incomplete.

When my uncle Najeeb died, they put his corpse in the concrete building next to our house. His friend Majdi went to the ice factory—by himself this time—and brought clear slabs of ice to help preserve the body from the intense heat until the burial. They planned not to tell anyone the body's arrival time or location, not even my mother and grandmother, but people gathered when they saw the ambulance parked in the neighborhood. My father hurried home, and hugged my mother close. It was the first time I saw her nestled in his arms. They wept together. I was observing them from the doorway, but I felt my tears moisten my sleeveless red sweater. I was overcome by a sudden nostalgia. This was one of the few moments I felt that we were a warm, loving family. I found myself grateful to my uncle Najeeb even in his death.

They washed him there quietly so as not to arouse the suspicions of the security forces who had informants crawling around the neighborhood. Even the expressions of mourning had to be fleeting and unsuited to the tragedy of Najeeb's passing. Neither my grandmother nor grandfather could mark the death of their only son. My grandmother didn't wail at the top of her lungs, and the women didn't cut off their braids and tear the clothes off their chests, as was the tradition for women in Raqqa. My grandfather repressed his tears, and they transformed into a poison that coursed through his bloodstream. This killed him only five months after his son's passing. My grandmother withdrew into silence. She used to say that God was punishing her with the loss of her son because she used to dance and show her body in front of men. I was afraid that what she was saying might actually be true!

I didn't see my uncle's corpse. But after the mourners returned from his burial, I went into the concrete building where they'd created an area to receive people for the funeral gathering. It wasn't in the neighborhood's large guesthouse overlooking the street. Security wanted everything to proceed with the least possible fuss. I crept out of the side door to the apartment and found the coffin. It was a rectangular but an irregular shape and made of cheap slabs of wood. There was a big spot of blood on the shroud wrapped around his head. His clothes were strewn around on the ground, spilling out of a blue bag: his green velvet trousers, navy blue cotton shirt, and his silver Citizen watch with the dark blue band was still working. The second hand ticked by gracefully. It was like a death knoll reverberating in my skull. I snatched it before anyone noticed and I've kept it with me ever since. I hid it from my mother, though she eventually saw it in my drawer. But she didn't take it; instead she clasped it close to her chest and burst into tears.

The light at my grandfather's house was extinguished. The neighborhood lost its joy with jolly uncle Najeeb's passing. Everyone mourned him, young and old, men and women. They postponed all weddings for a year, and didn't welcome people back from the Hajj in Mecca with decorations and drums as usual, nor did they write the traditional messages on the doors of their houses that year, welcoming them home.

When my uncle Najeeb was in prison, we also had no way to express our anxiety. We could only communicate in muted tones. All talk turned into whispers, even things that had nothing to do with his arrest or the accusation that Najeeb and his friend Nahil belonged to the communist opposition party. We weren't permitted to speak about Najeeb in front of any child in the neighborhood, no matter how well we knew them. Any kid might say something, and the mukhabarat asked children questions, often believing what they said in literal terms, not taking their imaginations into account. We had to act like everything was normal, as if Najeeb was just studying abroad, or on a vacation, or a work trip…He'll be home soon, and he'll get married, his children will fill the house. They'll storm into Karma's room and play with her powders and blushes, eye shadows and mascaras. They'll open the old rusted metal box where she keeps photographs and the edge will cut one of their fingers. Blood will pour out, and my uncle will come in smacking the box closed, "Ah, ah, bad box!" He'll clean the child's wound with rubbing alcohol. Karma will faint from the sight of blood. My mother will look up without interest, and then keep reading her book saying cynically, "That happened to a Jewish man once, and he died." This was the scene we hoped to someday witness while Najeeb was missing. During his absence though, we suspected that we might never again see joyful days and that our laughter and songs would transform into muffled moans.

I saw them on the day they came to take him for questioning. I was playing with Abboud in the neighborhood, and had gone inside to make cheese and jam sandwiches for us. This is what we used do when we got hungry while playing. We'd go into my grandmother's kitchen or ask my Auntie Maria who lived next door to us to give us something to eat: sandwiches with zaatar, or tahini and molasses. We used to avoid asking Anna for anything because she would realize that playtime should be over and that Abboud had to come back inside. When I came out of the kitchen, sandwiches in hand, I found my parents, grandparents, and uncle dancing to a song, "Ala Um al-Manadil." They were standing close to each other, in the living room that was quite dark because the shutters to the window looking out onto the street were closed. Light only seeped in through the courtyard door. They were all holding hands, like ghosts on a sinking ship. Nour El-Houda's voice crackled on the gramophone. I stood next to the door and my uncle called out to me to join them, but I didn't respond.

I was stuck in the doorway watching them, sure that they were a crazy family. My grandmother, the debkeh leader, stood up first and lifted up a bunch of tissues, which my grandfather had separated sheet by sheet, making each one into two over many hours. This was in the period when we were compelled to save resources during the Syrian government's official belt tightening policy of the 1980s. My grandmother bent over gently, her shoulders remaining straight with pride. Her chest was raised, her smile never left her lips. She couldn't break the rhythm no matter how sharp the movement. She had total control over her moods and movements. My mother danced debkeh unsmilingly, as if carrying out a military order.

Their movements were sedate and rhythmic. They pondered the words and melody; they flew away in rapture. My grandmother pulled her chest up high then folded it back down to her knees gracefully, causing enthusiasm to rush through the other three. Every so often my grandfather did a strange jump, like a rooster, but he stayed on rhythm. My uncle put Mama in the center and closed the circle around her, and moved it to another place. She started bending like a grape vine growing over a trellis. I rejoiced in her beauty, and bliss inhabited my body. It was the first time I saw this allure in her, it was as if holy oil had loosened her stiff joints. While all this was going on, there were three violent knocks on the outside door. Then someone rang the doorbell, holding down the button and not releasing it until my uncle went outside. We followed him, wondering who was knocking. They pulled him out of the house, simply, just like that. All the while we stood, devastated and defeated, watching them walk away.

My grandmother cried and my mother cried. My father and grandfather left the house, terrified, and didn't return until after midnight. Trying to summon some kind of logic, my grandfather said, "I am an Agha, my father was an Agha, and my son is not a communist. There must be a misunderstanding; this must be because of a malicious report." My grandmother had no obvious or special prayers or supplications for the situation. This was part of her sadness and loneliness sometimes, but she found a way to talk to God about it. She would spontaneously just say things like, "Oh God, I am so sad! Why are you doing this to me? Bring Najeeb back home to me today. I am mad at you, God. I am hurt, God, I want my son back, God..."

This was her character, she always said what she was feeling. She couldn't speak in eloquent proverbs or metaphors that would indicate something you needed or express a thirst for revenge. When one of her friends would mention a common proverb while she was talking, my grandmother would repeat it and memorize it. But she always failed to use it in the right moment. She had two or three Egyptian proverbs, which we never say in Raqqa. She would say the Egyptian version of expressions like, "Let's see what the future holds" and "All things come to an end." But when Najeeb was in prison she started repeating over and over, "The mother of a murdered man sleeps, but the mother of an accused man never sleeps..." My grandfather and father started going out for long periods of time together, searching for some kind of wasta, connections who could mediate on their behalf, any information about how to get him out, some clue as to which branch of security services arrested him, where he was being detained, or any of the circumstances about his imprisonment and arrest. They were trying to do this before the oblivion of prison swallowed up any news of him. This can easily happen to a person who is then forgotten. My mother just wept bitterly, the tears of someone who has lost a second self, carrying their weakness and errors.

My uncle Najeeb had a girlfriend who made me die of jealousy. I snitched on him when he talked to her on the phone, making a lot of noise, "My uncle is talking to his girlfriend on the phone, his girlfriend is on the phone…he closed the door and is talking to a lay-dee." I would say all this to Mama and then go repeat the same thing to my grandmother. They would both scold me for saying this, or just ignore it, since it wasn't acceptable for a man to be talking to a woman he didn't really know on the phone at that time. My uncle Najeeb used to break these kinds of rules, he did all sorts of forbidden things and no one ever took him to task for it. I always threatened to tell her parents. But I never met them. I never even saw anyone from her family, seeing as they didn't live in Raqqa.

My uncle Najeeb met Uruba in Aleppo, where she was his classmate in law school. Her father was a judge well known for his firm integrity and political commitment. He also was a friend of my grandfather's. They weren't close friends, but when he was assigned to work in Raqqa at the beginning of his career, they used to spend evenings together at home or at the farm, and have a drink. They would have lunch at my grandmother's house on Fridays. My uncle and Uruba were children at the time and the judge's family didn't live with him in Raqqa. He would go back to Aleppo on his holidays. My grandparents also used to visit them when they were in Aleppo, even many years after he left Raqqa. During those visits, they would stroll through the Montana Club and spend evenings together at the Aleppo Club. Over time the relationship between the two families became less close because of distance and being busy, but they always remained friendly.

Najeeb met Uruba again by chance. Their shared memories about an ancient history lent their relationship a certain intimacy. He wanted to get engaged but her father refused categorically. Her father asked her to stop seeing him before the matter reached the formal level of involving their parents. This was not only because the judge was a rising star in the Baath Party and it was suggested that Najeeb had communist sympathies, but also because he knew about my grandmother's history, which clung to her children like an immutable genetic code.

Comrade Uruba became an political figure active in the Baath Party, and intervened to release my uncle Najeeb at a critical and dangerous moment. This might have threatened her political future. But all she could do was return his body to us. She came to Raqqa for his funeral. It was the first time I'd laid eyes on her. She was slender and brown, average height with small, dark eyes and a pointed nose. She was wearing a black suit, with a knee-length pencil skirt, white shirt, high-heeled black shoes, and sheer gray stockings. She wore a short white scarf covering her hair, tied loosely under her chin allowing some black strands to show. Every few minutes she adjusted the knot of the scarf so it wouldn't fall off, displaying her shiny

French-tip manicured nails, long fingers, and veiny hands. She was a Member of Parliament, and premature age showed on her face. Her countenance betrayed a stoic sadness appropriate to her political position.

It seemed to be an overreach of her power to take such a gamble and offer condolences on the death of Najeeb, the political prisoner who opposed the party, which she was a representative of. My grandmother spontaneously greeted her, since she wasn't aware of this political equation, and she'd been totally out of it during the first days after the tragedy. If not, she would have eaten Uruba alive or thrown her out. But Urbua kept helping us with things related to the government whenever we needed mediation, or wasta, after Najeeb passed away. She continued to help us get things done without complaint. When one of the powerful people or thugs in the neighborhood burglarized our property, or a government employees tried to charge us extra taxes because of my grandfather's feudal past, or cut off the water to our land, or skipped our turn to have our telephone line installed, even when they tried to transfer my mother out of her government position…we would ring up Uruba. She would always find a quick solution to our problems.

I compared Uruba and Nada, his girlfriend during the holidays in Raqqa. The comparison always ended up in favor of Nada. Nada was the daughter of our neighbors. She was tall, full-figured, and had thick dark-blonde hair. Her braids were always pulled as tight as the silken ropes that the heroes would climb up in the Lady Bird children's book series. She had beautiful golden blonde tufts of hair at the top of her forehead. Her round green eyes were framed by unkempt bushy brown eyebrows. If a fashion model's representative had seen her, they would surely want to recruit her for their agency. Her body was firm, her waist slender, and her hips full. Her nose was well shaped and her lips red as a plum, round, prominent, and ready for a furtive kiss. Nada always seemed calm, standing in front of the large door to her house with its vast lush gardens and alabaster floors, or on the balcony, never looking directly into people's faces, her eyes moving nervously over the things she was studying.

Nada was born with a congenital incurable deafness, the result of which was that she grew up unable to speak. It was widely believed that the reason for this was that her parents were close relatives, though some people said that she'd fallen on her head as an infant. Still others thought that it was the evil eye. When we were small, we were certain that the reason was the pink rose that hung from the walls of their garden onto the street. People believed that this kind of rose was called a "terasheh rose," playing off the word for deafness, because it would deprive anyone who sniffed it of the ability to hear. It was a beautiful flower with no scent. Its petals were thick and velvety, and inverted like two pouting lips, like a person disagreeing with something. To this day, I avoid passing too near it and if I see one hanging down over a wall, I immediately cross the street.

Beneath her angelic exterior, Nada concealed a devilish passion. Her missing senses and experiences transformed into passionate desires. For this reason she ignored her three brothers and satisfied her effervescent body's demands, especially during the boiling hot summer afternoons when the streets were empty. Few people went out at that time, and those that did would have lost their focus and only cared about reaching their destination. Their brains felt like they would melt from the heat of the sun and the heavy, humidity-saturated air and their bodies oozed sweat.

The city smelled sticky—of rotting vegetables, kebabs, and desire.

Nada's lovely body wanted nothing more than to be embraced by uncle Najeeb. She loved him with all the silent parts of her body. She would devour him when they were alone. I heard the sounds of their panting in my grandfather's basement, where she joined him. He passed his afternoons there reading and taking advantage of the cool provided by the insulated walls whitewashed with lime. I could hear her secret moans and the sheer ecstasy almost allowed her to speak. Despite the fact I couldn't see anything, I felt terror strike my already-strained senses and I realized instinctively that something illicit was happening.

I felt something in the pit of my stomach and I was afraid to make any noise letting them know I was there. But then my uncle summoned me in a barely audible voice. He asked me for a box of Kleenex. I ran to get it and then stood outside the door, box of tissues in hand. Najeeb said that he had a cold. Then he sneezed and told me not to come too close so I wouldn't catch it. I was sympathetic, and took a few steps back. I forgot all about that moment, which had turned into an exciting memory, and which I recalled every time I went down into the basement or heard an animal panting, even a dog. My uncle walked out alone, pulling me by the hand, and we walked up the stairs into the house together. I went back down a little while later to spot traces of the incident…There was nothing but an innocent mattress and the scent of a man and a woman—excited hormones, clean sweat, and the sweet-scented girlish perfume she always wore.

Nada was seven or eight years older than me and she really loved me! At first I avoided her because I was afraid of her exaggerated movements. She stood too close when she was talking to someone, pulling on them violently, holding onto their bodies. She used to bite her lips powerfully, and pinch my cheeks. Sometimes when she should have been just be giving me a pat, she'd actually hit me. When I discovered all that chaos was because she couldn't hear, we became friends.

Nada's parents hired a private tutor for her, since there was no special school to teach deaf-mute children in our city. Nada read newspapers, magazines, and stories, and she really wanted to gossip. She knew all of the neighborhood gossip, family by family. Her body jerked violently when she spoke, but for me it sufficed to know the main lines of the story she was talking about. When she asked me a question and I replied, I realized that I was speaking like her. I acted things out with my body, exaggerating the movement of my lips, and moving jerkily. I would get exhausted quickly.

Nada's family was the richest in the whole area. Her father owned a transportation company consisting of small busses that drove people to the countryside. During school vacations, I used to go over to their house and watch videos with her. They were the only family in the neighborhood who had a video player. She wore cotton, short-sleeved, flowered jalabiya. She would lie down on the living room carpet, while I sat on the sofa across from the television. I would look at her elegant feet, legs thick as planks of wood, long fingers, fingernails, and the pendant that spelled out her name in gold. We used to turn on the air conditioning and binge on ice cream and local sweets.

I watched how she would get all involved in the films we watched. We cried together during *A Storm of Tears*, with Laila Taher, Omar Hariri, and Hala Fouad, as well as *Shame*, with Nour El-Sharif, Hussein Fahmy, and Noura. We cried even more at Naglaa Fathi, Farid Shawqi, and Mahmoud Abdul-Aziz's film that we watched many times. I always asked her about Lara. Where is Lara? The girl from the title of the film? She would get confused, think about this and then grow sad and silent because she didn't know the answer. She then asked me the same question in return, but I had gotten tired of explaining and so I gave up. Years later I learned that there wasn't a Lara in this film—I had been reading the title of the film wrong. I thought it was *Lara Loves the Sun* and believed that the grandchild who was born at the end of the film and died as an infant was Lara. But the title of the film was actually *A Love that Never Sees the Sun*, which is only different by a couple of letters in Arabic! Every time I wanted to tell her that I had found out the truth, I was afraid of the difficulty of communicating such a long explanation.

My uncle emptied the heat of July and August into her body. He treated her like a doll that couldn't speak, and was always available to play. But he was also generous with her and bought her gifts—a box to put her accessories in, green linen slippers, jeans, a cotton t-shirt with pictures of teddy bears on it. When he traveled for his studies, she threatened that she would throw herself into the Euphrates. She would come to my grandmother's house every afternoon, sit on the sofa and wander around the room. When she saw someone speaking on the telephone, she would turn toward them and ask if it was Najeeb on the line. She would come back inside the house with me or offer to make coffee.

She used to steal any opportunity to go into Najeeb's room. Then she would blush and tears would run down her cheeks. Sometimes she would react by hitting the wall and threatening to throw herself into the river. My grandmother would tell her, exaggerating the movement of her lips: "It's very cold now down by the Euphrates, wait until summer!" Then she would sit her down firmly and unbraid and rebraid her hair. Nada would calm down and relax, leaning back into the shelter of my grandmother's lap.

Nada's suffering moved me. I told myself, *She's right! How can she bear this separation? If I'd had a man like Najeeb I would have locked him in my room, in my heart.* He was like a man who comes from the impossible world of film stars—handsome, with strong, dark features. My man would have brown eyes with long lashes, dark and deep-set like eyes of saints who endured human suffering. He also would have an athletic body, tall with broad shoulders. Just looking at his chest would arouse the loveliest image of warmth and contentment. Najeeb's departure meant the end of nostalgia, determination, grace, and beauty. His passing wounded all of our hearts. Nada was truly his Mary Magdalene. She couldn't bear his final departure. Less than a year later, she made good on her threats and threw herself into the Euphrates.

In the days following my uncle's passing, I started losing my mother and grandfather every afternoon. They would go out and leave me behind. I knew that they were at his graveside. The cemetery had become our new home. When they took me with them the first time, the grave was still just soil. They'd cleared a large area and enclosed it with a green wrought iron fence. Inside they'd put a bed of flowers. My grandfather supervised the work, while my grandmother sat on a little straw chair and gave orders as if she were preparing a bridal chamber. I don't know how the little grave quickly became her garden with a door, lock, and key.

There were perpetually green vines and trees to resist weather conditions or possible absences.

The grave had a marble headstone, engraved with the words, "Those who fear their Lord will be led to paradise in throngs" (Q 39.73). I was oblivious to all that, busy playing with the children whose houses were near the cemetery walls. My grandparents paid these children to fill buckets to water the plants and wash the grave. They came and provided snacks for my grandmother to offer to beggars for Najeeb's soul. I would go with these local children and help refill the buckets and also play hide and seek with them, between the large, tightly packed graves. Someone would shout, "This is a young child's grave, go away." I knew that you weren't supposed to step on graves and that the dead might take offence, but the tombs were so close together that they nearly all touched each other on the uneven dirt of the ground. However, I tried hard to pass by them, stepping on the stones laid between them. If my foot touched the edge of a grave, my heart would fall from fear of disturbing the dead. But my experience grew with my daily visits and soon I'd memorized the path.

My grandmother set up a wooden bench, like those permanent benches in parks, which looked out over the deep green. She also installed a walnut-brown table in front of it and fixed it in the ground. We started coming every day to keep my uncle Najeeb company in his final resting place. We brought coffee, tea, and fruits, and would sometimes stay until evening prayers. Night would fall, the moon would rise, and we would still be there. We lived a lot of life in that cemetery.

My grandmother's lady friends would often join us, or my late uncle's friends would pass by. Perhaps acquaintances visiting their own dearly departed would be there and my grandmother would invite them to sit with us. She would pour coffee and say the fatiha for my uncle. My mother would read the Qur'an, carrying with her another book as well. She would eat her sandwiches and perhaps speak to some of the visiting ladies, asking them about those they'd lost and getting to know them. We washed the marble grave and my mother sat right at the headstone, putting her hand on it as if she were putting her hand on my uncle's head and stroking his hair.

I would look out at the clear moon until I saw its contours and fall asleep dreaming about its inhabitants. I'd cover myself with my mother's white shawl and perhaps my grandmother's as well, or one of their abayas. My mother wore her abaya only to visit the cemetery. I'd fall asleep listening to their whispers, and believe I was speaking to the moon's inhabitants or to my uncle Najeeb, who was giving me a speech from up there. I laughed in my sleep and they sometimes laughed too—my grandparents, my mother, and the guests. But their laughter soon turned to tears and wailing, which infected all of the visitors to the cemetery. No one there or elsewhere realized that this beautiful grave, located in a remote cemetery in northeastern Syria, belonged to a young man who was named after the famous artist Najeeb al-Rahbani.

Living next to the graves, I started getting used to the idea of death, which was merely a passage from over to under. My doll Natasha always came with me and I would wrap her up to protect her from the bitingly cold spring wind, or the cool breezes of summer nights. The weather in Hittin cemetery was generally milder than in our neighborhood, cool even at the height of infernal August. It was like the cold coming from Tasnim, the spring in paradise that God promised his most faithful believers, who were now spending the night relaxing and chatting in their other lives, just as I imagined.

My grandfather went to stroll around through the graves as if he were looking for a spot just for himself. Maybe he discovered the grave of a person forgotten by relatives. He met many people visiting their dearly departed, whose graves were still fresh and lined by large rocks. These rocks, covered by linden branches collected from the orchards announced the presence of a newly dead body. Sounds of mourning could be heard there. In the cemetery, you can always find one lone man or a woman wrapped in an abaya, sitting simply in reverence, or consulting with the dead after the world of the living had closed in on them. There would also at times be a young couple angry we'd invaded their privacy, and anxiously waiting for us to leave, anticipating one another's touch.

Auntie Maria read about the birth of the prophet for my uncle's soul. She clutched her book, holding it far from her eyes. She'd forgotten her reading glasses, and was forced to recount the story from memory. She raised her voice at the end of each chapter of the prophet's birth tale, "Perfume his grave God, with the scent of prayer, peace, and surrender to Him." We all stood up to pray and ask for patience. Sometimes I would awaken from my nap, and stand up confused, afraid that I'd missed the blessing of praying for the prophet. But the person who looks after the graves came and told her that her voice was awrah, or forbidden, she should keep it private. She forgot all about her heavy body and the pains in her knees, and attacked him, beating him with a bamboo pole and cursing both his mother and her forbidden voice. The prophet's birth had turned into a battle. The guard escaped, saying, "Your dearly departed was a communist atheist, and you shouldn't read the holy book for his soul." When my grandfather died, we found him a place near my uncle, and then we found one for my grandmother as well.

My mother and I went to the cemetery every Friday. We rarely missed a day, and only because of the weather. My mother was counting on longer absences, and so had entrusted one of the guards with looking after the place. She slipped him money, so he would wash the graves, water the plants, and not let anyone urinate nearby.

The cemetery remained our retreat. When I arrived there from faraway, I would run to our group of graves inside the iron fence. I would always long to meet my family and restore our missing intimacy. I used to sit at my grandmother's grave most of the time. I would cry and share my secrets with her. I would reassure her that I wasn't trying to kill her, and that if she didn't forgive me, God wouldn't help me out in life. I grew up like that, always moving one step closer to the grave. My family members who were under the ground now exceeded the number of those above it. When Daesh arrived they forbade visits to graves. Then they bombed them, and after that, coalition planes bombed them. These bombings shook up and scattered the headstones, unearthing the cemetery's inhabitants without them needing a resurrection.

Whenever there was an active spread of propaganda about the latest confrontations between the Syrian Democratic Forces (QSD) and elements of the Islamic State, Daesh, the intensity of NATO bombings of the city would increase, leaving it in bloody ruins. Corpses of people we knew would just lie in the streets. Hungry dogs would gnaw at them after a while. Entire families would be left under the rubble. Their nearest and dearest had to just leave them there, because it was impossible to move the debris. For a long time I believed that only eloquent people could write history, but the inherent evil of humanity is more powerful than any eloquence the human imagination could invent. I was terrified, but also felt disgusted and powerless. I was unable to make any decisions or persuade my mother to have an opinion about anything. We only had two options. One: leave with the likelihood of death, which was about equal to two: stay with the likelihood of death. Fawwaz, one of the reckless Daesh youth, came to our house one day and told us that we had to leave. If we didn't, he was going to just take it.

Fawwaz had grown up in our neighborhood. His mother was from our generation. She married young then left her husband and came back to live with her mother. We weren't really in touch with their family and my grandfather never made helping them out financially a priority, even though they subsisted on only few meager resources. My grandmother used to give them meat on the Eid, and sometimes would offer them seasonal fruits from our orchards. Fawwaz's grandmother was called Zakiyya. She used to sit in front of my grandmother's doorstep, and she'd bring her out a cup of coffee and a cigarette without inviting her into the house or inside garden. My grandfather used to pass her five liras to slip to her daughter, Umm Fawwaz. Zakiyya would give it to her and say, "Take this money from your uncle the Agha." Her daughter would always be very happy, but I didn't like it at all.

I don't know when Fawwaz grew up and became an adult. All I knew was that he'd dropped out of middle school to sell vegetables in the north of the city. When I saw him with his

Daesh look for the first time, I stopped to say hello. It was my first conversation with him since he was a kid and I'd ask him buy things for me from the corner shop.

"Fawwaz, what happened to you?

"My name is Saifullah. You shouldn't be speaking to me and you shouldn't be walking alone in the street without a male guardian."

"What do you mean a 'male guardian'?"

"Your father or brother or uncle."

"Fawwaz, are you crazy? You should know that I don't have any one of those left alive."

"Then go home, you deserve to be stoned…"

Of course I lost it completely. I couldn't believe what I was hearing. My mother said that both his grandmother Zakiyya and his mother who had remarried were now part of Daesh too. They encouraged him to loot the houses of people in the neighborhood who'd left at the beginning of this war, which had encircled us from both land and sky.

My mother tried to kick him out but he didn't move. She predicted that these were going to be their final days here and they'd go mad and loot everything before leaving. All reports indicated that the Kurdish forces were advancing toward the northern and eastern entrances to the city and confrontations were imminent. They had air cover by the coalition forces, which used to bombard us from the sky. Mama's notion that they were going to go mad and loot everything turned out to be correct.

At about nine in the evening, the Tunisian man who'd lived in the neighborhood for about a month and never spoken to anyone came to our place. He'd occupied the house of one of our distant relatives who'd left and moved to Damascus. He kept getting new cars—first a Jeep, then a Ford, and once he came with a Toyota complete with a rocket launcher. He wore a short black jalabiya and a black woolen cap, with long strands of black hair poking out. He had a mustache, which grew into his thick black beard, which itself grew long over the khaki armored vest he wore. It had many holsters for his Kalashnikov rounds, and many pockets for hand grenades.

The Tunisian man parked his Hyundai in front of our house, while his mother and sister were frolicking on the beach in Sousse, enjoying the summer sun and sea across from Europe, getting tan and absorbing vitamin D, which helps fight off depression and osteoporosis. The Tunisian man said to Umm Riyadh, "Whose house is this?"

"It's Doctor Riyadh's house"

"Where is he?"

"He went to the clinic, he'll be back shortly."

"Tell him he has to vacate this house because I want to live here."

"This is our house and we live here, where will we go?"

"Go live on the streets for all I care…"

After midnight we heard that the Kurds has reached the outskirts of the city, ten miles from our house, in the Maqass area where the road from Aleppo branches off, one road leading to Raqqa and the other to Deir ez-Zor. One of the QSD troops who was inside our neighborhood asked us all to leave, as a confrontation between Daesh, QSD, and the coalition was imminent. They don't really care if you stay or leave. They burn it everything to the ground, not caring about civilians, leaving the scorched earth behind them. About a month later, people started dribbling back in. They allowed it, but anyone who stayed did so at their own personal risk, knowing that the probability of survival was low.

About thirty women and twenty children gathered at Auntie Maria's and twenty-three men met in the basement of my grandmother's house. The women cooked in rotations, porridge made of flour and vegetables, pasta, or burghul—whatever they had left in their cellars. The biggest rations went to the men. Supplies started running out as the week drew to a close. The advance of QSD tightened a noose around the city, while Daesh bombed government positions, what was left of the schools, and two barely functioning hospitals. We heard exchanges of fire very close by. We felt the reverberations of terrifying explosions accompanied by bright lights and toxic fumes from neighborhoods a bit further away, just outside the city. But there were no rockets or aerial bombardments raining down on us.

Doctor Riyadh came back one morning. We saw him walking down the street from where we all were, piled up in the courtyard of his house. Our eyes were fixed on the open door through which we used to watch the street. He approached his mother, and my mother who was beside her. He motioned to us to go into his bedroom, which he'd prepared twenty years ago for the bride, whom he'd never married. The room was clean and tidy, with shiny wooden furniture. It didn't have a lot of things in it—as if he actually were a new groom. He took an apple out of the pocket of the hunting vest he wore over his jalabiya. It was a shiny yellow apple with a spot of red on it. He held it steadily—as if it were a precious jewel—and asked me to bring him a knife. We hadn't even seen a piece of fruit in a month, let alone tasted one.

When I saw it, it triggered nothing in me. I no longer loved fruit. We don't love what we have been deprived of. We'd given up on all our desires. Nonetheless, I got up and brought him the knife as he'd asked, since I didn't want to kill his joy from bringing home his hunt. He cut it into four pieces and gave each of us a slice. We sat together, him and his mother, me and my mother. Each pair of us on one side of the bed covered with blue cotton sheets, quietly nibbling on our quarter of the apple. I hadn't heard that crunchy nibbling sound for a long time. We didn't say thank you or anything else. Doctor Riyadh then left. My mother stood up and announced that we were leaving Raqqa that night. I thought she was kidding but she was decisive.

I said, "We can't leave alone, there are land mines on the outskirts of the city!"

Daesh had mined the borders of the city all the way to the bridges so that people couldn't leave, making us into human shields against the SDF and the coalition. Snipers were also stationed at the post office and fire station. No doubt leaving was a road to death. We never again heard from those who'd left, and I learned afterwards that many of them had died by sniper fire or land mines.

My mother said, "Everything is in the hands of God."

Our final warning from the SDF came around midnight. They told us that Kurdish forces had reached the clock tower, less than a mile from our house, where there was a street with a group of Daesh snipers, leading to the western road out of Raqqa toward Aleppo. This was our last chance to leave the city. It fell into Doctor Riyadh and Kamal's hands, and we all trusted their opinion. Doctor Riyadh pronounced, "We will leave quietly, everyone at their own risk. Whoever stays, it is also at their own risk. We've been waiting for the guarantee of safe passage by boat with the Kurds, but leaving individually is even more dangerous. 'Nothing shall afflict us, except what God has ordained' (Q: 9.51)."

Doctor Riyadh had met one of the SDF troops, who came from the people of contracts and solutions. He'd assured us of a safe passage, relatively speaking. How? No one knew, even him, but as Doctor Riyadh pointed out, everything was about covert agreements and secret plots. This was the meeting he'd left with an apple.

I had a deep desire to be done with all of this. I would live, or I would die…The important thing was to change the situation I found myself in. I gazed at the faces gathered around me, frightened, worried, exhausted faces. But no one was crying. We'd passed the stage of crying. Everyone was waiting silently. I said to my mother, "No one is more merciful than God." She nodded her head approvingly.

A mass of humanity had gathered in the neighborhood: people I knew and people I didn't know. It appeared that anyone who'd stayed in Raqqa had joined us to leave all together. It was like an epic poem about the Babylonian captivity. I'd wished that I wouldn't be bothered by bombing or terrorized by weapons, and I could sit, cry, draw, and sing all alone in the ruins. I was used to dead bodies, most of them were my loved ones, my family, and friends from school. I wasn't bothered by being crammed into a space with strange bodies and people I didn't know.

Raqqa was totally dark; the moon had almost become one with the land. We left in a long, long queue, one person lined up after the other. Auntie Umm Riyadh, who suffered from a chronic knee injury, was sitting on Kamal's motorbike with the motor turned off and he was walking alongside it, pushing it like a bicycle. All we had with us were ancient bags from back when there were shops. We carried hardly anything on us, only any money or gold we had—that's it. Before we left our house, I found a shirt and skirt of my mother's hanging on a peg. I grabbed them along with a few changes of underwear. We had only the shoes on our feet. We left everything else behind. I thought about bringing a little cologne, so we wouldn't have to smell our own sweat, and then changed my mind. We would just leave like this and God would sort us out.

Children carried nothing with them, except one boy who was holding a toy car, one little girl hugging a teddy bear, and another carrying her doll. Even these children were silent—not peep or whine out of them. We were a convoy of seventy people. The front was already at the edge of the neighborhood on Kuwatly Street, the site of a major historical demonstration against the signing of the Camp David Accords in 1977, when the protesters burned an effigy of Anwar Sadat. The end of the convoy reached Auntie Fatima's house in the heart of our neighborhood. We were in the last third of it. My mother was just in front of me and Auntie Umm Riyadh was ahead of her on the motorbike. Directly behind me was Hajj Ali who had resisted leaving with all his might. He said he would remain even if was the last one left in the city, but he'd been compelled in the end to come along with the rest of us.

I remember vividly how Hajj Ali bade us farewell—before he became a hajji by going on the pilgrimage to Mecca. He was called up to the Syrian Army as a reserve soldier to fight in Lebanon during the Israeli invasion of 1982. His wife cried and his daughter who was almost our age would go around the neighborhood every day singing patriotic songs for the army: "Eagles revolt across the land/ Eagles rise up in the sky/ Eagles protect our soldiers." It was like she was praying for her father's return.

When he returned home, they slaughtered a sheep in his honor and made mansaf for the entire neighborhood. We sprinkled candies over his head and my grandmother bought him a thirty-six piece set of dishes from Turkey. He didn't cry on the day his son died in the 2006 July War in Lebanon. After the funeral he asked me, "How are you, Lulu?" I told him, "May you have a long life Amo, I am sorry for your loss." He said, "Thank you, thank you" and began to laugh. He was picking up all the little children and playing with them as if his own son hadn't just died. Walking behind me in the convoy, he began weeping and wiped his eyes with his shirtsleeves. His long, twisted white beard was like a cactus and hadn't seen a drop of water in a very a long time.

The caravan advanced stealthily. Heads bowed like a herd of weeping horses, we advanced with nary a whinny or hoof fall to be heard. No one spoke. No one bade the city farewell or even stole a last look at its decaying corpse. No one wanted to remember anything, suffer, grieve, or even think about it. We just wanted to reach the bridge—there would be plenty of time for tears and sorrow afterwards. When we reached the clock tower where there were supposedly snipers, my heart started to pound in my chest. I was filled with strength. I wondered if it were possible for a sniper's bullet to hit me or injure my mother—picking the two of us out of a group of seventy people. Would it hit Auntie Maria? She was in her golden years; she'd lived a full life. I wanted to ask about snipers' etiquette. Was there one sniper? Does he snipe at one individual person or shoot many bullets at once? But I couldn't speak to anyone or even turn around.

The moist gusts of air redolent with the scent of gunpowder, death, decay, fear, and dirt surprised us. In the past, the air in this place used to smell of coffee. At that spot near the bus station, the fragrance of coffee emanated from the little café serving travelers. When I used to study in Aleppo, and travel at night, Mama would make me coffee in a small, old light green thermos with three blue lines at the top, so I could drink it on the road. She'd bought it a few months after I was born and used it to prepare my milk and baby cereal.

At the clock tower stood three armored vehicles that all of us tried to ignore. I stared straight ahead but, even though it was a clear night, I felt I was peering through a haze. Seeing is also thinking. When you don't think anything you don't see anything. I wanted to cross these fifty yards at any cost—except my or my mother's life. I lost my faith in the world at that moment. I implored God, "Why are you doing this to us?" I was really afraid of the empty space, of the idea that God had abandoned this place and was no longer there. I started screaming inwardly as I squeezed my eyes closed, "OhmyGod ohmyGod ohmyGod ohmyGod."

When I opened my eyes, we were on the wide, paved road near the cultural center. It was filled with holes and debris, fallen trees strewn along both sides. The country was like an overturned throne, the way books describe the smiting of Iram the city of pillars, or Sodom and Gomorrah the morning after. I couldn't have ever imagined that one day Raqqa would be left in ruins.

We crossed through the final area with snipers. We breathed a sigh of relief and I thought about the end of the caravan, praying to God to deliver them as we had been delivered. We experienced a great feeling of relief and reassurance when we reached the edge of the new bridge. I reckoned that the end of the caravan would have passed through the snipers' area by then. A feeling of joy washed over me. I wrapped my arms around my mother's neck, overwhelming her. She turned toward me with a rare laugh emerging from deep inside her. This was the first time I'd seen her face since we'd left. It was as radiant as the sun, and I felt an unmatched feeling of safety, as if we hadn't just escaped from the jaws of death. This was the same feeling of safety I'd experienced when we used to walk through the sunflower fields together.

We crossed the entire space in two hours. Pitch-black darkness began to give way to a thread of light that revealed that the bridge was in ruins, pieces lying everywhere like the bodies of ancient gods that had fallen on top of each other but remained sacred. We still had to worry about landmines, but they said that we would stay safe if we remained in the caravan line. The people at the front were guides from the SDF who know the road well. The caravan stopped, as the groups at the front had started boarding boats. Two ghosts behind me left and went toward the road to the right. There were ancient willow trees, which I knew well, at the entrance to the city of Raqqa. For forty years they've been bidding farewell to us when we travel, and welcoming us back when we return. We counted them when we were small: one, two, three, after thirty-five we would stop and enter the city…

Suddenly the earth lit up all around us. I swayed in place and then fell to the ground. I began feeling for my limbs, checking they were there. I could feel my mother's breath and her voice, "Yellah, Lulu." So I am alive and she's alive too! Terrified cries and then words transformed into quiet murmurs, "It's nothing…I'm fine." Shrapnel had hit some people. We caught our breath and the caravan kept moving forward. Ten feet ahead of me, I saw Ghada's body. She wasn't disfigured but her black abaya was burned. Ghada used to have curly hair and big thighs which she always stuffed into her jeans. She was older than me, and her brother Abdel-Latif was in my grade. She and her mother had left Raqqa with us. They'd gone to the side of the road to take care of their needs just after we'd crossed through the sniper area. I didn't see her mother anywhere. I grabbed her hand and shook it, "Ghada…Ghada." She was dead. I left her, since my mother was pulling me by the wrist, and we walked away. Thank God we had reached the bridge and survived. Each group of ten people would get into one of the five boats there to take us away. Our turn would come after the first two groups of ten. This is fine, I thought, and hugged my mother. She was small and frail; she no longer possessed that firm body full of bossiness, determination, and elegant, well-proportioned flesh. I murmured to myself, "In a few minutes we'll cross the river, leave this hell behind, and start a new life."

I wanted to hold onto the sides of the boat, climbing into it, grasping the boat's captain's and my mother's hands. When it was our turn, however, my strength drained out of me. I surrendered to my fate, to the others coming from the other side of the shore, to life. No pushing, everyone must take their turn and surrender to order. We began to distribute ourselves into the boats, my mother and I holding hands. We had to forget Ghada's corpse, which no one had buried. "Please God let someone bury her. God, please have mercy on her and don't let her be eaten by wild animals."

A family with children approached and began boarding the boat. We were just behind them. In front of me, the father's leg was submerged in the water. The captain shouted, "Women on one side, men on the other." The man tried to help his children and bumped into me. His son dropped something at my side. I bent over to pick it up; it was a cute little plastic horse. I couldn't tell in the weak light if it was black or brown. I stared at it for a bit too long. I wanted to reach out and hand it to him. He was looking at me, smiling sweetly. Everything around me lit up again, and a loud sound threw us all far away. I felt the incandescent heat and I thought that I was dead. When I regained consciousness I was bent over on myself and I couldn't find my mother, "Mama, Mama, where are you? Mama?" That's when I knew that I had lost her.

Some people had fled, but everyone who was still there circled around me. They dragged me by my arms, from where I was kneeling at the edge of the shore, screaming, thrashing my body back and forth like a mystic in a trance. No one could free my hands from my hair that I was clutching without even realizing it. They told me that another landmine had exploded near us, though the guide had been sure that this area was mine-free. I didn't reply. I got up and walked a little way toward the water shouting, "Mama…Mama…yellah." I was still hoping by some miracle that my mother might be alive.

I found my mother lying dead under the willow trees. Her legs had been sliced off—one from the knee down and the other from right at the top. I couldn't tell the right from the left, or even let the full picture enter my mind. Her face was not her face. Hot bloody flesh spilled over onto her burnt clothes. I threw myself atop her. I didn't know what my form, features, or voice was like, but we were not ourselves. I was not myself. I was looking at two people who could not be us—me and my mother. The boat's captain called out to me, then to the other people: "Don't go near there." I told them, "It's my mother, I found her dead…" No one came over. "I won't leave her," I gasped. The boat's captain paddled down the river to the closest possible point to me, "It's over. She's dead. Do you want to die too? We don't have time. It's daylight now and the Daesh fighters will come…"

"I need to bury her."

"It's not possible."

"I can't leave her naked body here." I thought of giving her my shirt, but how could I go without a shirt? Our bag was far away on the shoreline.

"We have to bring her with us in the boat."

"It would be shameful for her to take her the place of a living passenger. Don't worry, some good person will come along and bury her."

I shook my head violently, with anger, "No Mama, I won't leave you, Mama."

I told him to just take off if he didn't want to help me. So he left…

I was all alone. The entire world felt like it had gathered together to press down heavily on my heart. I cradled my mother in my arms. Now I was totally responsible for her—for her body, which had carried me inside it, her now cut-off legs that had taught me how to walk, her entire being.

The only thing that I could do for her was to cover her body with earth. I gave myself five minutes to mourn, and five more for my own thoughts. I decided to walk to Antar's house. He was the groomsman who used to sleep in the stable. I convinced myself that another landmine would not explode. I found his house the same as ever, a room on the edge of the river with a small enclosure walled-in with sticks next to it, giving off the smell of manure and horses' breath.

I called out his name and he came out terrified. He looked like the devil—short statured with a red beard, long shorts, and a short jalabiya indicating that he'd joined Daesh. He was surprised to see me. I reminded him who I was, and he remembered me though I was wearing the abaya and head covering that Daesh obliged all women to wear. We went back to being colleagues who worked at the equestrian club that we'd left twenty-five years earlier. I asked him to come with me and he did so like a lamp-bearer. He saddled a horse for swimming and helped me to ride. We wrapped my mother up in sheets from his place. She felt so light on my lap. The horse swam me over to the other shore, and Antar rode on another horse in front of me.

We splashed through the water between darkness and light. Raqqa and my mother's legs abandoned behind me, I found myself a stranger in the Euphrates for the first time. I began to cry. I wept, and blamed the world—people, governments, and oppression. I was all alone in the world; I didn't know where I came from. I wasn't sure if I'd been just spat out her with no genealogy or ancestry. Perhaps I simply fell from somewhere onto this spot where I am now, neither land nor water. I must safely lay to rest the severed limbs I am holding. Then I will be free. I will have settled everything and I paid off any remaining debts I had.

I felt tears wounding my cheek like sharp salty crystals. My mother's body was flaccid; *there is no might or power*. I asked her,

"Why did you do this to me? Get up! Who is left to look after me now?" She didn't reply; she didn't care. There would be time for blame when we got to shore. I regretted that I hadn't brought her legs. How could I have not searched for her body parts and just left them? I should have found them, clasped them to my heart, and held them there forever. I hoisted her onto the saddle in front of me like cargo, and found her to be a rag. Yes, she was a rag I didn't know and that didn't know me.

I smelled bread baking somewhere nearby, wheat bread. We hadn't eaten fresh bread in so long, the scent of fire clinging to it. I cried even more because I'd never thought to make my mother breakfast, as she was always the one who made it for me. From deep within the folds of my mind, which was losing its ability to concentrate because of such distracted fantasies, a quote from the plant scientist, Ernest Olivier, jumped out at me, "Were it not for the Euphrates, the world would never have known wheat, barley, and maize…"

Antar helped us on the descent, and people who I didn't recognize received and welcomed me. They prayed for her while I sat at their feet in a trance. We buried her in Kasra at the cemetery whose edges we'd walked by every time we'd crossed the bridge on our morning walks. I never once thought that one of us might be buried there someday. It has forever stayed with me that she died missing limbs, and I couldn't save her legs, which were as solid as they were when I was a tiny infant. She used to put a pillow over them and lay me down on it, rocking me to sleep. But I knew that God would do unto me as I did unto her. I'd deprived her of her mother and he deprived me of her.

CARMEN'S THREE MEN

I woke up at seven and took a shower. Everything was organized and easy to find in Carmen's little bathroom: a cupboard with white towels, two bottles of Pantene shampoo, another bottle of Dove for men, and Dettol shower gel. She had Colgate, Crest, and a third brand of toothpaste that I didn't even know. There were two Braun electric toothbrushes. A man frequented this house—that was clear from the bottles of aftershave. I had a lovely shower with plentiful hot water. But even the baths of a Sultan could not make up for the scarcity and torment that marked my last three years in Raqqa, where we used to go months without water. When it was available, we would buy it from tanks filled from the Euphrates so we could use it for only the most basic drinking, sanitation, and hygienic needs, which are a fundamental right of every human being. We were relieved if we avoided dehydration, rashes, and scabies. Who would believe that we had to do this in the twenty-first century, in a country of enormous wealth, that had Roman baths and mineral springs that kept elders youthful thousands of years before Christ? I made coffee in her automatic machine. Everything was so easy and convenient. I never needed more than a minute or two to figure out how to use the machines in her house. Such an easy modern life it is—much like our lives in Syria before the war.

Tingling, I drank my coffee. I pushed a button on the wall and a glass panel in the ceiling opened. The room was flooded by the outside world—lively sunbeams streamed in, carrying breezes heavy with warm humidity from the previous night's rain and warmth.

The apartment is small with a sloping roof, which is the building's rooftop. Inside, this slope is most pronounced in Carmen's little bedroom, right above her white bed. To me, the bed seemed large enough for two people. Clothes were stacked up on the armchair across from it, and there was a little vanity with a mirror for her perfumes and skin care creams. There were lipsticks strewn about everywhere, some of them collected in a crystal bowl sitting atop a little white table. I reached out to open a few. They all were neutral colors: beige, apricot, rose. Carmen says, "Try one, they're made of natural products and good for your skin." I opened one, and the fragrance of perfumed creams and femininity wafted out. I hadn't put lipstick on for years…three years perhaps. So when Carmen invited me to try her lipstick, I lost the path along my lips and applied the color outside of the edges. With Daesh rule, and the constraints they imposed on our lives, people entered a state of spontaneous asceticism. Anyway, who would be able to see your lips with you shrouded in black from head to toe, no one even able to guess if you're a man or a woman?

Certain products were also limited and shopkeepers couldn't sell anything to women who were there without a legal male guardian anyway. Daesh forbade this. In fact, even leaving the house without a male guardian was a risk that could have terrible consequences. You would be subject to penalty and punishment. Since my mother and I lived alone and had no such male guardian alive, we were unable to go out at all for four consecutive months. Sa'id, one of my mother's male cousins on her father's side, began helping us at his own risk. He brought us food and drinks and helped us out with other basic needs, like filling our water tank and putting gasoline in our generator. Of course we paid him for all of this. Our needs were rudimentary, and by the end we learned that a person doesn't need much to stay alive. We need only to breathe and to live without our bodies and homes being violated. That and staple foods will keep us alive.

There was a large French window in front of Carmen's bed. It was set into the wall and overlooked the street. There were a few books stacked up on the windowsill. A painting of a nude woman hung over the bed. You could see her back; she'd turned her head and was resting it on her shoulder. A profile of her face and breasts showed. She was holding a small bunch of violets. If a member of Daesh had seen this painting in Raqqa, they would have executed Carmen on the spot.

Next to the bedroom, there was a large dressing room, which had an enormous clothing rack like the ones that you find backstage at fashion shows. There were many rows of shoes and purses and a white wardrobe with shelves. The sitting room had a flat, high ceiling, far from the slope of the building's roof. It contained a taupe leather sofa, a lazuline blue shag carpet, and an oval-shaped white wooden table. This table held crystal bowls holding chocolate Easter eggs. It occurred to me that they might be spoiled, because Easter was four months ago! There were small crystal candlesticks and piles of books on a white desk. This room opened onto a little nook, which housed another small table for a laptop computer. You could feel the quiet solitude; there was no television or CD player in the house.

On the wall hung one large, rectangular painting of a port filled with boats, dominated by the color blue. There were framed pictures of her family at her wedding, others of her daughter Sarah as a child, as a young woman, and graduating from university. Sarah looked exactly like Carmen had when she visited us in Raqqa in the eighties—she had the exact same coloring and features. Carmen told me that she lived in Bonn and was studying for a doctorate in the behavioral psychology of dogs. I searched for a picture of Nicholas and couldn't find one that I thought might be him. I asked her if she had any photographs of him and she replied that she didn't. She'd had some in her mobile but she'd gotten a new one a few days ago. But she described him as an ugly old man.

The sitting room and small kitchen were divided only by a granite counter. I stood on the sitting room side and she stood on the kitchen side, both of us leaning on the counter facing each other.

Carmen wouldn't blow you away the first time you met her. She was the type of person whose beauty you discover slowly. Each time we met, I would learn something about her that I hadn't known previously. Her beauty consisted of, and grew with, interaction and time spent together. I wanted to help her prepare breakfast, but she shooed me out so I could finish my coffee. I tried to slip back into the kitchen where she was standing. She stated firmly: "It's my kitchen, get out."

I complied, thinking that she was a proud woman. Her kitchen was made up of gray cupboards, a round sink, a washing machine, and a small oven. She put a loaf of fresh bread that the baker had delivered to her on the counter top that doubled as a kitchen table. She peeled and sliced an avocado, squeezed an orange, and put slices of smoked salmon on a plate. She also served Landana cheese with truffles, as its packaging announced. A little electric pot kept our coffee warm next to us while we were eating. This was truly paradise compared to the long period of deprivation that I had just lived through. We ate our breakfast sitting atop two high stools, like in a bar. She was in the kitchen and I was in the living room. We began talking about my journey but the thing that gets women talking the fastest and breaks down any barriers is love stories!

Carmen is younger than her un-dyed gray hair makes her look. She said that she had made the decision to leave her red-brown hair color alone, and let time leave its mark on her. She had discovered lumps in her breast, and she didn't want chemical products to turn them into cancer. Her gray hair added something to her look. It made you feel that its owner was real, brave, and at peace with herself. Her complexion remained very pale, with a pinkish tinge. Her large, round eyes were blue and not conventionally beautiful, but the rest of her features were attractive. The skin on her cheeks was tight and glowing, just as it had been the first time I laid eyes on her. It made me long to reach out and stroke it, following the line of her prominent cheekbone. She wasn't as tall as you might have expected a German woman to be, but she was slender, her body tight and compact. Carmen didn't speak to me about the publishing house where she worked, and that she co-owned with her business partner. When I searched for her on the Internet, I found that she was a well-known novelist, among the best-selling authors in

Germany. She had published six novels and other books about writing. Her works were translated into many languages.

Carmen seemed to be burdened by some kind of disappointment, or so it appeared to me. She rarely laughed, and took up projects lazily, with a mix of inertia and sarcasm. Perhaps I was mistaken. I still can't distinguish between this prevalent German character trait of earnestness, and the unexpected changes people experience when they live through some kind of major event—failure, love, or loss. I can confidently say that you can't hide the disappointments of love. They show up in the tint of your skin, your speech, and the way you see things. The same is true of the glow that comes from love, when you are all embroiled in it. It shows—it makes our skin look healthier, it slips into our smiles randomly, and it shapes the sounds that emerge from our mouths.

I spoke to her about the war, loss, and the treachery of time. She talked to me about her family history, her Polish mother and Nazi father who had loved her sisters more than her. She told me how she was one of seven siblings and her mother was a famous poet. I was surprised because I had never heard of a woman who was able to birth and care for seven children and still have enough time and energy to write poetry! I had always thought of her and Nicholas as being alone in the world.

Her mother had later died of Alzheimer's disease. She also told me about her Palestinian Syrian husband Bassam, who she had met at the University of Damascus, and about their daughter Sarah. She told me how her father opposed her marriage to her Palestinian husband until the day he died. She said that when she first handed her newborn daughter to him, he looked into her tiny face and announced, "A little Yasser Arafat!" He boycotted her for many years but when he fell terminally ill, little Sarah cared for him in place of Carmen, and Bassam hosted him in his house, setting up a special room with all the supplies he needed, until his soul departed.

We kept talking until we arrived at one final man; I could see his features dripping from her eyes, his fingers grasping onto the tone of her voice. My intuition told me that Carmen was living through the very last stages of a draining love story.

✳

Carmen had come to Syria with Nicholas, and though she visited us in Raqqa several times while he was living and working there, she lived in Damascus. She was enrolled in the Arabic language program for non-native speakers at the University of Damascus, to complete the studies she had begun in Middle Eastern literature in Cologne. We spent a week together in Raqqa before she came back to Germany, after she'd finished her semester. Mama, Abboud, Nicholas, and I all went in Grandpa's Mercedes to pick her up when she arrived in Raqqa. She was an enchanting twenty-something-year-old woman; she had her red hair, a sturdy constitution, and was dressed in a flowing cerulean summery skirt and a sleeveless white blouse, that exposed her pink, freckled arms and a beaded turquoise necklace.

We held a feast in her honor at my grandmother's house. For lunch, we'd prepared stuffed eggplants, zucchini, and red peppers, as well as artichokes stuffed with lamb in a wild mustard leaf sauce. July was blowing hellfire on us; the temperature was hovering around 113 degrees Fahrenheit. The minute we took Carmen to the river, she stripped off all her clothes down to a black bathing suit she was wearing underneath and dove right into the water. The fishermen, passersby, and workers in the café all gathered around to gawk at her. This was an unusual scene, because women in Raqqa don't usually take off their clothes to swim in the river. The people standing on the bridge started whistling, cheering, and clapping. My mother was apprehensive about her at first, but after about an hour they became friends. My grandmother also really liked her and praised her beauty.

Carmen was unpretentious and kind to everyone. You could see genuine goodness in her eyes. The first time she went into the bathroom at my grandmother's house, me and Abboud stood behind the door waiting to hear her shout. The plastic seat of the toilet was broken in two. If you didn't know that you could easily injure your backside unless you were very careful sitting down. Of course we didn't tell Carmen this ahead of time and so set a trap for her. She fell for it. We heard a quick, sharp scream, and then the sounds of her talking to herself. Perhaps she was cursing in German. Abboud and I were overcome with the giggles. We heard the sound of the flush and then ran away. Carmen came out, red in the face. Every time we looked at her we cracked up uncontrollably in fits that nearly killed us.

We took her with us one day to a wedding of one of the girls in the neighborhood. She was absolutely thrilled to attend a real live ceremony that she had only read about in books. Abboud and I sat on either side of her. After a little while, they came in with a large tray of black henna, lined with lit candles. The young women started dancing with the tray taking turns holding it. They approached Carmen to decorate her with henna. But as soon as they came near, she reached out, took a piece, and popped it in her mouth. Of course we didn't stop her. Abboud and I simply waited to see what she thought of the disgusting taste of henna. She yelped and spat it out. Everyone there chuckled, pointing out that foreigners eat everything in sight, even the crumbs. But they manage to maintain their figures despite this. I rushed over to her with a glass of water, but the bitterness of the henna remained stuck in her throat until the day she left. She was sick to her stomach that night. She said it was on account of the poison she'd ingested. My grandmother corrected her saying that the tiny piece of henna couldn't have done anything, she fell ill because of the kebabs she insisted on scarfing down day after day.

Carmen met Palestinian-Syrian Bassam in Damascus. He worked as a teaching assistant in the Arabic Language Department at the university. They fell in love and married. He left Syria after winning a scholarship to study in Germany. Then they had Sarah. But it seemed as though he didn't emerge from his mid-life crisis unscathed. Carmen discovered that he'd had a relationship with a Syrian student who was a recent refugee, and he'd helped her to come to study in Germany. After a confrontation, Carmen decided to leave Bassam and live alone in her house. She wanted to enjoy what time was left in her own way. Honestly, for a second I felt ashamed of what Bassam did, as we were both Arab. I was even more grateful to her for hosting me, considering what my compatriot had done to her. But I tried to shake this silly, exaggerated, nationalist idea out of my head. What do I have to with their marriage and divorce? Why should I bear responsibility for its success or failure?

Carmen said, "Let's start from the beginning—I now know how to talk and write about betrayal if I have to. Betrayal distorts us. Betrayal is knowledge, knowledge distorts innocence, leading us through a tunnel filled with difficult questions: 'Why? What have I done wrong? What am I lacking? What is the alternative? What are its advantages?' This is followed by melancholy, submissiveness, and silence. Betrayal messes with our minds, and every day brings us closer to the brink of madness."

I started listening to Carmen's complex analyses of betrayal as if I did not know them very well myself, as if betrayal had not broken my heart and fed into my own sorrow. Her vocabulary was carefully chosen. It was like she'd studied this part of an Arabic dictionary. Sometimes I'd correct her, or add something and she would repeat what I'd said and add, "na'am, yes!" afterwards. For example, I would say, "al-irhaq," meaning exhausted, and she would say, "al-irtihaq, na'am, yes!" If she were ever truly missing a word, she would say it in English as a last resort.

This made me think back to Auntie Maria, my mother, and all of the many women I knew in Raqqa. When I thought about how they used to talk about things, I realized I had never heard the word "betrayal" from any of them. Words are what give meanings their harshness or gentleness. Perhaps their selection of vocabulary helped them to accept certain things. They didn't play the game of labeling things.

Words are truly harsher than deeds. For example, some people might tolerate physical relationships motivated by love. But when this is identified using the category of adultery, or *zina*, they are distressed. I wonder if Auntie Maria truly transformed into a different woman after her husband's physical relationship with a famous singer? Was she devastated? Proud? Better off or worse off? I have no clear conception of this, except that she preserved her joy and her beauty, at least up until the last time I saw her. I knew that my mother, on the other hand, took the stinging pain of betrayal with her to her grave.

Carmen will never be able to talk about this subject enough. If you so much as slightly hint at it, you will always be drawn into a conversation. It seemed to me that she hadn't recovered from him even one bit, though she claimed she had.

I would let her talk and enjoy the resonant sounds of her Arabic, especially her exaggerated pronunciation of Arabic letters and sounds. I would try to gain her confidence, as she would be my only support for a long time:

"We begin to fear for ourselves more than we did before, indeed we become cowards. We no longer dare to step outside of ourselves, because we lose the feeling of firm land beneath our feet, which we've been so sure of for a long time. After an earthquake, we don't trust the land; this is what it's like after a major betrayal. We lose our confidence in humankind. Perhaps the harshest thing is that we lose our confidence in ourselves. Have you ever broken your leg?"

"No."

Carmen had no idea how much speaking about injured legs pained me.

"When you break your leg you need time for it to reset and heal. Afterwards, you're afraid to walk. You lack confidence in your broken limb; it hurts. You need someone to encourage you; you practice a little at a time. You say to yourself, 'Other people who broke their legs walked again and went back to their normal lives,' you encourage yourself. Those people went through the experience of betrayal as well. The first stage of their healing will be listening to words, 'normal, natural.' Everyone betrays…"

I tried to be wise, mature, and find something to say: "Carmen, we have an expression for this thing you are calling an experience: What doesn't kill you makes you stronger!"

"Experience isn't necessarily a teacher, it might be a killer who stalks us, the snake lying dormant in our hearts that suddenly awakens, strikes, and slithers away once again."

"Forgiveness is a beautiful thing."

"A long period of reconciliation and forgiveness passed, but then suddenly I remembered that he had left for a new land, knew another body, its details, a whole other mood. He will compare the new land and old land. He will be impressed by the change even if it's a downgrade. He will enjoy the pleasure of discovery and that someone other than me fell in love with him. Watch out for men, they like to have their silly egos stroked and they will always love adventure."

"So what kind of betrayal was this for you? Was it the words? The physical betrayal?"

"I asked him about this relationship, in fact I used to talk to him about it every day, constantly. He would lie sometimes, other times he would omit details. He believed that he was limiting the harm this way. I stopped asking questions but I never asked the real question that ought to have been asked. We speak a lot but we don't always say the essential, important words that we really want to say; we never ask the questions that we want decisive answers to."

I ventured to reassure her that I was on her side and shared my feelings with her. My private, emotional life meant that I did know what she was talking about. But to be frank, my comments seemed beside the point because she didn't want anyone to share in this with her. She had something to say, and simply wanted to unload her baggage by talking about it. Perhaps she just wanted to close this chapter of her life, which appeared to have been exhausting her for a while now. Carmen wanted someone to listen to her and nod their head—that's all.

"Perhaps precise questions harm the person asking them and can even pierce their veneer of dignity," I said.

"That's because we know that we won't get the healing answer that we are looking for, the answer that we need to hear. But after that, every time I saw him smile, turn his phone over, or listen to music, I would say: 'that's for her, he's doing it for her…' When he slept I looked into his face and his eyes. I could see her there, blissfully peaceful, resting somewhere between his eyelids. Let him dream of her, but outside of my bed, my room, my house, and my life! At first, the best I could do was to get some pleasure from him. Perhaps that was the way to get him back. But her body was always there, inserting itself between him and me. I couldn't tolerate the duplicity. I couldn't eat, sleep, or write, I would just lie there thrown on the bed like a broken toy, just taking up space. I no longer wanted Bassam—to belong to him or for him to belong to me. It was resignation, not anger. I can distinguish between those feelings. I no longer wanted him. He undermined my self-confidence not only as a woman but also as a successful writer. He didn't appreciate my mind or my personality; he didn't make me feel exceptional. I thought this would be enough to make my man unsatisfied with other ordinary women. I'm a free and creative thinker; my mind can do anything…Once a professor of mine told me, 'A man never tires of a woman who has a mind of her own.' I knew that I could no longer be open with him and I needed to find a permanent solution. I need to have an unburdened, safe space where I can devote myself to other struggles in my life and to my writing."

"And what did he do? Did he want to break up or get back together?"

"He suggested that we stay together, tolerate and forgive each other, go back to the moment before this earth-shattering event. He swore that what they had was over, that it was only a fleeting relationship. Then he changed his tune, claiming that I was deluded, that what they had was nothing, and that I had to think more about it, to take our shared life of more than twenty years into account, as well as our love, which was still alive. He said that I was psychologically damaged. I thought about it, but it didn't take long. I had work to do. I needed to finish with all this and remain unscathed. I also don't like to torture myself with details and I don't like to torment others. If he found happiness outside my world, he should have it, why would I stop him?! My mother used to say, 'It's no use crying over spilled milk. We'll milk the cows and get the best, freshest milk.'"

"Ha ha."

"It's funny. You know Lulu, I was content with a wonderful moment, the lovely feelings which this experience introduced me to—for example, that feeling of discovery when I woke up one morning to find the mask had fallen off of the face of the man who'd been sleeping next to me for twenty years. I loved it as a moment of liberation too! No more burdens, responsibilities, or dividing up of time, energy, and income, successes and failures. All I have to worry about is myself and that's it—as I can't go back to the time before the hurt and the fear and as he isn't able to bring back my innocent laughter which gave me strength to take on the world. He can't give me back my youth! What they say about old age not being a matter of biology is true! Old age is the result of trauma. The biggest problem that betrayal produces is not a loss of confidence in your partner, but that we lose confidence in ourselves. Settling for simply reacting can be dangerous. I won't stay with someone whose presence over time makes me feel that I'm unwanted, or that I've been duped, or I'm stupid, lacking, or somehow less than…"

Carmen drew on many of her vocabulary words in Arabic, sprinkling in German as well and she was all confused. My mother's words came to my mind and I interrupted her, "Mama used to say, I want a man who doesn't try to teach me something every chance he gets!"

She echoed me as if she'd found the answer, "He always tried to teach me something…exactly!"

I felt proud, because I'd offered her something. "Did you look for another man?"

"I preferred to take a break! We need to rest our broken parts, not stress and exhaust them more. A broken leg weakens you, of course. Don't think that after a betrayal like that a woman becomes stronger! She loses her resilience. She seems stable, but stability isn't what she needs. Stability is not strength; strength comes from resilience. A girlfriend of mine once told me, 'Don't let him break you—you are strong, successful, famous, and beautiful. You're young—a woman in her fifties is still young. You're better than him…' Her comment saddened me. What if I was not beautiful, young, and all those things? I won't concern myself with him. And what concerns him is me going out with another man who will love me more than he did and care for me more than he did. Bassam isn't really that interested in me. He's only interested in me not finding another, better, man."

"Is she beautiful?"

"I have no idea. But no doubt her breasts are still perky, and even if I wear fancy bras from Triumph or Victoria's Secret, mine can't rival those of a young woman. We'd all feel so much more secure if only men thought that their man-parts would grow old and shrink too, and if every woman who is obsessed with her own youth knew that one day her breasts would be a pair of shriveled up apples on her chest!"

I told her about Auntie Maria and her indifference, sarcasm, and forgiveness—how to me she was a goddess.

She replied, "She sounds divine!"

Every time we talked, I wished that Carmen would just give up, and close the betrayal-file once and for all. She took me back to my darkest places, which I dread approaching. I'm not like her. I'm not a writer, but I do have my own dark places too. She says that she uses our conversations to help her writing. I don't know what a woman like me, with all the chaos and loss she's carrying around, can offer to a writer like her.

She said, "Lulu, do you know the first thing a woman does after a major betrayal? She changes her body because she's discovered that it is her only possession. She goes on a diet, cuts her hair, moisturizes her skin, puts on makeup…No medicine can heal betrayal; there are only therapeutic treatments. I've done them. The first thing is to burn all bridges with your betrayer-partner. This is an immediate action to be taken. If you go back to him, you will always be hurting. The second step is success, and this is the long-term part."

I mulled over this when I was not with Carmen. Do women in Raqqa look to the same therapies to get over this kind of situation? Or do they have other techniques? I do believe that they possess a greater ability to forgive or forget. Perhaps this is because such a thing wouldn't take on such enormous proportions for them. It is at the very heart of life, an everyday occurrence, their mothers and grandmothers have confronted this situation before. Women where we are from are stronger, more connected to the depth and substance of life. People betray each other, but they also forgive each other. Women don't cry about betrayal in front of each other. My mother never cried in front of me. Instead she changed into a violent, hateful woman until my father left, time passed, and she met Nicholas! Perhaps the problem is with those women who are compelled to stay with their betrayer-partners for some reason. They fail to forget, can never forgive, and this engenders misery.

This is why I couldn't sleep that night when Auntie Maria came. My grandmother's whole group came. The very first thing that pops into my mind is how my mother slept next to me that whole night. My mother occupies a particular place in my mind, an observer looking over my shoulder. Whenever I go through something, I think of her. She shows me the solution and leads me to the path, her own path, the path of perpetual loss. I don't want to follow my mother's example; I don't think any woman wants to follow her mother's example!

Carmen stopped me from helping her clean up breakfast. "Go away! Go drink your coffee. When I visit you at your place soon, I won't help you clean up breakfast." She showed me genuine friendship, that she was truly happy to be my friend, and that after she'd talked to me she was relaxed. She became even more cheerful.

"Carmen! Do people here think about love? Those people who are preoccupied with our wars and the refugees? What about those people who are just worried about feeding themselves day to day? Or the Germans who flew in the plane with me who had their heads buried in books and the police officers who I faced at the airport? And the ladies who I saw in the streets of Frankfurt rushing into banks and phone shops?"

"Oh yes, they think about it! Scratch the surface and there is love there. Though, if you don't get close to people you wouldn't know it. But everyone I know well either has just ended or just started a relationship. Or they're somewhere in-between!"

I said to myself that those people seem to have room in their life. They didn't escape a war, extremists didn't occupy their houses, they never saw their family dead, hanging from the gallows in public squares, which a few months previously had been used for picnics and lovers' trysts. Me, for example, I don't have clear ideas about love. In the flush of youth I never had it, out of worry for my mother, this also led me not to commit to my university studies—all for her sake. In order to study, I had to live in another city—Aleppo or Damascus—because there was no university in Raqqa. It wasn't possible for Mama to leave her job and come stay with me for so long. So I studied at home and only attended the final lectures at the end of term. Then she would come with me to Aleppo and stay while I took my exams. We lived there together in an old apartment Mama had inherited from my grandfather that held so many fond memories for her. I couldn't just kill her mother and then leave her all alone so I could study or live with some man.

After that conversation, Carmen started ending all her conversations with, "possibly," and "I don't know exactly." She doesn't use imperatives yet. She always repeats the word, "super," that she pronounces, "zuber," making it sound a lot like the word for penis in Arabic. This cracks me up. She sat on the sofa and stretched out her legs on the table in front of her. I could see her second toe folded over the first one, not giving it the chance to show through. She looked at her two toes, trying to separate them, staring at her feet as if surprised by them. I told her that when my mother found out about my father's betrayal, she said that he had "bitten her placenta."

"What?!" She asked me to repeat what she'd said.

"He bit her placenta. The placenta is the cord that nourishment passes through from the mother to the fetus in her womb."

"Ha!" she grunted, laying her hand on her belly and muttering as if she were turning the expression around in her own language. She then went silent. Her eyes turned to stone, gazing out at the sycamore tree through the faraway open window...A light drizzle dampened the cold morning air. I brought her a cup of coffee and she took it, remaining seated in the same spot until lunchtime.

In the evening, Carmen prepared to watch the live broadcast of the Germany versus Portugal match at the World Cup in Brazil. She said that I didn't have to watch the match with her if I wasn't interested in soccer. But I'd actually loved soccer since the 80s, our national team's glory years. In Syria, we all passionately followed the matches in the Mediterranean Games, Asia Cup, and the qualifiers for the World Cup. Watching these matches was part of the communal spirit in Syria back then that the satellite and broadcast monopoly channels damaged. From that time forward, the FIFA World Cup matches were festive events. Mama supported Holland, because she liked the team captain, Ruud Gullit. He had brown skin and fantastic dreadlocks. Baba cheered everyone on. I loved Malek Shakuhi, the Syrian team's goalie. I taped a picture of him blocking a powerful strike on the inside door of my wardrobe. Baba reprimanded me for ruining expensive rosewood and demanded I take it down.

Carmen sat down on the sofa in front of the TV and stretched her legs out onto a low stool, resting a glass of beer on the table beside her. She started watching silently. This was the first time I had seen someone watch a football match so calmly, with no excitement or cheering! She exhibited no enthusiasm and didn't clap during her team's attacks. She let out no cries of anxiety when the opponents counter-attacked. I felt like I was much more enthusiastic than she was. I sat in my chair next to her, amusing myself eating mulberries. I jumped up when there was a nice play by the German player, Mats Hummels, who scored a second goal for his team after the first, which had come from a penalty. I cheered for Thomas Müller who scored two consecutive goals. I felt sorry for the Portuguese goaltender Patricio, because the game was mostly played right in front of the goal he was defending. The matched ended with a 4-0 win for Germany. At the whistle, Carmen expressed her satisfaction by saying aloud, "Super!"

This was the most obvious emotion she'd shown the whole time. If the Syrian national team had won, I would have filled the world with my shouts. She, on the other hand, watched the entire match as if she were walking to work, watching a documentary on TV, or listening to the news. But she did say that we should dine out in a restaurant nearby to celebrate the occasion. When we were there she confided in me that she followed the match because she liked the coach, Joachim Löw. She loved his nervous movements and how he scratched his body parts and smelled their scent, and that all of this was captured on camera. She was not at all revolted; she cared only about his thick, black hair and the unusual folds under his eyelids, suggesting a fiery personality. She told me that she followed his twitter account and has written him complimentary messages there.

The restaurant was very nearby, two streets down. We went by car, and everyone was going out into the streets to celebrate even though it was so late. We shared a dish of fettuccine and an asparagus salad. We weren't hungry and I felt totally out of place. I hadn't sat with someone in a restaurant for years, since before the beginning of the war in Syria. I felt confused about how to use a fork and knife, until I saw them in Carmen's hand and remembered. Our lives were so lamentable when life itself was beautiful. The rest of the world was enjoying an effluence of safety and simplicity, while in Raqqa people were forbidden to leave the house.

"Soccer can help you to integrate, like going to university. Try to forget being a refugee. My mother came from Poland and she never forgot. She didn't study here, she never cheered for a local football team. She lived over there, on her own time and at her own pace. She was captive to her nostalgia and couldn't transform this into marketable, artistic power. She was more honest than she should have been with the poets who rode the wave of diaspora and asylum, leaving her behind as a third rank poet. Her work was rooted in her homeland, like her tears when she cut potatoes or when she heard Mazurka music. Don't repeat her mistake. Remember that your children will forget that you were a refugee. If I were in your place I wouldn't do what my mother did."

"What happened after you split up with Bassam?"

"Oh…I started seeing a therapist to cure my depression and regain to my old energy. I wanted to go back to working and writing. I was sitting and absorbing this experience to be able to write about it. But I was afraid to submit to the comfort that the notion of victimhood granted me. Being a victim means you take your time to heal. But healing doesn't just fall from the sky, you have to get up off the sofa and search for it before you fade into oblivion."

She wiped her lips with her dinner napkin, indicating that she was finished with her food. It had the restaurant's logo, an image of Italian filmmaker Federico Fellini, printed on it. She shifted the way she was sitting, refilling her glass of water. I noticed the wrinkles on her pink chest through the opening of her white blouse.

She continued, "I arrived in Heidelberg at noon one sunny July day, the kind people call a perfect summer day. They took off their heavy clothes, put on their straw hats, and went for a stroll down to the park along the Neckar River towards the ancient bridge, or they ate lunch at a sidewalk café in the old city. I found the group that I was a volunteer with waiting for me at the Auerstein Dependance Hotel. A Syrian man, Nader, and his German wife Olga were there. They had a plan to support Syrian refugees and integrate them into society, in cooperation with the Immigrant Foundation, sponsored by the Heidelberg Municipality. Our publishing house committed to printing and distributing their stories, and used all the proceeds for the project. We scheduled a musical-storytelling evening the following day to celebrate the launch of the books.

"Nader is a mechanical engineer who studied in Berlin in the late 1970s. He has German citizenship. Olga is his second wife. She worked a long time with an international relief organization for preserving culture in cities affected by war. They invited me to lunch at their home, not far from the hotel in Handschuhsheim. We walked on the wide, Heidelberg sidewalks to where they lived. They led me into a reception hall with displays of artwork by artists from all over the world who they had hosted over time. They held musical and cultural evenings in this room. Their little house, which was also like a museum, was located right above it.

"He had cooked us a chicken with vegetables and prepared a green salad with tomatoes. Lined up in front of me on the table in the kitchen were bottles of spices they'd brought home with them from Madagascar, Malawi, and Oued ed-Dahab in the Western Sahara... The music they played transported me to unexplored worlds. From the highest mountains in Kazakhstan to the sand dunes of the Sahara desert, it carried the patient soul of the Amazigh people, Arab melodies crossed with heavy metal. Most of these songs sing of people who have left their countries, powerless, and who've come to Europe searching for freedom, protection, and recovery. They transform their pain into souvenir shops. Their homelands become donation boxes and upturned hats into which donors throw their Euros, in ex- change for dabkeh, falafel, shawarma, and local sweets... I asked Nader to copy the music that he had available onto a flash drive for me and he gave it to me the following night.

"There was a man with us who was always silent. They intro- duced him to me as Gunter, a friend. I discovered later that he was Olga's first husband. She had no children with him. I assumed that Gunter, who was a psychologist, worked with them in the organization, by providing psychological support for refugees, for example. Gunter denied this, saying that he was a close friend who simply participated in their cultural activities. He specialized in working with separated couples. To me, it wasn't at all strange that the right things come when you need them—not necessarily in order—chance is what makes the world go round.

"Gunter seemed depressed. His thick dark hair was parted to one side and his skin was pale. He seemed to have lost a lot of weight for his heavy build and his arms hung limply at his sides. His eyes were always red with the exhaustion of insomnia. He observed his ex-wife and her partner with interest. He sat on the sofa, arms crossed and tense. I wondered to myself how he felt about his wife's second marriage, if he felt loving or jealous towards her. It seemed to me that he was not very interested in it. I kept examining Olga, who was wearing eastern-designed jewelry, large round silver earrings, and a wide bracelet studded with turquoise stones. These are things a person no longer feels they can admire as much as signs of a weak and desecrated world."

The things that Carmen said that were related to us got under my skin. How could she dare to say such things without taking my feelings into account? I felt insulted, choked on my tears, and I wanted to leave…But since I didn't have a choice, I had to invent a justification for her: She didn't mean to insult me. Carmen was speaking objectively and revealing her inner self to me. She is good hearted and a tortured soul. The most important thing is that she is an old friend, she'd visited our house in Raqqa, and she knew my mother, my grandfather, and Abboud. No one else in this place on the Rhine River knew my family except the two of them—her and Nicholas.

Carmen continued, "I knew that Gunter and Nader were friends before Nader married Olga. I knew he used to check up on her when she was with his friend. I understood this, but I couldn't participate in such a relationship. They say that after women leave a relationship they don't care about their ex-husbands any more, but rather blame themselves for their bad choices. When a woman regains her freedom, she moves on and erases the traces of her past. On the other hand, when a woman finds a new partner, she becomes more attractive to her man and he will pursue her and try to get her back. The prey that's escaped from the hunter. Honestly, I find that to be liberating, what do you think, Lulu?"

"I don't know," is how I replied to her because I really didn't know. I was happy to be friends with Carmen. Listening to her was like entering a pressure cooker—you mature completely in a very short time. I needed to have more experiences to make it to life's next stage. She was now my teacher.

Carmen kept talking after ordering a glass of red wine, a slice of goat cheese, and a piece of bread, having finished her main course. A cup of tea sufficed for me, but my hand kept creeping over to the bread and cheese. My appetite had been whetted. She ate and talked, licking her fingers. When I first noticed this I was disgusted, but then I just ignored it. This must be integration!

Carmen indicated that she was really pleased to be able to revive her Arabic skills because her work in translation between the two languages didn't require her to practice speaking. Both she and I also used many expressions in passable English.

"More than once I noticed Gunter looking at me and smiling. Honestly he was very handsome. It was difficult to resist his knowing sense of gloom. It was also hard to resist his ability to pass through other people's suffering, delve into their histories, evaluate their experiences, touch their souls, and change the way they organize things in their minds. His self-assurance was also enchanting, he listened really well and then concluded every conversation with his own opinion. He's not one of those psychologists who follows a certain pro-forma protocol or fetishizes strangers—the kind who always wear black as if they were hipsters, or who sport bowties all the time, or who maintain a formal appearance trying to show they are somehow supernatural. Never! Gunter was always well-dressed in an olive green linen blazer and dark blue jeans, with a freshly laundered white shirt. But his eyes remained permanently fixed and rigid as if he had conjunctivitis or perhaps some kind of allergy. Nader told me that Gunter was the best psychologist in Heidelberg, and that he'd treated one of the Bayern Munich players in the aftermath of a serious psychological crisis, which physically impaired him, after his girlfriend broke up with him. After lunch Gunter and I decided to go to the old city."

"You must visit Heidelberg, Lulu! Soon we will all go, you and me, and Nicholas. That was my first visit there, imagine… I am fifty years old and I hadn't managed to visit before, though it isn't far from Cologne, only three hours away."

"Carmen, you surprise me! How is this possible? Heidelberg is the city that the Internet sites I was able to browse took me to the most frequently when I was arranging to come to Germany. But it's normal—I didn't manage to visit every single Syrian city in the more than thirty-five years that I lived in my country!"

"See what I mean?" She replied, and then continued on with her story. "Gunter and I passed through the gate to the old city. I put my head in the helmet of the statue standing guard. All the tourists come here to stick their heads in it and take photos. He photographed me with a camera he was carrying on a strap over his shoulder. He said that he'd send me all the photos we'd taken by email later. He was a proficient photographer. He lay down on the ground, for example, trying to take a picture that captured my whole body, head to toe. His shirt came untucked, revealing his beautifully colored brown freckled skin. His flat belly had small folds, making it as soft as a delicious ball of pizza dough. We walked and walked, through streets lined with cafes and pubs. We went up to the castle on the funicular railway, and peered over the bridge. He turned my head toward the river saying, 'It is the most beautiful place in the whole world.' The red-brick roofs of the city were below us and on the distant horizon behind a thin film of fog lay the white peaks of Mont-Blanc in the Swiss Alps. He told me that once a group of businessmen were sitting there on the balcony after having designed what is now the famous Mont Blanc pen. They were puzzling over how to choose a name for it. Suddenly one of them looked at the mountain peak in front of him with its white protuberances and shouted, Mont-Blanc! It then became the brand and logo. This is how the moment of discovery often is, a moment of genius in which we pay attention to the things we normally exclude because we are used to them. I told Gunter, 'Perhaps you intend for us to change our angle of vision so we can see what is excluded from it, not change the actual things.'

"Gunter agreed without a whole rigmarole. I'm attracted to men who are won over by the truth! He took my hand gently, then left it and draped his arm over my shoulders, pulling me to his chest while we were walking for a few steps, as if protecting me from my history. Without him sitting me down on his psychoanalyst's couch or hypnotizing me, I told him everything, simply, with no fear, and with full trust in him. It's as if I were standing in front of a ghost, a mirror, or indeed even confessing in some faraway church to a priest who didn't know me, and who I didn't know. Believe me Lulu, I've never been to confession…not even once! But I imagined that confession would be comforting, not merely so that the Lord can forgive me, but so that I can feel my humanity and so a certain power can tell me that the sins I have committed are natural, that it's my right to be weak or break down, and I will get back up better and more valuable.

"Gunter said that I was a strong woman. I grabbed the edge of the bridge, and exploded. I told him that I was broken. I had no morals left except the basics—to condemn wars, injustice, and oppression. I told him that I had reached the point of a little bit of denial and a great deal of cruelty and just letting go. I told him that I'd used a spiritual intermediary to talk to my dead mother and that I'd had five abortions because a reader informed me that I would lose a young son when I reached forty years of age. I talked about how I was obsessed with Coco Chanel, Claudia Schiffer, and Joachim Löw. I related how once when a child asked me to chose a number between one and ten, I'd picked seven. That same child then told me that I was traditional—ordinary people usually picked five or seven. He said that when he chose, he would pick 2.4. The boy's words depressed me for a whole month.

"While tugging on my ponytail playfully, Gunter said, 'No doubt you once also danced with a man who perhaps danced with a girl who herself had once danced with the Prince of Wales?'

"He was making fun of me! Then he added gently, 'All this is nice, very nice,' and he cradled my head in his neck. When I told him about my sexual proclivities, he told me that I was what they call sapiosexual. He said that because of this I would inevitably be attracted to him, that I was lazy in school and I had a complex about the achievers, that I was egotistical to the point of harming and nearly killing them because they were like me. He added coldly, 'Surely one must shed some blood to reach the top, and surely there is a certain beauty in the psychological complexes that allow us to live life with passion.' He continued on, 'I'm not afraid of you having a psychological crisis, since you are aware of things and know what you're doing. Clearly, you want to write again. Write…going back to work will be your treatment…'

"We walked hand in hand inside the castle and its gardens. We went to a showing of *Romeo and Juliet* that a local troupe had put on to raise money for refugees. We drank a glass of Trollinger wine at the castle, which has stocked a huge wine cellar since the 13th century. Gunter didn't talk about himself and I didn't ask him anything. I thought of him as a doctor, and doctors ask the questions. You don't ask them about their own condition. I told myself that we had plenty of time, so I wouldn't preempt things with questions, which could slow everything down.

"A soft rain was falling, when we were walking on Chocolate Street. We went into a café and ordered a drink called Pleasure Elixir. He dipped his little spoon into his cup, and started to stir the chocolate to make it melt, 'Look, do it like this, this takes me back to fun times twenty years ago.' I don't drink chocolate and rarely even eat it, since I watch my weight. But I went with him where he was taking me, because sometimes we have to abandon our habits and find ourselves in places that have been previously closed to us. From that moment, I discovered the love of chocolate inside of me. I wish I hadn't. It is pure pleasure and now I can hardly restrain myself. We came down from the castle onto University Street, where we had to go to get back to the cultural evening. We sat close to each other on the bus, and a rainbow shone through the window…

"Gunter was sure to see me off the next morning when I was headed back to Cologne. It was a Sunday and that's a day to sleep in late but I found him at the hotel restaurant. He said that he would have breakfast with me and stay until the last moment. All of that meant that the excursion of the day before was not just a fleeting encounter showing a tourist around. We chatted and drank tea. He stressed that I wasn't suffering from anything and that I'd cured myself automatically by stepping up. He said I just needed good friends and to laugh more. He told me that the best people were perhaps friends from any happy period of life—childhood or university for example—people who we have loving memories of. Then he said that he had one other suggestion: I could come stay at the sanatorium there in Heidelberg and he could be with me every day. This startled me and I was really taken aback.

"He followed up saying, 'Perhaps I didn't express this properly. It's like a resort, with natural therapies and recovery programs, sessions where you confront your own psychological challenges that over time have become physical problems.' He told me that perhaps the joint pain I had been suffering from was due to this. I withdrew into myself, knowing the appeal of such labyrinths. You can't convince yourself later that you're actually OK and not insane.

"Gunter carried my little suitcase and put it in the backseat of my car. I got in and he closed the door. Morning dew covered the windshield. He stood outside across from the driver's side window and drew his finger across the glass, writing on it in reverse, the same way Leonardo DaVinci recorded all of his inventions in secret code: *Bleibe bei mir*, meaning Stay with me. Under this he wrote, *Bitte*, Please!

"I started the car and opened the windows, glued to my seat as if I both wanted and didn't want to go. I felt a fever overtake me, the color red sweeping over my entire body, staining even the whites of my eyes. This pleasant and unexpected surprise made my heart flutter and landed a broad smile I just couldn't hide on my face. He turned to my window and I noticed what he was wearing. He'd shaved his beard, rolled up the sleeves of his starched white shirt, and wore blue linen trousers and gray tennis shoes, making him look younger than fifty-five.

"He looked younger than me in fact, like Joachim Löw. Also like him, he'd tied his navy blue woolen sweater around his neck. I felt bliss. He took my hand, kissed it over and over and then took the other one. He nuzzled his face in them, like a little puppy rubbing its head on its mother's belly…Was this the beginning of a love story? Or would it be the taste of something that Doctor Gunter will turn into a medical condition? I don't trust psychologists! They will do anything to establish their clout and the validity of the theories they've studied, as if the human soul was a Lego piece, which you just have to put back in the right place. They build you up and tear you down; they change colors and sizes according to their own desires and convince you that it is the materialization of your own psychology. Honestly, I was nervous about being with Gunter. After he became my confidant, he was able to control my psychic self. But I loved that he loved my honesty and my weaknesses, that he was attracted to my strengths and healed my wounds.

"About a week later, he called me, and told me that he'd been reading *Bahia*, a little book I'd written about my experiences in Brazil, where I'd once lived for a year. I'd forgotten about our encounter, I considered it a lovely little flirtation that had stirred some confidence in us both, but wouldn't go any further. But delving into the hidden depths of a writer by exploring their characters, thoughts, and language is a serious step in getting to know an author. I still don't know what made Gunter read my book so soon after we'd met. No, it's not because he loves to read. He never really had much time for reading—he's completely preoccupied with the frightening world of his patients."

Carmen slept late. I went to investigate and passed by her door twice cautiously, but she didn't wake up. I stood in the doorway, looking at her, and she opened her eyes. You could see her small bare shoulders, the white sheets wrapped around her like a rose enveloped in spirals of petals. She had two or three pillows under her head, and she was hugging another in her arm. All of her pillows were so soft and their softness made it difficult for me to sleep. It's as if the heavier our worries in life, the heavier pillows we need—so they can carry our burdens, thoughts, and memories. I needed those hard, raised cushions stuffed with wool, instead of pastel pink and pistachio green pillowcases filled with polyester or feathers, like the ones Farhan had brought back from Saudi Arabia embroidered with the words, "Good Morning" and "Sleep Well!"

After we'd had our coffee, Carmen opened the kitchen cupboard and took out three bars of what was no doubt fancy chocolate. I have no position on chocolate, but I generally prefer white. I took a piece. It was white chocolate with orange. I wished that Mama had been here with me—she also loved white chocolate.

She continued her story about Gunter, which I listened to eagerly, refilling my coffee cup every time I emptied it.

"Less than a month later, Gunter visited me here in Cologne. We didn't leave the house. I sat on this same chair and he stretched out on the sofa that you're sitting on right now. We talked endlessly. I had not been alone with a man in a room for more than a year. For the twenty years before, I had only been with Bassam. Thus, when he came close to me, I was afraid I wouldn't know how to act, how a man and woman should touch each other. I was also afraid of what our bodies looked like. He was ardent—as if he'd planned for this. His breath was warming and becoming sporadic; he grabbed my hips. But I wasn't ready. I felt my body was heavy and had lost its sense of gravity. Life had crushed it.

"I began to push him off me, crying. But he calmed my delusions and started whispering reassuring, pleading words in my ear so I wouldn't be afraid. When I looked in his eyes, I found dozens of people: the dead, incompetent, arrogant, frustrated, injured, addicted, and treacherous…In his repressed cry, I could hear the shouting of the tormenters and the echoes of wails. In fact, I was afraid of myself and sad about the condition I was in, lacking confidence in my own body. Gunter helped me with the touch of his delicate fingers, which he ran over my naked back, until I dipped my fingers into his legendary, doughy body and kissed it!

"Before this happened, I believed that we were in a race to see who would take advantage of the other first. Would I transform him into material for my writing or would he make me into a case study? I didn't often allow myself to open up and get close to anyone. I truly feared knowing myself too well. If I dared to delve too deeply into my dark and hidden places, I imagined

I might be capable of anything—robbing, murdering, stealing other women's husbands. I would be completely without morals. But the notion of competition vanished on this very sofa, safe and secure in his arms, I told him about my father and mother…

"It was the beginning of September 1939. A group of beautiful women in the Polish city of Gdansk went to the Sopot Club on the water. The young Marion, who later became my mother, was one of them. She was about sixteen years old, the daughter of a handicraft salesman who owned a little shop in the city's Long Market, the most important commercial center in the old city. He employed a group of women who worked in their homes embroidering red and yellow poppies and blue lilium flowers on sheets, pillowcases, and folkloric blouses. My mother and my grandmother also did embroidery work, and he sold it to tourists coming from Western Europe.

"At the end of the summer Gdansk is unparalleled in its charm. It is full of sun, cherries, Baltic seagulls, and cool northern breezes. You can drink Tyskie beer and nibble on goat cheese. My mother and her girlfriends had no way of knowing that this was the last time they would gather in their motherland Poland, that had always been a place of conflict between Prussia and France, Russia and Germany. It was occupied, liberated, and then an international zone. Senior European military leaders had passed through it over time—Napoleon, Hitler, and Rommel. Children would stop playing and raise their heads to the sky, startled by the buzzing of warplanes. The war, later known as World War II, would annihilate more than 60 million people, and mark all of our lives.

"Things accelerated in Gdansk. They started executing people who were defending their homes and workplaces. Nature contributed to this dismal scene: gray clouds filled the sky and the sun disappeared as a squadron of Astuka German fighter planes flew overhead. People remained on the coastline to stop the advance of the war, and tried to keep their daily lives going, because if the war broke out nothing could stop it.

"Marion put a short green linen dress on over her damp bathing suit, grabbed her canvas bag, and started running, her long red hair trailing behind her. She was headed for home; it would take about fifteen minutes to reach Ghoun Miasto, where their house and father's shop was located in the back streets of the merchants' quarter. When she passed in front of the great Saint Mary's Church, fear compelled her to step inside for a moment and pray. She did that from time to time, hesitating before this Gothic basilica, with its seven gates. It had stood with indifferent solidity through a series of wars and attacks that had besieged it since the fourteenth century. It is like all objects of glory, which are rebuilt after they fall, earning themselves a new life that we call an era.

"This church remained confused by whether it was Catholic or Protestant. Sometimes it served one community, sometimes the other, and yet other times both together. But its true identity was derived from its red stones, its winged arches, and how it looked after the downtrodden. It remained ignorant of the intentions of those people who used their fertile imaginations to invent pretexts for war. Marion knelt before the golden icon of the Virgin Mary. There were many local people from Gdansk there, no tourists or strangers.

"The local city authorities had mobilized the youth to volunteer. Church cellars and back gardens had begun to fill with aid. There were no more candles you could use to make a vow.

Marion called on God to stem this flood, and protect her home, family, and country. Heart heavy, she left. But her prayer wasn't fulfilled. She thought this was because she hadn't prayed in so long, and she felt ashamed of her opportunism, even though she used to donate to the church regularly. She also was from a family with strong religious roots, which were confirmed after the communist tide swept through Eastern Europe, making attachment to the church a way to resist the Russians.

"Everyone knew that Hitler's consolidation of his position in Europe meant control of Gdansk, and that a civil war would break out. The allies wouldn't permit him to take this sensitive Baltic corridor and they also believed that Poland was for the Poles, regardless of their German or Russian origins. No power could deny their right to exist and abolish an entity that had already been created, not once they'd savored the sweet taste of an independent homeland!

"Marion crossed in front of colorful facades of German buildings, whose power she felt looming over her. The movement in the main street of the old city didn't feel normal. People were sheltering in their houses because they could see low-flying planes, the kind that prompted children to run out and wave to the pilots, sure that they could see them from inside the cockpit.

"She reached her father's shop. Her mother Jacquelyn was stacking up what was left of their merchandise far away from the door. She piled it all up onto a big table, draping a white sheet over it. There wasn't a lot left because there hadn't been many orders, or even much tourism at all lately. Moving things home seemed absurd. Their German origins gave them some protection from Hitler's attacks, but bombs and planes don't have sensors to detect your origins, affiliations, or feelings of loyalty.

"Marion asked after her father. Her mother told her that he was with her brothers and sisters at home organizing the supplies, covering the roof with stones, and preparing the cellar to live in…The war may drag on and her father wanted to prevent her brothers from joining the defense. Someone would do it; it didn't have to be them. Before they locked up the shop, they heard a loud bang in one of the nearby neighborhoods behind ours. Everyone was sprawled out on the ground in the street. Most of the youth of Gdansk had taken a course in disaster preparedness and first aid. The relatively nearby explosion shook the whole area, and people started running in every direction. Marion felt her heart squeeze tightly in her chest. She and her mother ran as fast as they could, their feet dragging their bodies forward. The smoke grew more intense and the smell of things burning became more piercing the closer they got to the house. Her heart pounded harder against her ribs, as if announcing that the disaster had affected her personally. This is what happened: the neighborhood had been destroyed by shelling, killing her father, sister, and brothers. Her senses were paralyzed, her memory frozen. Her mother started to hope aloud that some of the four of them were not in the house. The destruction was so extensive that a search and rescue operation under the rubble was impossible.

"When evening fell and no one had returned, they understood that the two of them were alone in the world. Local volunteers came and moved the remaining people to the places they wanted to go. Marion and her mother went to Auntie Liz's house in the western countryside, down a road filled with horses and cars stuffed with refugees. They mourned there. The war had intensified, causing a struggle between Soviet and German supporters. This split the soul of Gdansk. It was ready for a battle between Russia and Germany. The Polish navy headed for England. The Air Force was destroyed, but despite this, Polish forces fought bravely. The pilot Stanislaw Skalski alone shot down eighteen German planes. Kazimierz Rasinski was tortured and murdered by the Germans for refusing to reveal Polish communications codes. Intellectuals and members of the political opposition were transferred to detention camps, where they were tortured. Many Jews were shipped off to Palestine until only a few elderly members of their community remained.

"Warsaw surrendered in early October after Juliusz Rómmel's forces fell. Marion and her mother Jacquelyn left for Germany, after making a declaration of loyalty to their German roots. They were in fact loyal only to life. They were searching for shelter, equally hating all parties. They moved to the north with a convoy of refugees and priests who were carrying Saint Mary's church's bells to deliver them to Lübeck. There was a church of the same name there and it would always remind them of where they came from. They worked in a little factory making marzipan candy out of almonds and sugar. Their earnings weren't enough to cover their food and lodging, however, so they moved to Frankfurt after train travel was reestablished.

"Jacquelyn found employment at a tailor's shop; Marion worked as a volunteer in a hospital to ensure they could store up provisions. Marion was passionate about reading; she'd developed political sympathies for confronting the German spirit, and tried to express this in poems laden with symbolism that she published in the local press. She had a group of comrades whom she spent Saturday evenings with in a pub near the hospital. They traded political opinions and aspirations, under the guise of fun and dirty jokes. All of them were on alert to detect which one of them might be an informant. Marion spent years living in the shadow of war and had acquired an extra layer of beauty, shaped by her sorrow and principled struggle."

✳

"There wasn't much cloth available. Clothes got tighter and dresses got shorter. A military spirit prevailed over how civilians in the street dressed. Marion wrapped a bright blue turban around her head, tied it with a velvet bow, and wore her short gray skirt with a white shirt. She went on her evening shift at the hospital where Heinz Schacht, the failed Messerschmitt pilot, was healing from his injuries after spending two days in a coma. His airforce squadron was bombed while still on the ground, and he was injured by burning shrapnel from the shelling. His grief over his destroyed plane was unbearable, and he regretted surviving, considering how diminished his once powerful air fleet was. The fleet's reputation and abilities had been denigrated and humiliated.

"Most of the men in the hospital ward were sleeping, others were moaning and groaning. Many had lost limbs; bandages wrapped around their bodies had turned them into mummies in a Pharaonic cemetery. Only Marion emanated life. She sat on a chair on the side of the room stretching her legs out onto the edge of Schacht's bed in a half-reclining position. She recited her poem:

'The comrades surrounding me are full of passion
You left my womb, with no souvenir or star
Like a burnt-out Panzer tank
In a room redolent with formaldehyde…

I will trade almonds with you on a gray bed,
Between the music and giggling of the palace genies,
I will jump like a poppy seed in your soup bowl
Like a lost herring,
And you will now open your eyes and see me
You will open your eyes and draw a rose!'

"The only possible outcome was that their love would flourish—as it does in most intense circumstances…like war. You defy death and create unexpected destinies, because with defeats and disappointments, people's bodies are aroused by cauldrons of absurdity and desire that push fear into hiding.

"When the war was over for good, and Marion and Heinz confirmed that he hadn't been castrated and all his parts were working (unlike so many others), they married and had the seven of us! We lived in a big house in Cologne, which had been half-destroyed by filth and squalor. My grandmother Jacquelyn kept working as a seamstress in a fashion house and lived with us until she passed away. She was afflicted by dementia in her final days. Whenever she heard the sound of a click or a knock, she'd quickly scoot her body, which had remained healthy for a woman in her eighties, under the kitchen table, growling, 'Hitler is here, Hitler has come!'

"She used to make Polish cakes stuffed with rose petal jam, cheese, and poppy seeds, while telling us about the astronomical clock, which they'd left in Saint Mary's Basilica. It told the time, date, the phase of the moon, the holidays, and the future. The astronomical clock was the centerpiece of mysterious love stories of the Gdansk people. It was because of this that Nicholas became attached to the galaxies. It is why, from his youth, he seriously researched Johannes Hevelius, the city's seventeenth century astronomer. It is by studying the details of his life that he stumbled upon al-Battani.

"My mother carried on writing anti-war poetry, while my father remained a Nazi and never abandoned this ideology. This was a silent and repressed struggle between the two of them, which could turn to hatred at times, making him lose the desire to continue on with the family. My mother never forgot her roots. When we had become an army, she and her mother remained a counter-force—their memories, language, and sorrows different from ours.

"When my father died of old age, we put an announcement in the paper and the Wehrmacht soldiers who were left gathered to mourn his passing. The house transformed into an old people's home. They put on their uniforms and medals, and we made a lot of food. They sang the anthems of the Third Reich, re-opened ancient memories, and filled the air with the aroma of the elderly—full of their wrinkled mouths, shiny dentures, and yellowing breath. My mother was searching their eyes for her history, transforming her back into a young girl. Once again she was Marion in her floral-print dresses, wide-brimmed straw hat, and strong constitution like Marlene Dietrich. They gave a eulogy in his honor, in which they remembered the heroism of the late Heinz Schacht, his bravery, his loyalty to his beliefs, and his flight in the skies over Gdansk on the first day of the war. They recalled how he out-maneuvered the Polish pilots and dropped his bombs over the city center…

"My mother said that her brain exploded when she heard this last sentence. In that cursed moment, she had discovered that the man whom she'd lived with for more than half a century had been the one who destroyed her house, murdered her family, orphaned her, and displaced her and her mother as refugees in another country. Harsher yet was that he'd passed and she couldn't take revenge on him or even ask him about it so that he could comfort her with his denial. She couldn't cry while punching his chest full of criminal arrogance.

"After the moment of truth, my mother retaliated against us. She boycotted us. She no longer spoke with anyone. I felt that we were a living, daily symbol of her violation—her violated youth, body, and blood. I used to beg her to speak. I screamed at her to say something. I paid Sarah to talk with her…Bassam used to feed her and take care of her needs. She would accept this from him lovingly. The doctor said that she was afflicted by Alzheimer's disease. But I never believed it. She memorized many poems and I heard her repeat them in a child-like voice. She used to sit next to me, holding a framed picture of me she'd taken from above the fireplace, saying, 'Look, my daughter is a famous novelist, look at her picture.' My mother didn't have Alzheimer's or anything else. She hated all of us and that's it. She withdrew from us and died."

"Gunter soothed me like an inexperienced child does with a bird they've caught in a trap. He was perplexed, as I lay in his arms wracked with sobbing lamentations. He asked me the wrong kinds of questions like what my favorite color was, or if I could write about what was happening to me. I couldn't answer; all I could do was weep. I didn't heal lying in his arms. My head would always butt up against the barriers between us. I tried to talk to him about this but he said there were no barriers. None at all! I asked Bassam the very same question, and also asked Danny later. Lulu, I don't need a psychologist to tell me that I am suffering from my father's cruelty and that a girl who hasn't had enough love from her father will never get enough love from any man in the world."

I could see my own father's face: his dark skin, his curly black hair, his round brown eyes, his broad nose with a thick mustache under it, hiding his delicate lips, and his always clean-shaven oval chin. Later, after Carmen left, I began to cry myself because I remembered how I used to tell him that I didn't want to grow up because I didn't want him to get old. I used to tell him that if he died, I'd bury him in the back garden of our house and talk to him as if he were still alive. But I realize now that I couldn't bury him, and how I wished I could sit him on the sofa, talk to him, feed him, and wipe his dirty shoes.

During the war, most people had to live with their dead relatives still in their houses and cellars, until bombings would ease up and they could bury them in their back gardens. Back gardens were the most appropriate; people could talk to the dearly departed every now and then and let them know what was happening. It was as if the trees were growing to honor them, as if they were there when their families were sitting outside, watching their favorite television programs, and when they got back into bed at the end of a long day. I wish I could've been able to bury Mama in the garden of our house. We had three gardens and I couldn't bury my mother's legs in any of them.

I didn't know if Nicholas had told Najwa anything about his family's difficult story. Perhaps he didn't so as to keep his personal suffering private. Or maybe he didn't consider her someone who could journey with him into these unexpressed deep feelings. Or perhaps he wanted to keep her separate, like a feminine joy from a distant world with no bearing on this fantasy.

Carmen continued her story,

"Gunter wasn't content with our connection after I'd let him into my inner world. He'd made me surrender to him without resisting and this made him suffer. This wasn't because of love but rather his power to control my psychic being. He was stingy in expressing his feelings to me, to the point that he didn't tell me stories. I liked him to tell me stories: I knew he had many and his voice reminded me of my mother's. Despite her domestic burdens, my mother used to gather us every evening and tell us tales from the Brothers Grimm. He deprived me of my mother's voice. It was sick cruelty, the opposite of love.

"I was always careful to call what we had love or healing, but something inside told me that this was dangerous. Our gut feelings never lie. He deprived me of spontaneity by reprimanding me when I called him. He'd call me back later telling me that he really missed me and that it was just his long working hours keeping him from me. At night I would turn my phone off and sit and write. When I analyzed my attachment to him I started to withdraw. It was attachment to a threat, pulling me towards my own strengths and protecting me from falling into the pits of despair.

"His way of counting every word and movement alienated me, as did how he looked at everything through the lens of psychoanalytic theories. He taught me about boredom and patience, probability and statistics. He trained me to wait for long periods, the exhaustion of having expectations and being weak. When I needed urgently to speak to him, I wouldn't be able to reach him. But then he would suddenly broadcast his love for me. He always was preoccupied with his own concerns. I know friends of my brother Nicholas, who work at NASA, the busiest place in the world. They have girlfriends who they make love to and also share their concerns. Generally, Gunter was busy with his own concerns until I started ignoring his calls. I was preparing for the impending end that I felt was coming, accompanied by some great sabotage."

She pointed to her heart, "But then suddenly he was dead."

I asked innocently, "He committed suicide?"

She looked at me with surprise, "He was murdered."

"How?"

"I don't know. All I could think about was that my phone number was recorded in his call register. I wanted to contact Olga and Nader but I needed to remain silent. I was gripped by an insane anxiety for months until I was sure that the whole story had peacefully faded away. God had saved me from a terrible evil. What would have happened if we'd have stayed together? I would have been swallowed up by a vortex of police and investigations. Perhaps I would have been dead. No one called me; I wasn't even registered at his clinic. I couldn't believe that I'd ever known a man was murdered!"

The intensity of the last thing Carmen said paralyzed me. What if she'd known that she was talking to someone who'd killed her own grandmother? Indeed what if she'd known that she'd welcomed an even bigger murderer, Abboud, into her home? She'd cared for him and helped facilitate his move to Cologne. I believed that Carmen truly needed psychiatric treatment and that I had to hold onto myself in this strange country where the easiest thing to do was hand a refugee over to a psychiatrist.

Carmen said that all she needed now was a well-lit place to sit and write. She told me that after I came back from walking around the city that day, she'd be waiting for me with a surprise so I shouldn't be late for dinner, which we'd fixed for six o'clock that evening.

Cologne's streets welcomed me with open arms. I'd never before had the chance to be alone, free as a bird separated from its flock, who'd survived predators on the ground and in the sky, and only had a distant memory of flight. I walked in and out of shops, sat in sidewalk cafes, and watched people walking by. I spilled coffee on my white blouse, but I didn't care about anything anymore, to the point that I couldn't remember if spilling coffee augured good or evil!

I bought a few things at Primark, a shop that Carmen had mentioned because its clothes were a good value for the money. I got a bright blue lace dress, casual trousers, gold sandals, sporty shoes, and three blouses, one of which was silk. I also picked out two handbags—one for daytime and one for evening, pajamas, and underwear… I didn't have any decent clothes except a few simple things I'd bought in Damascus under shelling. My journey from Syria had happened so quickly, I preferred to travel only with the money that Mama and I had taken out of Raqqa and the gold I'd sold before leaving. I had enough money saved to put some into the bank to use for my studies. Eventually, I would receive a monthly stipend that Nicholas had arranged for me through the university, and then my financial situation would be stable.

I wished so much that Mama were with me! She would have enjoyed shopping in Cologne, we would have loved walking around the sidewalks under the vaulted archways together and sitting on the terrace of a café, drinking delicious coffee. She would have invited me for a fancy lunch saying, "Come on, just for you, let's go to the best restaurant in the country!" If I could have ever imagined that she'd have the chance to live in this enchanting place with Nicholas instead of ending up in such an unexpected tidal wave of misery, I would have let her do whatever she wanted. I wouldn't have worked so hard to derail her plans.

I let myself enjoy the beauty of Cologne's streets and its ancient architecture. I cried. Doctor Abu Malai, who was my fourth year Art History teacher, taught me that true beauty can make us cry. Historical immortality holds a poetry within it that moves something deep inside us, he used to tell us. We may not cry when we lose someone beloved, but we weep bitter tears when contemplating ancient ruins. This is how we honor the memory of our loved ones and make up for our dry eyes after losing them. If beauty is linked to glory, we'll be in God's hands, and we can't cry if we're in God's hands!

I still feel overburdened. I cry because my heart and memories cannot absorb so much beauty. Loneliness envelops me—I don't have a mother to write letters to, I don't have a boyfriend with whom to share this captivating place. Beauty overcomes us and, without a helper or loving assistant, it weighs heavily on us. I thought: this is the beauty of freedom—from taboos, traditions, history, family, and fear. Fear is a disfiguring emotion. Fear for my mother and worrying about her had constrained me. I never expected to find freedom after her passing. I even felt liberated from the sin of my grandmother's death, which had lodged itself in my deepest darkest depths.

On the narrow wooden steps of the building, in front of the door to Carmen's apartment, there was a white wardrobe. I opened it and found shoes. I looked into the mirror hanging there and saw my skin was clear. My circulation was better and my body felt more limber—as if this walk had helped me lose a few pounds. I misted myself with a few spritzes of the eau de cologne that I had bought the day before and tucked my sunglasses away as I entered her building. The scent of a delicious meal filled the air: vegetables stir-fried with garlic and ginger.

I tentatively pushed the apartment door open and walked inside. No Carmen! Behind the counter stood a man wearing an apron, his back to me. Surely this couldn't be Nicholas; it was a young man with reddish blonde hair, and a toned body.

"Hi," I offered warily.

He turned all the way around and stood still, staring at me for a moment. Then he stepped toward me, untying his apron and placing it on the counter.

"Hi? Ha ha ha ha, Hi??? Lulu, my Luluuuuu!" His booming voice spoke in Arabic, in an old-school Raqqan local accent—not one person of the younger generation speaks this way! He approached me and lifted me up in his arms, laughing louder and louder. When he put me down and my head was again level to his chest, he squeezed me tightly and his laughter faded. He clutched at me, hurting me more and more with his squeezing, as if he were juicing memories, his childhood, and a lost place out of me, as if he were seeking to recover that which we had been forcibly removed from, like a missing finger.

He swung me left and right so hard that my legs wrapped around his and went numb. I had given him all my strength…

Those minutes that he held me tight against his heart made me come to terms with the pack of wolves that had been snapping at my heels for almost forty years now: loss, war, fear, alienation, betrayal, immigration, sorrow, pain, forgetting, disrespect, being an orphan, being a refugee…For a few moments he let me escape our galaxy, and then he put me back down feeling much lighter and much more beautiful. He kept breathing in the scent of my clothes, while I whispered his name into his neck over and over again, "Abboud, Abboud, Abboud…."

Carmen was really happy that evening. She kept looking over at us with tears in her eyes. She prepared the table on which Abboud had placed the food he'd cooked: ginger chicken, veal steaks with asparagus, grapefruit salad with lettuce and walnuts, and Käsekuchen for dessert.

I quickly changed into a blouse and trousers I'd just bought. I put on some of Carmen's makeup and tried to tame my messy hair. I joined them at the table, where Abboud was lighting three white candles.

"He cooked for you," Carmen said, "A man who cooks for you is a man who loves you!"

I laughed and felt my face go hot. Abboud leaned over and hugged me until my shoulders popped, "Of course I love her." He spoke to Carmen in German and I didn't understand, but I pulled away from him a little bit.

Of course I knew that he loved me, and he loved the old days when Lulu was his neighbor and childhood companion. Today I am less than this; I couldn't be anyone's girlfriend. I am nearly a refugee and very weak. Love needs energy and strength. Historians call what separates me from those people "cultural and civilizational differences." Abboud will help me, empathize with me, but nothing more. I'm also not willing to show contrition in front of other people. If I want to survive I'll have to fashion a parallel life without burdening anyone. Currently, I can't think about anything except safety and this lovely friendship, so much so that I no longer am even curious about his private life—does he have a wife? Kids? Of course a man so handsome would be a ladies' man. And I, on the other hand, am all over the place and not even in competition.

I thought about Carmen's loyalty and generosity. We'd caused her fall on her bum in the toilet and forced her to eat disgusting henna, and yet she fed me the best food, provided me with a safe haven, and reunited me and Abboud. She and Nicholas had helped him, when he first came from Prague to Cologne. She helped him find somewhere to live and gave him her old kitchen cabinets as well as some good extra furniture she had at her place.

Abboud became a well-known chef after studying in the hotel and hospitality industry in Prague. Then he worked under the famous German master chef Joachim Wissler in a restaurant at the Altes Schloss Bensberg Castle near Cologne. He is one of the chefs who have a three-star rating in the Michelin Guide. Abboud traveled to Dubai for a year as the head of the kitchen for the Radisson Blue hotel. He came back to Cologne to work for the same Radisson chain. He also launched a channel on YouTube where he shows off his dishes and now has more than a million followers!

Just recently he'd published a book in German with Carmen's publishing house called, "Colorful Family Dishes." The book became very famous and was translated into English, Czech, and French. It is a cultural history of food, the relationship of cuisine to identity. He showed me some clips from his YouTube videos: there is a beautiful girl putting an apron on him, as he holds his custom-made knives, which as Carmen pointed out have Swarovski crystal handles. At the end of the show, two young women appear at his side dressed in revealing clothes, throwing cream—which they have squished in their hands—at each other.

Now Abboud is working on the launch of his own brand of eco-friendly, gourmet cooking utensils. But despite all this he found the time to cook for me, saying that he would make anything at all for me. I asked him about his mother, Anna, and he told me she's now a volunteer musician who plays in a band on the Charles River to raise money for Syrian refugees. He said that we could go together and visit her in Prague as soon as we got the chance.

After dinner we moved to the sitting room. I was so happily emotional that my voice quivered whenever I spoke. Though I was spent from exhaustion and all of the surprises of this lovely day, I stayed up with Abboud all night. I folded my legs under me on the sofa and we sat talking, drinking tea, and laughing. I stole glances at his frightening beauty, not believing that he was sitting next to me—red hair which the children in our Raqqa neighborhood used to compare to rust, neat beard, creamy, freckled skin, and brown eyes, round as hazelnuts. I searched my memory for someone who looked like him and then I figured it out—he's a carbon copy of Prince Harry, the son of Prince Charles and Princess Diana.

He wrapped a blanket around me. Cologne's chilly night-time breeze had crept in through the kitchen windows, carrying the damp green scent of trees and impending rain. Abboud slipped under the cover, holding it tightly to keep us both fully covered. He clung to me. I told Carmen that he's cooked liked a professional since childhood and how once he made me a genius pumpkin soup when I had a stomach virus. It was so good Mama even asked him how he made it. I told her how he used to bring me honey straight from their hives whenever I had a cold. He'd also gotten me addicted to pickled sardines—once when he'd come back from Prague, he fed them to me, and afterwards I asked him for them every day until I'd finished all the tins he and Anna had brought back. Whenever he traveled he'd bring me pickled sardines. We would wrap the little fish, along with a hot pepper, inside of a piece of pita bread and eat them sitting on the sidewalk, enjoying the spicy burn in our noses.

Carmen laughed, "A woman might forget a man who brings her honey, but you never forget the man who taught you to eat pickled sardines."

She got up to go to sleep, while Abboud and I were still deep in conversation about Raqqa. I hovered between laughing and crying. He cradled me in his arms, wiped my tears, and held my hand between his open palms. He kissed my fingers one by one and stroked my hair gently as if I were a tiny baby. He offered me condolences on the death of my mother, and made me forget the crime we committed against my grandmother. Abboud was the only living human who made my soul feel that there was a heaven.

Carmen woke me up at eight the next morning and prepared breakfast, then we were going to go out to the country to finish buying everything I needed before meeting Nicholas. I felt so much love and regret toward him, as if he had been my father or my mother had actually run away with him. Ethical concepts in life appear simple and flexible, once you cross the invisible line thirty-five degrees north of the equator. It was still too early to go out. We opened the skylight in the sitting room to let in the sunlight. Carmen gazed out through it, as we sat on her sofa next to each other, talking and drinking her carefully selected coffee.

"My relationship with Daniel was stormy. It came at the wrong time and lacked the necessary lead up. It was like eating a cold watermelon in the height of winter—delicious but not something you need. We had known each other less than two months, but Daniel convinced me that we had met two years previously at the Frankfurt book fair, where he happened to have attended a reading of my book *Silver Spoon*, dedicated to my grandmother Jacquelyn's memory. He reminded me that he'd bought the book and asked me to sign it. I didn't really remember but I pretended that I did. At the time I was feeling refreshed, since I had recovered from my miserable relationship with Bassam and overcome my sick attachment to Gunter. My neck surgery had been a success and this seemed auspicious. I felt strong and reborn, but with my memory making me an expert in life's twists and turns. I was ready to move beyond my previous mistakes and breakups. I had a plan: I wouldn't create problems; trivial details wouldn't stop me; I wouldn't ask a lot; I would remain at a safe distance from the world.

"Danny told me that when he'd seen me speaking at the podium, it was as if I'd emerged straight from inside his heart to sit down in front of him. What could be better than being born from inside a man's heart? This guaranteed that any distance between the two of us would simply disappear. Months later, one of my Twitter followers sent me pictures of himself in the places I talk about in my books: Warsaw, Sao Paolo, Bahia. I wrote back to him, 'Wonderful! I hope you enjoy.' He responded, 'Together!'

"Later I would discover that this follower was Daniel himself, magically making this 'Together!' happen. I'm someone who takes thousands of readers with me to places they don't know, and I make them enjoy things through my imagination. They see them through my words, my late nights, my feelings, and my tears. I found that he was taking me with him, playing the role of teacher, guide, and assistant. I could feel him leading me by the hand, with me complying, walking with him through unknown worlds, ancient cities, deserted harbors. We sat together in little sidewalk cafes, in alleys that no one knows except tourists who like to enjoy life and see the world, even on limited resources. Everything seemed new and fresh when he said, 'Together!' I am always alone. 'Together' opened up my life for me. It made me happy and still warms my heart to this day.

"Danny burst into my life full of impulsiveness and instincts. This confused me and I didn't know how to receive his overflowing love. But his love repressed me. Up until now, I have not been able to write about it; it's as if my receivers are disabled and can't transform his powerful signals into a reply. You could say that I can't fit this powerful stream of emotions into my weary heart. With him, I was closer than I ever had been to being myself. It was as if I were a pair of weak windshield wipers that remain dry and unused, but are suddenly surprised by a rain shower. Not naturally strong enough to push it away, what is there to do other than stop the car and wait for the weather to calm down?

"His way of being in love overwhelmed me, as I was facing up to the extent of the injury that continued to dog me. Before him, I felt mutilated by love. Love can do that sometimes. Bassam mutilated me with his betrayal, Gunter with his stinginess. I repeated one mantra: 'I am tired, I am tired.' He used to greet my exhaustion with extremely active feelings, which only exhausted me more. Our emotional strength was not well matched to each other. Truly, it never occurred to me that a person could reach such a level of exhaustion and laziness that even a great love could not budge them. He told me that if someone in this world loved him like he loves me, he would be the happiest person on the face of the earth. He was puzzled about why I was depressed, just as I was puzzled by how he could be so happy, and have so much love. I was depressed by disappointment, betrayal, and waiting. I wasted my feelings on the wrong people. By the time I met the right person, I'd become a living corpse. A fifty-year-old woman remembers nothing but her depression.

"I sometimes rejected his love hysterically. When he called me, I would scold him, telling him that he was wasting my time and invading my privacy. He would tell me that he missed me and that we had to meet up. At that time we were still just talking on Skype, because he wasn't even in Germany. I treated him like Gunter treated me. I refuted all the reasons he loved me: whimsy, a lack of ownership, falling in love with the characters in my novels…He would answer, 'Listen Carmen, just listen. I forgot about your books completely once we talked. You are closer and more beautiful when you leave the printed word behind.' He said, 'It will make me fly like a butterfly.'

"My arthritis medicines make me feel like a baby elephant. I started to love butterflies and searched for them in gardens. I went on YouTube to watch them fly. He read books about the psychological make up of writers, their moods, what they love and what they hate, the reality of writing…All of this was so that he could treat me as well as possible. He was in a hurry, hungry for love and affection. He had lost his two younger brothers, one after the other, from a sudden illness and was left all alone. How would I, who was so exhausted and weak, possibly fill the role of two young men at the pinnacle of their beauty, strength, and joy? How could I make up for such a great loss? I was far from up to the task of doing something like this. I feared fresh new failures and wanted to protect myself. I have the right to protect myself at fifty, when age turns from your ally into your enemy. I told him that I had to undergo a surgical procedure on my neck, that I had sciatica, and that my menstrual periods had stopped. He told me, 'Even if you were only a bag of bones, you would still be my soulmate…I love you.' I replied to him once again with my short mantra, summing up my state, 'I'm tired.' He then said, 'Fine. When a metal is subjected to pressure, by a force whose source is known, we can treat it. But when the forces are chaotic and unknown, and we can't specify their source, we are unable to treat it. I am sad for this rare metal. I beg you, Carmen, tell me what will make you happy. I only want you to be happy.'

"Daniel is a construction engineer and had many projects on the coast of the Caspian and Black Sea in Azerbaijan and Georgia. His mother is Georgian and he inherited her Caucasian traits, dark eyes and thick hair, which is still jet-black in his late fifties. He has a regal stature, a snowy white beard, and a square, upturned mustache like the janissaries used to wear, waiting for their falcons to land at their sides. When I asked him about this strange style, he told me that it was all the rage in Eastern Europe and was going to Hollywood next.

"Danny organized a trip for me to the phosphate city project his company was undertaking in Batumi, Georgia. He told me that the virgin forests and the strong sun there would cure me of my exhaustion, and would make me find myself again. He said that he wouldn't come on the journey with me and we didn't even have to meet if I didn't want to. He also said that it was a gift from a passionate reader to his favorite author. I could join in with a team of journalists who were learning about the projects there. I agreed and I went. I discovered much more about him there than what I'd found searching the Internet. He is an important businessman, the kind in magazines and films, who had shares in transnational corporations, and was protected by bodyguards and guard dogs. His mornings might happen in one hemisphere and his evenings in another—but he still had time for love and read the books of a poor woman like me."

Poor! I laughed with Carmen, looking around at where we were sitting and talking. I couldn't have dreamed of a life nicer than hers. She has a car, a house, a job, and has written influential books. Her daughter is a beautiful young woman. I got a lump in my throat: My house was more beautiful than hers. It was large, well furnished, and looked out onto the Euphrates. When Carmen visited us in Raqqa, she found it to be an antique masterpiece. It is true that it was just one story tall and wasn't as fancy as my grandmother Karma's house. But it had a huge garden, with plum, pear, and lemon trees, wild roses and jasmine. We also had a big padded porch swing, trimmed in blue and white. The floors were tiled in marble, and Mama had picked out all our furnishings from the famous Taurus shops in Aleppo. Baba let her choose whatever she liked, and didn't get involved at all except to pay the bills. The bed was round, which at that time was really unusual; there wasn't even one other circular bed at the time in the entire town. Our house's one problem was that it was located at the center of a civil war. Daesh bombed it, destroying one side. Its walls cracked as a result of repeated bombardment by both alliance and regime airplanes, shattering all the windows. We left before we were able to repair them.

Carmen and I drained a full pot of coffee during our conversations, each of which followed directly upon the last. She suggested I bring over a tub of ice cream hidden in the back of the freezer.

"Are you sure you want me to go into your kitchen?"

"I think so…" she said, tossing a little sofa cushion at me in jest. I brought over two glass dishes and two spoons. I opened the container of mulberry and cream flavored ice cream to scoop it into the dishes, but Carmen started digging right into the container and eating with gusto. She said that dishes were superfluous, as we would just have to wash them afterwards. "It's fine," I said and scooped some into my dish. Only a few moments later she had polished off the rest of it and started licking her spoon. I was delighted by her childish gluttony and good appetite. She said that we had to finish up our chat because we had a long day of work ahead.

"We arrived at the coastal city and walked around this project's sites, which was the purpose of our visit. We had lunch in a restaurant on the Black Sea, where each member of the delegation chose whichever fish they wanted from the fish market under the restaurant and they prepared it. The waiters cooked them quickly on a grill and served them to us with fresh salads and wine vinted in the famous winery, located right in the nearby vineyards. When we got back to the hotel I found a big basket from Danny with a bottle of Caucus mountain honey and sweets made from grape molasses, one was mint flavored, another cherry, and a third had natural flavors. I called him to thank him and let him know I'd arrived. He said that we would have dinner together in the hotel casino, which was right across from where I was staying. I would be his guardian angel in a game of Blackjack. I told him, 'Let's rather have coffee in the hotel this evening because my ankle is hurting a lot and I can't walk.' My Achilles tendon had started bothering me all of a sudden, perhaps because of the travel and the long stroll."

"Evening fell over Georgia's lush forests. The sun's red disc plunged into the sea. My blood came to life and started circulating through my veins, feeling clean and warm. I was aware that I was about to have a first encounter with an amazing man who loved me. I really wanted to see him face to face—to enjoy the evening with him. I prayed to God that my ankle would feel better and I would be able to walk. My body had let me down at the wrong moment. This showed that I was starting to get old!

"Despite this, I put on a long, black, muslin sleeveless dress, which trailed on the ground, and red coral earrings. I applied sparkling foundation, with a little dark blush, black mascara, and pink lipstick. I couldn't wear any of my shoes, so I went barefoot and sat in the lobby. When Danny arrived, I'd propped my leg up on a little table, which I'd asked a hotel worker to bring me. He greeted me in celebration, not hiding his unbridled joy. He was genuinely magnificent, my heart pounded at the very sight of him and this elated me. He didn't shake my hand, or hug me, but rather knelt down, held my ankle in his hand, and began massaging it, as he looked into my eyes and whispered with overblown seriousness: 'It's going to get better…' A man was holding my foot the first time we met.

How could I anticipate his next move? Stranger yet was that my ankle really did start feeling better.

"We went on talking for a long time and he kept massaging my foot. He ran his hand over my toes, stroking the layers of my red nail polish."

I looked at her feet, and she had the same nail polish on I think. It was very enticing!

She continued, "Danny suggested that we walk on the beach, because walking on the warm sand might help my foot. He took off his shoes too. I leaned against his arm, and we both walked barefoot, alive with passion. My God, what was this wonderful life that Danny was helping me live? It was like a dream. He beseeched me to love him and let him be near me. He'd memorized entire passages of my novels and talked to me about my thoughts and ideas. I told him, 'You should pay attention to your projects and your work.' He responded, 'It's all good. I'm successful; everything is going fine. I draw inspiration for my projects from you and your ideas, and engineers do the rest.'

"He made me laugh. The next day, he sent a car and driver to take me to the yacht club. He was waiting for me there in neon colored shorts, a white t-shirt, and sporty sunglasses. This man was super-attractive—any woman could fall in love with him. He drove me to a little wooden bridge and said, 'Here we are, give yourself to me and we will fly away together.' I looked around and there was a group of small-engine gliders and tourists wearing life jackets seated behind the glider pilots. The two blades on the side skimmed the water and the glider took off into the sky. Danny told me he owned this group of gliders and he would fly with me. I didn't hesitate. A young man helped me into a life jacket, which I put on over my bathing suit. I sat behind Danny, holding onto the metal pole in front of me, my feet planted on the sides of the seat.

"As we took off from the sea, a spray of salty water flew in our faces and on our bare legs, refreshing us. Then we flew up into the sky. We ascended slowly, the sea and the city growing tiny beneath us. When the plane settled at a certain altitude, Danny turned off the engine and we glided, moved only by the wind…I gazed at the world all around me: space, the beautiful red-tiled buildings, the fancy hotels, the enchanting blue sea, the dolphins jumping and playing in the water. I rested my cheek against Danny's back and felt him tremble. Powerful gusts of wind attacked my face and hair, preventing me from hearing what he was saying. He spoke to me using sign language, his hands hidden inside driving gloves. It never occurred to me, even in my novels, that one day I would ride on a flying carpet with such a handsome prince! This journey was the happiest moment of my life. It made me reclaim my youth—I'd realized that I was more desirable than before, with a unique joy. He signaled that I should prepare for a rough water landing. He turned on the motor and we flew a bit, then the skis of the plane slapped the surface of the water powerfully, soaking my clothes and hair. My heart leapt into my throat…Afterwards we reached the wooden bridge where we'd started."

I didn't even notice that I'd clasped my hand over my mouth. I was right there with Carmen, riding along with her as she rose and fell, as if I were there in the glider, "Carmen, you're crazy! How could you trust him like that? You flew in a glider plane in a foreign country the first time you met this man in person! Weren't you terrified?"

"Actually," she replied, "I was scared of one thing. When

the engine was off, and the plane was calmly gliding in the sky, I thought, 'What if Danny were to drop dead right now, while we're up in the air?' If he'd had a stroke, for example, how I would I land the plane? I swear to you that was the only thing I was thinking."

"My God, you are truly mad! But then why are you sad? You should really be the happiest woman in the world. If I were you I would be with Danny without a second thought. Be with him Carmen, I'm begging you!"

She stared at me and sighed. The spark in her eyes, which had been there throughout the story, quickly dimmed. They became sad with the loss of their final joy.

"I can't kid myself. I reached a new breaking point on this journey with him, and I cannot handle any more breaking points, or any of their consequences. This is what Danny couldn't understand. I couldn't deal with how he refused to understand this. He surrounded me with love and splendor, but I didn't want a torrential love that would bind me to him and then break me. Break ups in your fifties can't just be repaired like when we were in our twenties. Watch out, Lulu! He also has a family, and a wife. They don't live together but she and he move back and forth between Georgia and Frankfurt."

I put my hand on her shoulder soothingly, and she asked me not to worry about her. She said that she was not in love as much as exhausted from her escape from paradise.

This long talk made me love Carmen more. She took me on little trips, introduced me to people, and taught me that there are people who can leave paradise for their own self-preservation. At that time, I only had heard of people being expelled from paradise! She gathered up her hair and wrapped it behind her neck in a small bun. She said calmly, "There are wonderful men in this world but we can't have all of them in our lives, just like we can't land on all the sides of the dice in one throw."

THE BIG BANG

Abboud called me in the middle of the day, saying that he was going to pass by so that we could shop for things I needed, and we would eat dinner together at six PM. I had already finished everything I needed to do with Carmen and so all I had to do was spend time with him before I left with Nicholas for Munich. It might be some time before we would meet again. I told him this and suggested that we spend the day at his place. When he came to pick me up, I was wearing an open-backed, short-sleeved navy blue dress that Carmen had insisted on buying me the day before when we were shopping in Neumarkt. I stood in front of the mirror to see how the back looked. I craned my neck, but I couldn't really see. The dress was elegant; I hadn't worn such nice clothes in a long time. I also went with her to her Turkish hairdresser, who gave me a cut and style. This helped my hair, which had suffered from neglect, and especially from the lack of water and healthy food during the last siege of Raqqa. He gave it an oil treatment and then arranged it to flow down over my shoulders. It came out looking shiny and healthy again.

Before I put on my cream-colored, high-heeled shoes with their red, Louboutin-style soles, I decided to paint my toenails with Carmen's burgundy polish. I started with my right foot and rested it against the edge of the bed. Abboud was suddenly there in the doorway, arms folded across his chest, leaning against the doorframe and staring at me silently. I was startled when I saw him and stopped polishing. He said, "I'm waiting for you, do you need help?" I sat up properly and smiled. He came over, took the small brush from me, and began painting my toenails. I was overwhelmed with surprise and excitement.

"I love doing things with you that I've never done but that I'd like to have done."

"Abboud, don't make stuff up. What about the girl who dressed you in an apron, and the two naked girls who doused each other in cream?"

"That's work! Nothing equals the pleasure of watching you give yourself a pedicure, or you slowly putting on your silk stockings, lifting your leg in the air. Would you believe that I've imagined those two exact scenarios since we were young?"

"I don't believe it actually. You've never given any indication of that..."

He reached over to Carmen's vanity and picked up a makeup brush. He began passing it over my face—from my forehead to my chin, down my neck to my chest, which was covered by my dress. He traced a path with the brush down my shoulders to the back of my neck and I felt tiny butterfly wings fluttering against my body, making it tremble. I closed my eyes, my body contracting a little, trying to resist melting into a puddle. I shifted slightly and he started moving the brush down my back a millimeter at a time, feeling every inch of my skin until it reached the last possible point before the dress's opening. I could hear the sound of his breathing cutting through the silence. My lower parts relaxed, then tensed right up, and then relaxed again. I turned over and got up off the bed, "Don't do this to me, Abboud, I'm not like you. I don't live in Europe. I haven't ever been with a man. I don't have anyone to put an apron on me."

He replied miserably, "Fine. Has no man ever come near you?"

"Don't say it like that, Ab…"

He interrupted, "So don't say this to anyone else. They'll think you have serious mental problems."

He threw the brush on the bed, and it bounced off onto the parquet floor with an echo. He grabbed me, hugged me close with one arm, swiftly kissing my neck, "Come away with me!"

Honestly, I was so excited that I had to grab hold of the door handle of the closet so I wouldn't fall over. Despite being so enthralled by him, I replied to his comments snippily, "I'm not from here and I'm not like this. I use different standards to assess situations than you do. Wait until my nail polish is dry. Then we can go!"

As children, Abboud and I used to quarrel while we roamed all around Raqqa together, going in and out of people's houses. We would buy sodas and potato chips from the little shops, where we'd open up freezers to find the drinks warm and food spoiled because of the long electricity cuts. I never expected that he had such bold fantasies about me.

This is how I wound up inside the old building that I had been gazing out at since I'd arrived in Cologne three days earlier. It was the very same apartment with a white window frame and organza curtains. I expected his apartment to smell of kitchen spices, but instead it smelled masculine, of sleep mixed with the natural scents of a young man's body. It smelled of dirty laundry, a damp bathroom, and pine-scented cologne...He pulled back the curtains and opened the windows. He guided me in front of him, resting his hand on my back right at the opening of my dress every so often. He walked his fingertips up and down me, pressing against my flesh and gently kneading it. It seemed to me that he might keep moving me around his apartment forever. But I need to sit down right away because my knees could no longer carry the weight of my body, I could hardly even talk, "Abboud, come on..."

He plopped me down on the sofa and hugged me tight, as if we had just been reunited and hadn't just spent the entire night together in Carmen's apartment.

"Oh Lulu, I never ever thought that you would visit me here! All of Raqqa is here with me today, my father, grandmother, aunties...the whole neighborhood..."

His father had died before the war and his grandmother had passed on a bit before that. His curious auntie had married a widower when Daesh first came, and his step-mother Safaa had taken her two children to the countryside. Their house was closed up for good.

Through perseverance, Abboud was able to buy this place that was surely worth a lot. It was on the Rhine in the center of Cologne. The solid building dated to the pre-Second World War era. It was made of white stone and its neo-Gothic architectural style gave it small balconies and winged arches over the windows. Abboud had hung his diplomas on the walls of the large living room, as well as pictures of people who looked to be from the artistic and culinary worlds. There were pictures of him with many beauty queens—Miss Ecuador, Miss Guatemala, Miss France…He'd given a series of lectures at the last Miss World pageant, about cooking: bringing local dishes to the world stage and respecting the special resources of local environments. He told me the story of his successes with pride. I interrupted him with a question that had been burning within me since childhood, that had tortured me my whole life, and which I'd never before been in the right circumstances to ask:

"Abboud, how could you murder my grandmother, Karma?"

"What do you mean by, 'murder my grandmother'?"

"I mean on that night when my grandma died, you jumped up in her widow and stuck your head inside wearing a nylon stocking over it. You frightened her, she had a heart attack, and died. Have you forgotten?"

He scooted away from me a bit, rested his hands on his thighs, and stared out into a space as if he were replaying the events in his mind. It seemed as though he'd forgotten about his crime.

"What are you talking about, Lulu, surely you're joking?"

"No, I'm not joking. I haven't been quiet about this for my whole life only to joke about it now…Abboud, I've been carrying around the burden of this crime to this day. I live with fear, regret, blame, and sorrow. I lost her because of your murderous stupidity and what you did. We're criminals, Abboud…you're a criminal. How can you just forget all about it, go abroad, live happily, and be so successful? My whole life was disrupted by your stupidity and your crime."

"No, no, no, no, Lulu. You are truly mad! What crime are you talking about? I'm not a criminal, or a murderer. And the murderer of your grandma? I left everyone and killed Nana

Karma? God rest her soul, she was dear to my heart. I was completely enchanted by her. I used to search her face, house, and stories for the signs of the dancer they said she once was."

Oh my God, enough with this. Enough shocks and surprises! So he knows she was a dancer, how? Everyone knows the truth, but me, I am the only one who is living with delusions! I put my hand on the side of my head to protect it from exploding, "I know that you didn't do it on purpose, but you did do it!"

"Lulu, don't make me crazy. When I climbed up into her window I didn't see her. She wasn't in bed. Your grandmother had fallen in her kitchen and died there. That's what I remember everyone saying at the time. She had a stroke in the kitchen. That was her diagnosis. She'd fallen down in the kitchen and was paralyzed. They took her to the hospital in an ambulance and my father rode along with them. I remember very well how he rushed back quickly. I searched the streets for you but couldn't find you. I figured that you were sleeping. I didn't even see her that night, Lulu. You've gone crazy."

It was as if someone were confronting me with the reality that I was not me, I was not from this world, I was not a daughter of these people, and that I was not even alive, but dead, and I had to wake up and face my own resurrection.

"Abboud, what are you saying?"

"I'm telling you the truth, Lulu"

"All my fears, tall those hose, dark days, God's retribution on me by taking Mama away from me…"

"Retribution, what retribution, Lulu? Your mother died because people die. My father died too, millions of people die every day because life ends in death. This has nothing to do with rewards or punishments."

"I've lived my life based on the fact that I helped you kill my grandmother."

"That's actually your problem."

Abboud was now absolved of any wrongdoing, and I'd lived a quarter of a century based on an illusion. I'd self-flagellated over this illusion, I was afraid of my own footsteps, and paralyzed in my decision making. I walked around with the terrible certainty that God would never help me and never be on my side. What about my deep sorrow for how I treated Mama, my constant sense that I'd created her tragedy and couldn't enjoy being with her? I felt guilty instead of safe whenever I looked at her. All of this disappeared instantly…

Abboud listened to me, confused. He rested his hand on my forehead and patted it as if he were trying to rearrange my thoughts. Then he leaned his head back, uncrossed and crossed his legs, and lifted one to my face.

"Get your foot out of my face…"

My mind started slowly free falling, since my life had just been emptied of its core issue. I was like a torture victim who was lost without her torturer, "What will I do now?"

"You will change what you believe…How could you have thought that for so long? Why didn't you just ask me? I was right there in front of you! Lulu? Come here, come, you poor thing… I could have reassured you on that very day, come here…"

He wanted to wrap me in his arms, and I screamed in his face, "Get off of me. Go away, you're a criminal!"

Aghast, Abboud drew back a little, "If you say that again, I'm going to get really angry with you."

"You'll get angry with me? I've lived my life angry and tortured, avoiding the black hole in my heart. I feared getting close

258

to myself, my inner feelings. I built barriers against the world so no one would discover how fragile I was inside because I was a murderer. I couldn't be close to my mother, I didn't make friendships, I didn't allow myself to love a man or get married because everything would result in me being punished for my crime. You tell me you will get angry. Get angry, brother, be angry!"

Abboud was silent. He started staring at the walls, then closed his eyes, like he did when confounded by a scientific fact. Then he got up and said, "I'm going to make you a cup of tea."

I shouted, "That's not what I want!" and I got up, looking for the door.

"Where are you going?" He followed me and grabbed my arm, "I'm not going to let you go, Lulu, even if you are crazy. Don't go! We aren't in Raqqa any more…"

I tried to get free of him shouting, "Let go of me, let me go now! Get off me," while beating his chest with my free arm.

I wanted to leave and walk alone in the streets until my feet melted. I fell down and couldn't get up. I wanted to flee my whole entire life, the one in which I woke up every day trying to forget I had killed my grandmother. I spent every single moment of every single day waiting for punishment or forgiveness. That is all I'd done in my life. I clung onto my mother so I wouldn't lose her or she me, as retribution for what I had done. I never fully committed to my studies, pursing a masters or doctoral degree, as she wanted me to. I never fully committed myself to my work at the museum that I loved so much, waiting for my inevitable punishment. I believed that when my father died in Greece without me being able to go and see him was the retribution. Then when the war started I believed that was a part of it too. The same is true of when Daesh came, when our house was bombed, when we left Raqqa, when my mother lost her legs and left me alone. My punishment is not finished, though. Will it end now? Will it end with me learning this fact that blew up everything in my past? How should I start building a new life for myself on a new set of facts now that I am nearly forty years old?

I'm lost in my thoughts, telling him hysterically, "Leave me, leave me alone," while hitting him on the chest as if I were split in two.

"I'm not going to leave you, I won't ever leave. You are my responsibility. Come here, hit me again, come on, again…"

I hoped that Abboud wouldn't leave me, I didn't have anyone else in the world, "You don't know…"

He cut me off putting his mouth to my ear, "I do know, really I know. I'm sorry for everything you've been through. I understand what you've suffered and what you are suffering through now. But it happened. You built your life around a misunderstanding. It happened. It's going to be OK; don't worry. As Nana Karma used to say, 'Shh calm down' in that Turkish way of hers, 'Ya wash.'"

When he said "shh" it was so soothing, I smiled. His voice was low, calm, and gruff. My voice was sharp, high pitched, and trembling.

"Lulu, you can't keep torturing yourself, you deserve to be happy."

I began to calm down as I felt that he understood my suffering. He was playing the role of the confident, wise man whose stability and certitude I needed. I wanted him to help me through the difficult transition from from being a criminal to being innocent.

I stood in the doorframe at a short distance from him, hid my face in my hands, and began to sob…

Abboud wrapped me his arms, and led me back to the sofa. Weak and empty, I surrendered to him. My God, even the foundation upon which my life was based had now collapsed. I wanted Abboud to understand the pain of my transition from one reality to another, opposing, reality and the suffering that was awaiting me, as I adapted to this.

Abboud and I didn't do anything. We didn't eat, drink, or even talk. We just sat together on the sofa and that's it. I listened to his even breathing, his regular heartbeat, the grumbling of his stomach. He encircled me in his arms to protect me from the consequences of the truth and the pain of change. I think that he fell asleep while I was still resisting surrendering to the reality, which still seemed like a terrible fantasy. Indeed, it was like something from a fairy tale, "I fell asleep and woke up to find I was someone else!"

There started to be quite a few heavy things that I had to forget. In fact, I had to forget my whole life. I had to come to terms with myself before I could come to terms with the loss of my mother, my new country, strange people, a new language, preparing to have Nicholas in my life, Munich, work…Abboud said that he was really worried about me. My nerves couldn't take all this stress and change. He proposed that I stay with him, in his care for a while before I moved to Munich. He even offered to speak to Nicholas about this when he came tomorrow. He followed up, "You have enough pressure on you and you clearly need to rest, Lulu, so you can start your new life with new energy…"

All I had to do was comply. He was right. I started to catch onto the idea that I was insufferable. Why did I shout at Abboud, hit him, and accuse him of being a criminal? What does he have to do with how I'd lived up until now? Why did I make him bear the burden of the wrong idea, or stupid fantasy, which I'd built my life upon, while he was supporting me, talking to me, and reaching out to help me? I should be grateful that he was giving me his time, his care, and that he was worrying about my nerves, helping me think through my future. He didn't owe me anything. We didn't share a dangerous secret, we hadn't participated in a crime, there wasn't even a crime committed! I told him that and apologized. He continued to be generous. He drew me to his chest, "Stop it, Lulu, what are you saying? I am you. I've been so sad ever since you pulled away from me and left me alone. I was always confused about that. I don't want to leave you like you left me. I don't want you to be confused and suffer. I don't want you to be alone, the way I was. Those days were hard on me. I couldn't be with you or with Mama. Whenever I asked Auntie Najwa about you and the reason you'd grown so distant, she'd say, 'I don't know, perhaps she's busy with her studies.' You ran away from me, I thought you didn't love me any more…"

"So why didn't say anything or ask me about it?"

"You didn't give me the chance. All of this torture, Lulu, because we didn't speak to each other! If you'd only told me about how you suspected Nana Karma had died, or I had known the reason for you cutting me off and being so distant, perhaps life would have gone differently. We should have spoken to each other about it. We should have talked."

The storm passed. It had destroyed what was left of my ship but had deposited me on a beach. I didn't want to guess how much damage there was, or think about repairing it. I wanted to catch my breath and simply surrender to the emptiness. Abboud said that we were both hungry, but we didn't have food. Because he didn't cook at home, he didn't have any provisions. He suggested that we go out to eat. I told him that I wasn't hungry, that I would throw up if I ate. He lay my head on the pillow, lifted my feet up on the footstool in front of the sofa and told me to breathe deeply. I felt better a few minutes later. He went out to get some food, but he had to run a quick errand nearby first. I apologized for making him do all these things but he stopped me and put his hand over my mouth. He told me he was putting everything in his life on hold for me, announcing, "In life, first things first."

He covered me with a thin blanket, handed me the remote control for the television, and encouraged me to have a nap on the sofa. Then I heard him lock the door. I tried as hard as I could to doze off but I failed. I began flipping through all the satellite channels. There wasn't an Arabic channel, but Muhammad Faris, the first Syrian astronaut, was talking on a French channel and memories flooded through me like horses escaping from their stables.

We didn't sleep at all that night. Everyone had gathered in Auntie Maria's living room. My grandmother went to sleep at midnight then got up at four thirty in the morning as if an alarm had woken her. My mother came along for Nicholas's sake. Abboud and I were playing with Auntie Maria's grandchildren in the garden, which had a big basin of flowering plants right in the middle. She had a green thumb and loved roses.

Some of her seedlings blossomed into Nile roses, and her coral seedlings dropped their flowers on the wooden supports that Auntie Maria had propped up between the bushes to help them grow. The scent of her nightshade plants filled the air. She also had grape vines climbing on a wooden trellis with a crisscrossed roof above it. We always picked the grapes before they were ripe and sprinkled salt on them. Even if they were hard, we ate them anyway. She used to tell us to leave them and let them become grapes. But we preferred the challenge of the sour taste that would make our tongues swell.

This was a rare chance for me to stay up late with Abboud, legally. We used to call these "days of grace"—a holiday, wedding, or funeral…On any important group occasion, our families would let us stay up late together, even until morning, without restrictions on when we came home. It was the night before July 22, 1987, during summer vacation. We lined up on the terrace in the courtyard in front of the pantry to play the color game—I'm thinking of a color that begins with the letter…C…coffee-colored, H…hazelnut-colored, P…pine-nut-colored. We would invent names for all the colors that God had created. At that same moment, and it can be determined precisely—at two in the morning Damascus time—Soviet astronauts, comrade Aleksandr Viktorenko and comrade Aleksandr Aleksandrov, entered the Soyuz M3 spacecraft, along with Lieutenant Colonel Muhammad Faris, the Syrian astronaut. He had been training for two years in a facility called City of Stars, thirty miles from Moscow. Together, they ascended to the Russian space station, the Mir. Faris would carry out thirteen experiments that would lead to developments in scientific research in agriculture, chemistry, physics, and geography.

Nicholas drank chamomile tea in Auntie Maria's big living room, where there were two cobalt blue velvet upholstered sofas side by side and a group of mattresses, covered with brown bedspreads dotted with large beige flowers, on the floor. We called this kind of furniture, which most houses in Raqqa had, "Arab style." Nicholas walked in and out of Auntie Maria's house completely freely. He might go into the kitchen and make sandwiches or dinner or pour some drinks. He sometimes helped her tidy up and clean the carpets. She was really fond of him and thought of him as one of her children, many of whom had gone abroad to the Gulf to work. Two of her married daughters lived in the new suburbs on the west side of town. Zeina had stayed with her and became a pharmacy student after her husband Amo Hadi, died.

I asked Nicholas, "Will Muhammad Faris go to the moon?"

"No," he replied, "Space isn't the moon!"

"Will he come back?"

"Here's hoping!"

I didn't like his neutral tone. It added to my anxiety about the astronauts' possible fate. Nicholas didn't care about this journey as much as I'd expected. I overheard him speaking to my mother, telling her, "The Russians are nerds!" Until this point she hadn't cared too much about it either. The television broadcast patriotic songs on a special program because of it, and most Syrians were awake awaiting the five AM blast off. We felt that all the socialist countries were one big happy family. This made Abboud proud and happy: the Russians were our uncles.

My grandmother came in looking for company that evening. Auntie Maria laid out plastic bowls filled with fruits and vegetables: cucumbers, peaches, apricots, and plums. We all spent some time outside in the courtyard or standing at the front door, and then went back inside to watch the moment when Muhammad Faris and his comrades were strapped into the rocket, preparing themselves mentally and physically for blast off. He would travel fifty yards into the air with them and then break off. No one knew what would happen when each of them broke off separately. Would they return or die in space?

I spoke to Nicholas, trying to break the wall of ice, which re-formed every time I managed to melt it. Why did he treat me with such coldness and arrogance? Which of us had attacked the other? Who had stolen from whom? He knew that I detested him, and I knew that this was his way of avoiding me. I besieged him with questions as if he were solely responsible for this journey into space. I trusted his knowledge absolutely. He led me to believe that he knew the secrets of black holes and had the answers to all puzzling, cosmic questions.

"Will they go out and swim in space? Will they stop on any planets?" It struck me that in Arabic, we use the same word for Earth and land and it's strange to talk about the "land" of a planet, since none of them by definition are Earth. So I phrased my question as, "Will they stop on the surface of any planet?"

"No, they won't go out and swim around in space. They'll only leave their spaceship when they attach to the Mir space station. This should happen two days from now. It is

250 miles above Earth. Their colleagues have already been living up there for about a year."

"Why are we going into space, to other planets? To search for a place to live when Earth is full?"

"Actually, it's to learn about history—the history of the Big Bang, the beginning of all creation. We go into space to know more about Earth!"

"History?"

"History."

"What if one of them dies up there in the spaceship? Will his colleagues bury him on the surface of the nearest planet? Or will they just throw him out in space?"

"Perhaps, but they wouldn't have the heart to do that. There are no graves in space. Perhaps after a while NASA will find a solution and companies will bury the dead in space in an environmentally friendly way. They would probably put a corpse in a well-sealed body bag, freeze it in deep space, then dry it with nitrogen while continuously shaking it so that it crumbles into tiny pieces, and eventually disintegrates into powder, which can be put in a jar and attached to the outer part of the spacecraft."

I didn't like this image—it bothered me that it didn't have the dignity that an astronaut deserved. The announcer on the live broadcast showed us the first stages of the journey. His buoyant voice got everyone excited. We took our places as he began praising our nation, especially Syria's openness to the world, even far beyond Earth's borders. Euphoria, pride, and fear were the emotions flooding my heart. I was truly afraid for the three astronauts, not only the Syrian one. My grandmother started grumbling, "Oh, here we go, now the hypocrisy soap opera begins. Where do these words come from anyway, aren't they tired of this yet?"

Auntie Maria stretched out her legs, so that her dress was hitched up, exposing her pale skin. Then her clean, neat, painted fingernails appeared and she covered up what was exposed with a prayer rug she'd taken from the closet behind her.

I was practically stuck to Abboud on the little sofa whose cover had slipped off. It had golden fringe and a picture of Romeo and Juliet hugging each other. I fixed the cover and went back to sit down again so I could be attached to Abboud without anyone noticing how close to each other we were. The room was packed with viewers, sitting in rows as if we were in a cinema. Auntie Maria said, "My God, I hope they come and go safely…May God be good to their wives and children…what if they don't ever come back?"

My grandmother was silent. She wore a nightdress with a dark blue. light cotton robe over it. She wrapped a beige scarf over her hair, which hung down over her neck and covered the open part of her nightie. She'd begun covering her hair like this after my uncle died. I didn't change my clothes that evening and neither did Abboud. We were still wearing our shorts and t-shirts, which we'd been playing in since the afternoon. The announcer's voice got louder. The rocket launcher was fired up. It looked like the flame under an old-fashioned lamp, or heater, like the kind that the Bustani family still had because they didn't trust automatic washing machines.

At one minute to five, we heard Muhammad Faris shout from inside the rocket ship, "Ya Allah!" This gave me chills, and the rocket separated from its stand, rising higher and higher into the sky as we all applauded. Everyone in the room, even my grandmother who seemed to have been ignoring the whole thing, was repeating, "Oh God, Ya Allah." The announcer was chasing the rocket, saying, "Go with God, be safe, the heavens are opening their doors to you, the skies are embracing Syria." The camera turned at that very moment toward all the Russian generals at the station back on land. They were clapping just like we were, laughing and cheering. The spaceship rose higher and higher, the fire that had propelled it slowly dying down. We breathed a collective sigh of relief. Suddenly, the rocket's passengers appeared on the screen. I heard Auntie Maria gasp and start to pray, calling on God with a series of her own personal imprecations. I could hear my heart pounding, and I was afraid, but it was a fear accompanied by pleasure. Total silence descended upon us. But my fears were allayed when Muhammad Faris appeared, with his bushy mustache and black hair, wearing his smart blue uniform with its shiny silver military stripes, a helmet atop his head. The Syrian flag was hanging behind him, and I was filled with pride. I locked my arms in Abboud's. He said, "Ouch..." and scooted over a little.

The image changed to show the president of the Syrian Arab Republic sitting in front of a stately desk with a bookshelf behind it. He began speaking full of emotion and pride. The president's measured joy was impaired by his stringent paternalism, his happiness not yet freed from the laws of Earth, as he asked the astronaut:

"Colonel Muhammad, what are you seeing now?"

"I can see my beloved country Syria, I see it strong and beautiful, just as is it truly is."

Despite being carried away by everything happening around me, I noticed my grandmother walking out of the room muttering under her breath. No doubt she was cursing. She found everything even the least bit patriotic indicted in her son's murder. I don't know if she could ever forgive, but she didn't appreciate seeing anyone who reminded her of her pain. She never wanted to to look into the eyes of even the lowliest employee connected to the state security services. They had killed her son. Before it happened, the wife of an important army officer took my grandmother's gold and money in exchange for arranging a visit with him in prison. But she didn't keep her promise. Instead my grandmother received threats, that things would get worse if she continued pursuing the matter. 'What could be worse than losing Najeeb?' my grandmother always used to say. She lit a cigarette and carried on. She sat in her nightgown on the raised threshold of one of the rooms in the house, and started smoking. She gazed at the thin thread of smoke trailing upwards. Perhaps she was imagining a meeting between the spaceship and Uncle Najeeb's soul up there in the heavens.

I felt badly for the other Syrian astronaut, the reservist, Munir Habib. He had received the same training, but they chose Muhammad Faris instead. I guess they decided that the name Faris, meaning Knight, was more appropriate for an astronaut. I wondered what Munir Habib was doing now Was he disappointed because he wasn't chosen? Perhaps he was relieved, since he survived this possibly-deadly adventure. Sometimes it seemed to me that the whole idea of going up into space was colossally stupid! Perhaps it was a mix of those two feelings together, but I was really sad for his sake nonetheless. I felt it was actually fair that they named a middle school in our city after Habib. Out of sympathy for him, I asked my mother to transfer me to that school but she said it was too far from home.

The Euphrates River, which borders our city at a distance of three miles, did not know that there was a scientific experiment in space that carried its name. We would have a home in orbit, even if our homes on Earth were destroyed. The passengers aboard the Soyuz were in space for seven days, twenty-three hours, and five minutes. Muhammad Faris conducted thirteen experiments. The Euphrates experiment included tests with remote sensors, in which satellite pictures of Syria were taken to study air and water pollution, ground-water basins, and soil-salinity ratios.

When the broadcast cut off, I noticed my mother and Nicholas were no longer in the room. My heart sank. I heard my own heart thumping in my chest, and a big bang went off inside of me.

I half reclined on the beige suede sofa and turned to the window next to my head. I could see the Rhine through the birch branches so intertwined their tips weren't visible. From here, one column of trees becomes a dense forest. The leaves started losing their green, yellow, red, and orange color, fading to a dark blue. I pulled up the thin woolen blanket, which Abboud had covered me with, to cover my stomach. I noticed that he had put a fresh glass of cucumber and lemon juice beside me. It had three red cherries floating in it. I loved the atmosphere he'd created. The air was a little cool, but filled with tenderness and caring. Such unprecedented tenderness felt like true generosity. We both knew that we wouldn't stay together. Perhaps he was just being as hospitable as possible and that was it. His actions mirrored the changing of the seasons. They give lavishly and then pull back, leaving emotional imbalance, illness, and depression behind.

Muhammad Faris, who we remembered from the spaceship but was now speaking to the French television host, had hardly changed at all. His body had aged and his hair was white. But he spoke with his same thick Aleppo accent, which was the living language of the people thirty years before. I could hear it booming through my television screen, subtitled in French. The interviewer asked him about his journey into space. He replied, "The space ship blasted off so fast—at 78,000 miles per hour, so it could break free of the of earth's gravitational pull and go into orbit. Then the vehicle had to speed up to 55,000 miles per hour to avoid the sun's gravitational pull and to reach the stars."

As he was speaking I was searching for my mother in the emptiness of Abboud's room. The sound of a foghorn shook the calm of this falsely reassuring evening. My eyes flooded with salty tears, because I hadn't found her, but I was going to meet Nicholas the next day…in less than twenty-four hours.

Muhammad Faris owned a pricey women's clothing and bridal shop in his hometown of Aleppo. Whenever I passed it while shopping in Azizieh, I wondered if the astronaut would be sitting at the cash register, or selling things to clients, or at least sitting in the shop. But I never saw him once in the boutique called Faris in Space. I never found the things you would need to go up into space, like a space suit, as my childhood mind thought I might at the time.

Muhammad Faris said to the interviewer, "Space is total darkness. Any light there is very diffuse, and only forms 2.5% of universe, despite the existence of billions of galaxies. Ninety-seven percent of the universe is dark matter. Earth is more beautiful than the moon and the other planets. It is a small planet suspended in a huge universe, one of God's many creations. No one who sees it from out there could possibly believe it is beset by violence and war." At the time, Muhammad Faris was awarded the Order of Lenin by the Soviet Union. He achieved the rank of major general and taught at the military academy. The French interviewer asked him about his break with the Syrian regime and belonging to the revolution. He spoke to her about how he fled the country with his family for Istanbul.

"What will you do now?"

"Not much. I smoke my argileh, I sit in coffee shops and my friend's houses."

He was disappointing. I was sad about the decline of his strong body, which had helped him be chosen over more than fifty other army pilots. He got to see what so few humans ever do. His body helped him to penetrate the Earth's atmosphere, go beyond the danger zone, and reach the plasma of existence where the outer shell of the spaceship melted away and scattered because of a temperature exceeding six thousand degrees Fahrenheit. How could he now be depressed, damaging his body by sitting and smoking? He kept up his good fitness throughout the entire journey. His Soviet comrades said that he trembled when they flew above Syria. When they landed on Earth, he was the most balanced of his peers. He slept for seven hours then woke up and played tennis. He also said that the most beautiful thing on Earth was Syria.

I looked out the window and couldn't see the moon. The sky was dark, and light filtered in from the street lamps. I hadn't seen the moon once since arriving in Germany. Had it even appeared in the cloudy Cologne skies? I rang Carmen and she told me that she was going to do some writing and we could have dinner together somewhere near her house afterwards. I declined, apologizing, I told her that Abboud and I would make something to eat, and that I wanted to be with him that night.

When my mother and I felt desperate during the ISIS siege of Raqqa and the bombardments by coalition forces, we used to think about how we could possibly leave. Many people we knew had left Raqqa for Turkey, and then on to countries accepting refugees—Greece, Italy, Holland, and France... The most welcoming of these was Germany, which for the two of us meant Nicholas. Whenever the shelling started up again, we would regret having stayed. I used to beg my mother, crying and pleading to leave. I didn't want to die under the bombs. I wanted to escape like other people had—at least to Aleppo. We didn't have a man with us, which made it all the more difficult to leave.

Every time we tried to figure this out, we found all the exits closed and the city besieged once again. That's when we surrendered. Mama said that we had to contact Nicholas and use any means necessary to locate his address. I realized at that moment that they hadn't been in touch in a very long time. She was convinced that he would help us nonetheless. I wanted to leave Syria in a way that would avoid the stigma of refugee status, so I could ensure my ability to return legally. I wanted to realize her old dream of me completing my studies, as she had planned for back during the archeological dig at Tel al-Bi'ah that Stephanie was running. The only reason I failed to pursue that dream is because I didn't want to be so far away from her. She told me, "I must go and settle down in Germany. It will be somewhat safer there than in Aleppo, then you can follow me. Or we can go together if we both can get visas." When it came to the story of Nicholas, the only feeling I had was regret for not seeing her as a woman. I didn't appreciate her anguish, feelings, and needs. My presence in her life was a cause for misery, since I prevented her from being happy. I believed that I had taken her mother from her, but I was certain that I'd kept her from the man she loved with my arrogance, selfishness, and childish way of thinking. I made one inevitable choice.

It would be easy for me to find Nicholas, if I could get a good Internet connection. I was searching for quick salvation so I didn't hesitate. I often went to an Internet café in the neighborhood. It was across the street from the house, but I had to take a thousand things into account just to get there. I might encounter one of the members of Daesh who followed women, as well as men, to surveil and punish them for more or less anything they did. It took me two trips to find Nicholas's address and email on University of Munich website. I wrote him a letter in Arabic. I reminded him who I was, and told him about the impossible circumstances we were stuck in, the life Mama and I were leading. I told him that I wanted to leave. I received his reply the next day, a welcoming letter and assurance that he would do everything in his power to help us get visas. Most likely, he said, this would involve a request for me to work with him as a research assistant on a project to do with the history of the region where he'd worked previously and that was now threatened with being destroyed. This plan would take advantage of my specialization in history and my work at the museum. My mother would then join me in the not-too-distant future. He said that I must begin studying

German at an accredited center in Aleppo or Damascus in order to get a diploma attesting to my language skills. This would bolster his invitation. His message reassured us. I know Mama spent that night lost in memories. For just a moment, she forgot about Daesh, the coalition, and the regime…bombardments and shelling…public whippings and the sharia courts…water tanks, and how we had to buy electricity by the ampere once the war stopped the government-provided electricity service…She closed her eyes with images of the old train car days and nights in her mind.

The next time I wrote to Nicholas, my mother was no longer there. I had buried her and left for Damascus where our friends helped me get set up for six months so I could catch my breath. I began pursing my travel abroad in earnest from Damascus. I started studying German but couldn't get the official certificate, because the in-person interview for my travel visa was fixed at the embassy in Beirut before the course had ended. Nicholas sent me a sincere letter of condolences and expressed that he was absolutely ready to host me at his house, pay for my studies and expenses, and find me work, so I wouldn't need anything else. I asked him to intervene so I could get a scholarship from one of the NGOs so I could complete my studies. He really did organize everything so I could arrive at the place where I am now.

Carmen told me that he would get in from Munich in the afternoon but he had to go straight to a meeting at work. We would meet him at dinnertime, at around six PM. I was exhausted from everything that had happened the day before, especially the slap in the face about the truth, which I was now aware of. I was also exhausted by Abboud and being near him—his compassion, warmth, touch, and scent, as well as our memories. I was simply spent. My body awoke hungry and protesting at the deprivation caused by an imposed period of slumber. Carmen and I headed for the west side of Cologne to the expansive wooded area that rings the city. A light drizzle spotted our windshield and Carmen asked if I was excited to see Nicholas. I told her that my feelings were completely neutral—I wasn't happy, sad, or excited.

Worrying about what had happened the day before made me less nervous about our meeting. After all that, it was hard to say anything could make me feel more worried or afraid. Often you go through things because you simply have to. I just want to finish with everything so I can find myself, and a routine that will center me. I told her that Abboud had made fun of me for not having had relationships with men. She replied, "So let him be the first then!" I told her sharply that I wouldn't simply let him enjoy me just like that! She slowed the car and threw me a puzzled look out of the corner of her eye, "You will enjoy him too!" I was quiet and turned to look out at the green meadows.

I would have liked to be more prepared to meet Nicholas. I would have been had I not been so exhausted. But I tried to appear coherent and full of life, studies, and research, in order to be worthy of the effort he'd put into me. All I did was put on my bright blue lace dress and gold sandals, which I'd bought from Primark, and applied some of Carmen's makeup because I hadn't bought any of my own. The colors didn't suit me, but I chose neutral shades. I searched for a kohl pencil, and she said she didn't use one. In the end I found a worn-out eyeliner that had to be at least ten years old and burned off the end to make it work. I traced two curved lines around my eyelids. I found that kohl wasn't too thick-lined around my small eyes, in fact, it made them look gray rather than black. My hair was still mostly black, but my skin had become clear and rosy from eating so many wild mulberries and blueberries, which contain powerful antioxidants. I walked everywhere with a little dish of berries and devoured them constantly. This was something I'd dreamed of my whole life and hadn't been available to us either before or after the war.

The journey didn't change my size, however. I was still five foot-two inches tall. I didn't know how much I weighed but I'd slimmed down a little. I wasn't as well-proportioned as I used to be. As Auntie Safia used to describe me, "A fish with no bones," making a joke about me being not heavy. I wore a strand of my grandmother's pearls around my neck. My mother often used to wear them, and I thought that it might put a bit of emotional pressure on Nicholas, reminding him of Najwa, Karma, al-Battani, and the train car. This in turn would prevent him from considering giving up on me. When Carmen saw me all ready to go, she exclaimed, "Super!" I was sure that I really did resemble my mother and this was enough for me to feel that I was looking incredibly beautiful.

Abboud had asked me the day before to stay with him. He said that he would look after me and take care of me, better than anyone else in the whole world. He said that he would help me to study German quickly, and then help me choose what I would do after, for example, follow Nicholas or study somewhere else. He insisted that I needed not to force myself into things I didn't like just for the sake of getting a scholarship. He himself could cover all of my expenses. It was difficult for me to hear this from him, because I felt like he was offering me charity. But at the same time it was reassuring because I still had some support in the world and more than one option. But I decided to go with Nicholas and take the scholarship.

When we arrived at the Astoria Club, the rain had changed to a torrential winter flood, even though it was July. We pulled out our umbrellas and walked briskly to the club. The bright floodlights of the vaulted entrance greeted us. On the two facing walls of the entrance hung rows of black and white pictures of generals. Carmen said, "The club was originally a military park for army generals during the Second World War, these are pictures of some of them." We arrived at a giant bar, with more black and white images on the walls, this time movie stills featuring actors in war films, like: *Cross of Iron*, *The Night of the Generals*, and *Das Boot*. The larger wall was devoted to Sophia Loren, including oversized black and white photographs in thin black frames from a professional photo shoot. We were surrounded by endless remnants of the war. There was no color that could erase this memory, except to turn people into eternal beauty—like Sophia Loren's iconic beauty. You can see this in the classic picture of her wrapped in a white bed sheet as if she were asleep, her naked shoulders and top of her breasts peeping out. There is also the photograph of her walking out of the sea toward the beach with the waves crashing behind her, and the one of her in jeans shorts holding her foot, as if she'd stepped on a thorn. All pictures of her are magical.

Mama had inherited her passion for the star of *Two Women*, and *Yesterday, Today, and Tomorrow* from my grandmother, Karma, who felt they were closely related because of their common origin in Palestine. She used to speak of her courage, pointing out that she'd been hit in the chin by shrapnel as she was heading to a bomb shelter, and how this injury didn't at all mar her beauty. This had happened in her native village Pozzuoli, near Naples, which was the target of repeated bombings by Allied Forces in the Second World War. She also remarked how she'd washed dishes in her grandmother's pub and then later had fabulous success, making her a wonderful example for all children of war.

We sat at a table on the inner terrace looking out over Adenauer Weiher Lake, which had been named in honor of the first German Chancellor after the war, who led his country out of its rubble to an economic miracle. A bevy of swans glided by, as bright rays of evening sun poked through the retreating clouds, lending this lake an aura of peacefulness.

There were elm and birch forests on the opposite shore of the lake. The deeper you looked into them, the more mysterious they seemed, and the more they guarded their secrets. I tried to lessen my anxiety by looking into Carmen's eyes, while she was examining the menu. She'd put on mascara and taken care with her radiant makeup. She wore a knitted gray jersey dress, with a navy blue scarf draped over her shoulders. She was also wearing the red coral necklace that I'd given her as a gift. It was from my mother's jewelry collection, and I couldn't imagine a better person to gift it to. She pulled me through this, she really did!

I thought to myself about how Carmen had gotten herself out of the depths of pain and despair, worked through her parents' epic tragedy, her emotional downfall, and what she called her escape from paradise. Would time really pass and I'd become just like her, sitting atop a mound of destruction, drinking a cup of coffee and talking to people about my grandmother who I discovered I hadn't murdered and about my mother whose legless corpse I carried on a horse as if we were living in the time of Hyksos? Would all of this happen while I was sitting in a restaurant, wearing a dress made by Escada, waiting to throw myself upon the mercy of my former enemy?

Nicholas had crushed me when I was a child. He snuffed out a light in my little girl heart that I could never rekindle. His galaxies and stars, al-Battani, and his mother's poems made my childhood miserable. After that summer, I spent long nights tending to the burns left by the bitter tears I'd shed in the saddle room. This damaged my mother and me both.

Carmen rapped her fingers against her glass, to get my attention. "Hey…" she said, pointing at the wooden bridge that connected the lake to the side entrance of the Astoria. An elderly man, tall and slightly hunched over, was moving calmly toward us. He was wearing a beige raincoat. He walked as if he were counting each step he took, tapping the bridge with the tip of his black umbrella. His beard had started to go white; his long gray hair hung down to his shoulders. He looked like Poseidon emerging from the sea.

I left Carmen and headed over to the door, careful not to smack right into the clean, clear glass. I don't know who opened the door. Was it as the waiter or was it simply an automatic door? The important thing is that it opened. I was immediately assaulted by the scent of damp trees, the screeching of geese, and the stinging cold. I went back to get my shawl, and stood in front of the door that was no longer open. I once again crossed the terrace that separated the closed dining room from the lake. I moved as if sleepwalking, my eyes fixated on the head bobbing toward me, boldly carrying my life's black box and all its codes and images, truths and fantasies, laughter and tears. I noticed that I was starting to shrink into myself. Back when Mama taught me to walk across the ancient bridge in Raqqa, she always said that if I lifted my head high, kept my back straight, and shoulders pulled back I'd be six inches taller. This is just what I needed to confront Nicholas's confidence and resist the German summer chill.

I approached the wooden bridge. Nicholas was so close to me. His hazel eyes were still disturbing, like a black hole singularity, where all the laws of physics break down. But I had to admit to myself at this decisive moment that I'd never doubted the kindness of this man's heart. I saw this kindness in my mother's laughter, and then in her tears after he left. I was certain that his heart, like the heart of ancient cities, would never change. I touched the pearls hanging around my neck. On my mother's amputated legs, I walked over the bridge to meet my former enemy.

Translator's Acknowledgements

The translator would like first to acknowledge the cheerful and detailed assistance of the author Shahla Ujayli, who has been a wonderful partner to work on translation with. Translating a difficult and complex novel like this was a pleasure in her company. Thanks also to the wonderful team at Interlink for continuing to publish high quality fiction in translation from Arabic.

I would also like to acknowledge my research assistants at McGill University, who helped on his project, Sarah Abdelshamy and Caline Nasrallah, the latter of which worked hard with me on revising and finetuning elements of this translation. Thank you Caline for attention to detail, creative translation solutions, and positive energy in working together. This translation was partly completed under the auspices of the Women's War Stories project based at McGill University and funded by the Social Sciences and Humanities Research Council of Canada, who I would also like to acknowledge here. Thanks to my colleagues and co-researcher on this project Malek Abisaab, and also Rula Jurdi Abisaab. Heartfelt thanks as always to my friend and colleague Yasmine Nachabe Taan who has always been there to work, and think, and live together through my many translation projects, with her support and suggestions.

The bulk of the translation of this novel was done in a small Lebanese mountain village overlooking the mountains of Syria. A huge merci to the people who make this place into a productive, creative, and inspiring summer workplace. Thanks to all of the Nachabe-Fakih-Merhej-Taan family for their hospitality and conversation that adds so much to my work. Thanks for patience and conversations with Amanda and Tameem Hartman, constant companions in both language and translation, always.

This translation is dedicated to the women who have lived through wars and tell their stories, in many languages.